THE FIRST PHONE CALL FROM HEAVEN

MITCH ALBOM

ISIS

LARGE
PRINT

First published in Great Britain 2013
by
Sphere
An imprint of Little, Brown Book Group

First Isis Edition
published 2017
by arrangement with
Little, Brown Book Group

A catalogue record for this book is available
from the British Library.

ISBN 978–1–78541–327–8 (hb)
ISBN 978–1–78541–333–9 (pb)

Published by
F. A. Thorpe (Publishing)
Anstey, Leicestershire

Set by Words & Graphics Ltd.
Anstey, Leicestershire
Printed and bound in Great Britain by
T. J. International Ltd., Padstow, Cornwall

This book is printed on acid-free paper

For Debbie, a virtuoso with the telephone,
whose voice we miss every day

The Week It Happened

On the day the world received its first phone call from heaven, Tess Rafferty was unwrapping a box of tea bags.

Drrrrnnn!

She ignored the ring and dug her nails into the plastic.

Drrrrnnn!

She clawed her forefinger through the bumpy part on the side.

Drrrrnnn!

Finally, she made a rip, then peeled off the wrapping and scrunched it in her palm. She knew the phone would go to answering machine if she didn't grab it before one more—

Drrnnn—

"Hello?"

Too late.

"Ach, this thing," she mumbled. She heard the machine click on her kitchen counter as it played her outgoing message.

"*Hi, it's Tess. Leave your name and number. I'll get back to you as soon as I can, thanks.*"

A small beep sounded. Tess heard static. And then.

"It's Mom . . . I need to tell you something."

Tess stopped breathing. The receiver fell from her fingers.

Her mother died four years ago.

Drrrrnnng!

The second call was barely audible over a boisterous police station argument. A clerk had hit the lottery for $28,000 and three officers were debating what they'd do with such luck.

"You pay your bills."

"That's what you *don't* do."

"A boat."

"Pay your bills."

"Not me."

"A boat!"

Drrrrnnng!

Jack Sellers, the police chief, backed up toward his small office. "If you pay your bills, you just rack up new bills," he said. The men continued arguing as he reached for the phone.

"Coldwater Police, Sellers speaking."

Static. Then a young man's voice.

"Dad? . . . It's Robbie."

Suddenly Jack couldn't hear the other men.

"Who the hell is this?"

"I'm happy, Dad. Don't worry about me, OK?"

Jack felt his stomach tighten. He thought about the last time he'd seen his son, clean shaven with a soldier's tight haircut, disappearing through airport security en route to his third tour of duty.

His last tour of duty.

"It can't be you," Jack whispered.

Brrnnnng!

Pastor Warren wiped saliva from his chin. He'd been napping on his couch at the Harvest of Hope Baptist Church.

Brrnnnng!

"Coming."

He struggled to his feet. The church had installed a bell outside his office, because at eighty-two, his hearing had grown weak.

Brrnnnng!

"Pastor, it's Katherine Yellin. Hurry, please!"

He hobbled to the door and opened it.

"Hello, Ka—"

But she was already past him, her coat half buttoned, her reddish hair frazzled, as if she'd dashed out of the house. She sat on the couch, rose nervously, then sat again.

"Please know I'm not crazy."

"No, dear—"

"Diane called me."

"Who called you?"

"Diane."

Warren's head began to hurt.

"Your deceased sister called you?"

"This morning. I picked up the phone . . ."

She gripped her handbag and began to cry. Warren wondered if he should call someone for help.

"She told me not to worry," Katherine rasped. "She said she was at peace."

"This was a dream, then?"

"No! No! It wasn't a dream! *I spoke to my sister!*"

Tears fell off the woman's cheeks, dropping faster than she could wipe them away.

"We've talked about this, dear—"

"I know, but—"

"You miss her—"

"Yes—"

"And you're upset."

"No, Pastor! She told me she's in *heaven* . . . Don't you see?"

She smiled, a beatific smile, a smile Warren had never seen on her face before.

"I'm not scared of anything anymore," she said.

Drrrrrnnnnnng.

A security bell sounded, and a heavy prison gate slid across a track. A tall, broad-shouldered man named Sullivan Harding walked slowly, a step at a time, head down. His heart was racing — not at the excitement of his liberation, but at the fear that someone might yank him back.

Forward. Forward. He kept his gaze on the tips of his shoes. Only when he heard approaching noise on the gravel — light footsteps, coming fast — did he look up.

Jules.

His son.

He felt two small arms wrap around his legs, felt his hands sink into a mop of the boy's curly hair. He saw

4

his parents — mother in a navy windbreaker, father in a light brown suit — their faces collapsing as they fell into a group embrace. It was chilly and gray and the street was slick with rain. Only his wife was missing from the moment, but her absence was like a character in it.

Sullivan wanted to say something profound, but all that emerged from his lips was a whisper:

"Let's go."

Moments later, their car disappeared down the road.

It was the day the world received its first phone call from heaven.

What happened next depends on how much you believe.

The Second Week

A cool, misting rain fell, which was not unusual for September in Coldwater, a small town geographically north of certain parts of Canada and just a few miles from Lake Michigan.

Despite the chilly weather, Sullivan Harding was walking. He could have borrowed his father's car, but after ten months of confinement, he preferred the open air. Wearing a ski cap and an old suede jacket, he passed the high school he'd attended twenty years ago, the lumberyard that had closed last winter, the bait and tackle shop, its rental rowboats stacked like clamshells, and the gas station where an attendant leaned against a wall, examining his fingernails. *My hometown*, Sullivan thought.

He reached his destination and wiped his boots on a thatched mat that read DAVIDSON & SONS. Noticing a small camera above the doorframe, he instinctively yanked off his cap, swiped at his thick brown hair, and looked into the lens. After a minute with no response, he let himself in.

The warmth of the funeral home was almost smothering. Its walls were paneled in dark oak. A desk with no chair held an open sign-in book.

"Can I help you?"

The director, a tall, thinly boned man with pallid skin, bushy eyebrows, and wispy hair the color of straw, stood with his hands crossed. He appeared to be in his late sixties.

"I'm Horace Belfin," he said.

"Sully Harding."

"Ah, yes."

Ah yes, Sully thought, *the one who missed his wife's funeral because he was in prison.* Sully did this now, finished unfinished sentences, believing that the words people do not speak are louder than the ones they do.

"Giselle was my wife."

"I'm sorry for your loss."

"Thank you."

"It was a lovely ceremony. I imagine the family has told you."

"I am the family."

"Of course."

They stood in silence.

"Her remains?" Sully said.

"In our columbarium. I'll get the key."

He went to his office.

Sully lifted a brochure off a table. He opened it to a paragraph about cremation.

Cremated remains can be sprinkled at sea, placed in a helium balloon, scattered from an airplane . . .

Sully tossed the brochure back. *Scattered from an airplane.* Even God couldn't be that cruel.

7

Twenty minutes later, Sully left the building with his wife's ashes in an angel-shaped urn. He tried carrying it one-handed, but that felt too casual. He tried cradling it in his palms, but that felt like an offering. He finally clasped it to his chest, arms crossed, the way a child carries a book bag. He walked this way for half a mile through the Coldwater streets, his heels splashing through rainwater. When he came upon a bench in front of the post office, he sat down, placing the urn carefully beside him.

The rain finished. Church bells chimed in the distance. Sully closed his eyes and imagined Giselle nudging against him, her sea-green eyes, her licorice-black hair, her thin frame and narrow shoulders that, leaned against Sully's body, seemed to whisper, *Protect me.*

He hadn't, in the end. Protected her. That would never change. He sat on that bench for a long while, fallen man, porcelain angel, as if the two of them were waiting for a bus.

The news of life is carried via telephone. A baby's birth, a couple engaged, a tragic accident on a late-night highway — most milestones of the human journey, good or bad, are foreshadowed by the sound of ringing.

Tess sat on her kitchen floor now, waiting for that sound to come again. For the past two weeks, her phone had been carrying the most stunning news of all. Her mother *existed*, somewhere, somehow. She reviewed the latest conversation for the hundredth time.

"*Tess . . . Stop crying, darling.*"

"It can't be you."

"*I'm here, safe and sound.*"

Her mother always said that when she called in from a trip — a hotel, a spa, even a visit to her relatives half an hour away. *I'm here, safe and sound.*

"This isn't possible.

"*Everything is possible. I am with the Lord. I want to tell you about . . .*"

"What? Mom? What?"

"*Heaven.*"

The line went silent. Tess stared at the receiver as if holding a human bone. It was totally illogical. She knew that. But a mother's voice is like no other; we recognize every lilt and whisper, every warble or shriek. There was no doubt. It was *her.*

Tess drew her knees in to her chest. Since the first call, she had remained inside, eating only crackers, cereal, hard-boiled eggs, whatever she had in the house. She hadn't gone to work, hadn't gone shopping, hadn't even gotten the mail.

She ran a hand through her long, unwashed blond hair. A shut-in to a miracle? What would people say? She didn't care. A few words from heaven had rendered all the words on earth inconsequential.

Jack Sellers sat by his desk inside the converted redbrick house that served as headquarters for the Coldwater Police Department. It appeared to his coworkers that he was typing up reports. But he, too, was waiting for a ringing.

It had been the most bizarre week of his life. Two calls from his dead son. Two conversations he thought he would never have again. He still hadn't told his ex-wife, Doreen, Robbie's mother. She had fallen into depression and teared up at the mere mention of his name. What would he say to her? That their boy, killed in battle, was now alive somewhere? That the portal to heaven sat on Jack's desk? Then what?

Jack himself had no clue what to make of this. He only knew that each time that phone rang, he grabbed for it like a gun-slinger.

His second call, like the first, had come on a Friday afternoon. He heard static, and an airy noise that rose and fell.

"*It's me, Dad.*"

"Robbie."

"*I'm OK, Dad. There's no bad days here.*"

"Where are you?"

"*You know where I am. Dad, it's awesome—*"

Then a click.

Jack screamed, "Hello? *Hello?*" He noticed the other officers looking over. He shut the door. A minute later, the phone rang again. He checked the caller ID bar. As with the previous times, it read UNKNOWN.

"Hello?" he whispered.

"*Tell Mom not to cry . . . if we knew what comes next, we never would have worried.*"

Once you have a sister, you never stop having her, even if you can no longer see or touch her.

10

Katherine Yellin lay back on the bed, her red hair flattening against the pillow. She crossed her arms and squeezed the salmon-pink flip phone that had once belonged to Diane. It was a Samsung model, with a glitter sticker of a high-heeled shoe on the back, a symbol of Diane's love for fashion.

It's better than we dreamed, Kath.

Diane had said that in her second call, which, like the first — like all these strange calls to Coldwater — had come on a Friday. *Better than we dreamed*. The word Katherine most loved in that sentence was *we*.

The Yellin sisters had a special bond, like tethered children scaling small-town life together. Diane, older by two years, had walked Katherine to school each day, paved the way for her in Brownies and Girl Scouts, got her braces off when Katherine got hers on, and refused, at high school dances, to take the floor until Katherine had someone to dance with too. Both sisters had long legs, strong shoulders, and could swim a mile in the lake during the summer. Both attended the local community college. They cried together when their parents died. When Diane married, Katherine was her maid of honor; three Junes later, the positions were reversed. Each had two kids — girls for Diane, boys for Katherine. Their houses were a mile apart. Even their divorces fell within a year of one another.

Only in health had they diverged. Diane had endured migraines, an irregular heartbeat, high blood pressure, and the sudden aneurysm that killed her at the too-young age of forty-six. Katherine was often described as "never sick a day in her life."

For years, she'd felt guilty about this. But now she understood. Diane — sweet, fragile Diane — had been called for a reason. She'd been chosen by the Lord to show that eternity waits for the faithful.

It's better than we dreamed, Kath.

Katherine smiled. *We.* Through the pink flip phone she held to her chest, she had rediscovered the sister she could never lose.

And she would not be silent about it.

The Third Week

You have to start over. That's what they say. But life is not a board game, and losing a loved one is never really "starting over." More like "continuing without."

Sully's wife was gone. She'd died after a long coma. According to the hospital, she slipped away during a thunderstorm on the first day of summer. Sully was still in prison, nine weeks from release. When they informed him, his entire body went numb. It was like learning of the earth's destruction while standing on the moon.

He thought about Giselle constantly now, even though every thought brought with it the shadow of their last day, the crash, the fire, how everything he'd known changed in one bumpy instant. Didn't matter. He draped himself in her sad memory, because it was the closest thing to having her around. He placed the angel urn on a shelf by a couch where Jules, two months shy of his seventh birthday, lay sleeping.

Sully sat down, slumping into the chair. He was still adjusting to freedom. You might think that after ten months in prison, a man would bask in liberation. But the body and mind grow accustomed to conditions, even terrible ones, and there were still moments when Sully stared at the walls, as listless as a captive. He had to remind himself he could get up and go out.

He reached for a cigarette and looked around this cheap, unfamiliar apartment, a second-story walk-up, heated by a radiator furnace. Outside the window was a cluster of pine trees and a small ravine that led to a stream. He remembered catching frogs there as a kid.

Sully had returned to Coldwater because his parents had been taking care of Jules during his trial and incarceration, and he didn't want to disrupt the boy's life any more than he already had. Besides, where would he go? His job and home were gone. His money had been depleted by lawyers. He watched two squirrels chase each other up a tree and kidded himself that Giselle might have actually liked this place, once she got past the location, the size, the dirt, and the peeling paint.

A knock broke Sully's concentration. He looked through the peephole. Mark Ashton stood on the other side, holding two grocery bags.

Mark and Sully had been navy squadron mates; they flew jets together. Sully hadn't seen him since the sentencing.

"Hey," Mark said when the door opened.

"Hey," Sully replied.

"Nice place — if you're a terrorist."

"You drove up from Detroit?"

"Yeah. Gonna let me in?"

They shared a quick, awkward hug, and Mark followed Sully into the main room. He saw Jules on the couch and lowered his voice.

"He asleep?"

"Yeah."

"I got him some Oreos. All kids like Oreos, right?"

Mark laid the bags between unpacked boxes on the kitchen counter. He noticed an ashtray full of cigarette butts and several glasses in the sink — small glasses, the kind you fill with alcohol, not water.

"So . . . ," he said.

Without the bags in his hands, Mark had no distraction. He looked at Sully's face — Sully, his old flying partner, whose boyish looks and openmouthed expression suggested the ready-to-go high school football star he once had been, only thinner and older now, especially around the eyes.

"This the town you grew up in?"

"Now you know why I left."

"How are you getting by?"

Sully shrugged.

"Look. It's awful. What happened with Giselle . . ."

"Yeah."

"I'm sorry."

"Yeah."

"I thought they'd let you out for the funeral."

" 'Navy rules rule the navy.' "

"It was a nice service."

"I heard."

"As far as the rest . . ."

Sully glanced up.

"The hell with it," Mark said. "People know."

They know you went to prison, Sully thought, finishing the unfinished sentence. *They don't know if you deserved it.*

"I tried to come see you."

"Didn't want to be seen."

"It was weird for the guys."

"Doesn't matter."

"Sully—"

"Let's drop it, OK? I already said what happened. A million times. They believed something else. End of story."

Sully stared at his hands and punched his knuckles together.

"What are you planning next?" Mark asked.

"What do you mean?"

"For work?"

"Why?"

"I know a guy near here. College roommate. I called him."

Sully stopped punching his knuckles.

"You called before you saw me?"

"You're gonna need money. He might have a job."

"Doing what?"

"Sales."

"I'm not a salesman."

"It's easy. All you do is sign customers back up, collect a check, and get a commission."

"What kind of business?"

"Newspaper."

16

Sully blinked. "You're kidding, right?" He thought about all the newspapers that had written about his "incident," how quickly they had jumped to the easiest, fastest conclusion, reprinting each other's words until they had devoured him, then moving on to the next story. He'd hated the news ever since. Never paid for another newspaper, and never would.

"It lets you stay around here," Mark said.

Sully went to the sink. He rinsed out a glass. He wished Mark would go, so he could fill it with what he wanted.

"Give me his number, I'll call him," Sully said, knowing full well he never would.

Tess sat cross-legged on soft red cushions and stared out the bay window to the large front lawn, which hadn't been mowed in weeks. This was the house she had grown up in; she remembered, as a child, curling in this very spot on summer mornings, whining to her mother, Ruth, who sat at a bridge table, reviewing her paperwork, rarely looking up.

"I'm bored," Tess would say.

"Try going outside," Ruth would mumble.

"There's nothing to do."

"Do nothing outside."

"I wish I had a sister."

"Sorry, can't help you."

"You could if you got married."

"I was already married."

"There's nothing to do."

"Try reading a book."

"I read all the books."

"Read them again."

On and on they went, a jousting conversation that in some form repeated itself through adolescence, college, adulthood, right up until Ruth's final years, when Alzheimer's robbed her of her words, and ultimately of the desire to speak at all. Ruth spent her final months in a stony silence, staring at her daughter with her head tilted, the way a child stares at a fly.

But now, somehow, they were talking again, as if death had been an airplane flight that Tess thought Ruth had taken but later found out she'd missed. An hour earlier, they'd shared another inexplicable phone call.

"It's me, Tess."

"Oh, God, Mom. I still can't believe this."

"I always told you I'd find a way."

Tess smiled through tears, remembering how her mother, a health food devotee, used to joke that even dead, she'd make sure Tess was taking her supplements.

"You were so sick, Mom."

"But there is no pain here."

"You suffered so much—"

"Honey, listen to me."

"I'm here. I'm listening."

"The pain you go through in life doesn't really touch you . . . not the real you . . . You are so much lighter than you think."

Just the words brought Tess a blessed calmness now. *You are so much lighter than you think.* She glanced at the photo in her hands, the last photo of them together, taken at her mother's eighty-third birthday party. You could see the price the illness had exacted — Ruth's hollowed cheeks, her blank expression, the way her caramel sweater drooped on her skeletal frame.

"Mom, how is this possible? You're not using a phone."

"No."

"How are you speaking to me?"

"*Something has happened, Tess ... There's an opening.*"

"An opening?"

"*For now.*"

"How long will it last?"

A long pause.

"Mom? How long will it last?"

"*It won't.*"

Miracles happen quietly every day — in an operating room, on a stormy sea, in the sudden appearance of a roadside stranger. They are rarely tallied. No one keeps score.

But now and then, a miracle is declared to the world.

And when that happens, things change.

Tess Rafferty and Jack Sellers might have kept their calls secret, but Katherine Yellin would not. *Proclaim the good news to all mankind.* That's what the gospel said.

And so, on a Sunday morning, twenty-three days after Cold-water's first mysterious phone call, Pastor Warren stood before his Harvest of Hope congregation, flipping pages in his Bible, unaware that his sanctuary was about to be transformed forever.

"Let us read together from Matthew, chapter eleven, verse twenty-eight," he announced, blinking. The print was blurry, and his fingers shook with age. He thought of the psalm: *Do not forsake me when I am old and gray.*

"Excuse me, everyone!"

Heads turned. Warren peered over his glasses. Katherine was standing in the fifth row. She wore a brimmed black hat and a lavender dress. In her hands, she clutched a piece of paper.

"Pastor, I'm sorry. The spirit of the Lord compels me to speak."

Warren swallowed. He feared where this was going.

"Katherine, please be seated—"

"This is important, Pastor."

"Now is not the—"

"I have witnessed a *miracle!*"

A small gasp rippled through the pews.

"Katherine, the Lord is with us all, but claiming a miracle—"

"It happened three weeks ago."

"—is a very serious matter—"

"I was in the kitchen, Friday morning."

"—best left to the leaders of the church."

"I got a phone call—"

"Really, I must insist—"

"—from my *dead sister!*"

More gasps. She had their attention now. The sanctuary was so quiet, you could hear her unfold the paper.

"It was Diane. Many of you knew her. She died two years ago, but her soul is alive in heaven. She told me!"

Warren fought to keep from shaking. He had lost control of the pulpit, a sin, in his mind, of the highest order.

"We first spoke that Friday morning," Katherine continued, reading louder as she wiped tears with the back of her hand. "It was 10:41 a.m. And the next Friday, at 11:14 a.m., and last Friday at 7:02 in the evening. She said my name . . . she said . . . 'Kath, the time has come to tell everyone. I'm waiting for you. We are all waiting.'"

She turned to the rear of the sanctuary. "*We are all waiting.*"

The congregation mumbled. From the pulpit, Warren watched them shifting in their seats, as if a wind were blowing through them.

He rapped his palm on the lectern.

"I must insist!" *Rap.* "Please! Everyone!" *Rap, rap!* "With all respect to our fellow congregant, we cannot know if this is real—"

"It *is* real, Pastor!"

A new voice came from the back of the church. It was deep and gravelly, and all heads turned to see a tall, burly man in a brown sports coat, standing up, his large hands on the pew in front of him. He was Elias Rowe, a longtime African American congregant who owned a construction business. No one could recall him ever speaking to a crowd — until now.

His eyes darted. When he spoke again, his voice was almost reverent.

"I got a call, too," he said.

21

The Fourth Week

No one is certain who invented the telephone. Although the U.S. patent belongs to the Scottish-born Alexander Graham Bell, many believe he stole it away from an American inventor named Elisha Gray. Others maintain that an Italian named Manzetti or a Frenchman named Bourseul or a German named Reis or another Italian named Meucci deserves credit.

What few dispute is that all these men, working in the mid-nineteenth century, explored the idea of transmitting vocal vibrations from one place to another. But the very first telephonic conversation, between Bell and Thomas Watson, standing in separate rooms, contained these words: *Come here. I want to see you.*

In the uncountable human phone conversations since then, that concept has never been far from our lips. *Come here. I want to see you.* Impatient lovers. Long-distance friends. Grandparents talking to grandchildren. The telephone voice is but a seduction, a bread crumb to an appetite. *Come here. I want to see you.*

Sully had said it the last time he spoke to Giselle.

He'd been awakened at 6:00 a.m. in his Washington hotel room by a senior officer, Blake Pearson, who was supposed to fly an F/A-18 Hornet jet back to the West Coast. He was sick. Couldn't do it. Would Sully cover? He could stop in Ohio if he wanted, see Giselle for a few hours — she and Jules were there visiting her parents — then continue on. Sully quickly agreed. It would break up his two weeks of reserve duty. And the unexpected family visit would make the long hours of flying worthwhile.

"You can be here today?" Giselle said sleepily when he'd called her with the news.

"Yeah. In, like, four hours."

"You really want to?"

"Of course. I want to see you."

Had he known what would happen that day, he would have changed everything, never flown, never talked to Blake, never even woken up. Instead, his last telephone conversation with Giselle ended much like the world's first.

"I want to see you, too," she said.

Sully thought about that now as he turned the ignition in his father's Buick Regal, a nine-year-old car that mostly sat in the garage. That was the last time he'd flown a plane. The last time he'd seen an airport. The last time he'd heard his wife's voice. *I want to see you, too.*

He steered out of his parents' driveway and drove to Lake Street, the main drag of town, passing the bank and the post office and the bakery and the diner. Sidewalks were empty. A store owner stood in his doorway, broom in hand.

Only a few thousand people lived in Coldwater full-time. The summer tourists who fished the lake were gone now. The frozen custard stand was boarded shut. Most towns in northern Michigan buttoned up quickly come the fall, as if preparing for winter's hibernation.

A bad time, Sully realized, to be looking for work.

Amy Penn was hoping for something big. When the TV station asked if she could work a few weekdays, she thought yes, good, politics — or even better, a trial — anything that might lift her from the swamp of weekend news. She was thirty-one, no longer a kid in this business (although friends told her she was pretty enough to pass for twenty-five), and to get to a bigger job, she needed bigger stories. But big stories were hard to find on weekends in Alpena County, which were mostly reserved for football games, charity walks, and various fruit festivals.

"This could be my break," she'd excitedly told Rick, her architect fiancé. That was Thursday night. But by mid-Friday morning, after rising early, choosing a chartreuse skirt suit, blowing out her sideswept auburn bangs, and applying a hint of mascara and bold lipstick, Amy found herself in a window-less office at the station, hearing a story that was straight out of the weekend file.

"There's a woman out in Coldwater who says she's getting calls from a dead sister," said Phil Boyd, the station's news director.

"Really?" Amy said, because what do you say to that? She looked at Phil, a portly man with a scruffy reddish beard that made Amy think of a Viking, and wondered if he was serious — about the story, although the beard also warranted the question.

"Where's Coldwater?" she asked.

"About ninety miles west."

"How do we know she's getting calls?"

"She announced it during church."

"How did people react?"

"That's what you find out."

"So I should interview the woman."

Phil lifted an eyebrow. "That's a start."

"What if she's crazy?"

"Just bring back the tape."

Amy glanced at her nails. She'd done them special for this meeting.

"You know it's not real, Phil."

"Neither is the Loch Ness monster. And how many news stories have been done about that?"

"Right. OK."

Amy rose. She figured they would kill the piece once it proved laughable.

"What if it's a waste of time?" she asked.

"It's not a waste of time," Phil replied.

Only once she'd left did Amy guess what he meant: It's not a waste of time *because* *it's you*. It wasn't like they were using someone important.

What Phil had not revealed, and what Amy had not thought to ask, was how *Nine Action News* became aware of an event so far away.

It happened through a letter, which arrived mysteriously on Phil's desk. The letter was unsigned, no return address. Typed, double-spaced, it said only this:

A woman has been chosen. The gift of heaven on earth. This will become the biggest story in the world. Coldwater, Michigan. Ask a man of God. One call will confirm everything.

As news director, Phil was used to crazy mail. He mostly ignored it. But Alpena was not a market where you tossed aside "the biggest story in the world," at least not one that might help the ratings upon which Phil's job depended.

So he pulled up a list of churches in Coldwater and made a few calls. The first two had voice mail. But on his third try, Harvest of Hope Baptist Church, a secretary answered, and — *ask a man of God* — Phil requested to speak to the clergyman in charge.

"How did you find out?" the surprised pastor had said.

A phone today can find you anywhere. On a train, in a car, ringing from your pants pocket. Cities, towns, villages, even Bedouin tents are looped into the circuit, and the most remote of the world's citizens can now hold a device to their ears and speak.

But what if you don't want to be reached?

Elias Rowe climbed down the ladder and grabbed his clipboard. Cold weather would soon move his construction work indoors, and this remodel was one of the few jobs that would bring in money once winter came.

"We can start drywall Monday," he said.

The homeowner, a woman named Josie, shook her head. "I have family all weekend. They don't leave until Monday."

"Tuesday, then. I'll call my drywall guy."

Elias grabbed his cell phone. He noticed Josie staring.

"Elias. Did you really get . . . you know?"

"I don't know what I got, Josie."

Just then, the phone vibrated. They glanced at each other. Elias turned away and hunched over as he answered. His voice quieted.

"Hello? . . . Why are you calling me? . . . Stop. Whoever this is. Don't ever call me again!"

He squeezed the disconnect button so hard the phone squirted from his grip and slid onto the floor. Josie looked at his big hands.

They were shaking.

The town of Coldwater had five churches: Catholic, Methodist, Baptist, Protestant, and nondenominational. In Pastor Warren's lifetime, there had never been a meeting of all five.

Until now.

Had Katherine Yellin never stood up that Sunday morning, what happened in Coldwater might have passed like so many other miracles, held quiet, wrapped in whispers.

But once exposed to the public, miracles change things. People were talking — church people in particular. And so the five lead clergymen gathered in Warren's office as Mrs. Pulte, the church secretary, poured coffee for everyone. Warren glanced at the faces. He was the oldest by at least fifteen years.

"Can you tell us, Pastor," began the Catholic priest, Father William Carroll, a stout man in a clerical collar, "how many people were in services that Sunday?"

"Maybe a hundred," Warren said.

"And how many heard the woman's testimony?"

"All of them."

"Did they seem to believe her?"

"Yes."

"Is she prone to hallucinations?"

"No."

"Is she taking medication?"

"I don't think so."

"Then this actually happened? She got a call of some sort?"

Warren shook his head. "I don't know."

The Methodist minister leaned forward. "I've had seven appointments this week, and every one of them asked if it is possible to contact heaven."

"My people," added the Protestant minister, "asked why it happened in Warren's church and not ours."

"Mine, too."

Warren glanced around the table and saw that every clergyman had a raised hand.

"And you say a TV station is sending someone here next week?" Father Carroll asked.

28

"That's what the producer said," Warren replied.

"Well." Father Carroll put his palms together. "The question is, what are we going to do about it?"

The only thing scarier than leaving a small town is never leaving it at all. Sully said that once to Giselle, explaining why he'd gone out of state for college. Back then he thought he'd never return.

But here he was, back in Coldwater. And on Friday night, after dropping Jules at his parents' house ("We'll watch him tonight," his mother said. "You relax"), Sully went to a bar called Pickles, a place he and his high school buddies used to try and sneak into. He took a corner stool and ordered whisky with beer chasers, one and another and then one more. When he'd finished drinking, he paid and walked out the door.

He'd spent the last three days looking for work. Nothing. Next week he'd try the nearby towns. He zipped up his jacket and walked a few blocks, past countless bags of dead brown leaves awaiting collection. Off in the distance he saw lights. He heard the echo of a crowd. Not ready to go home, he walked in that direction until he reached the high school football field.

His old team was playing — the Coldwater Hawks, in their scarlet-and-white uniforms. From the looks of things, it was not a good season. The stands were three-quarters empty, the small crowd mostly families, with kids running the steps and parents using binoculars to find their sons in the middle of a pileup.

Sully had played football as a teenager. The Hawks weren't any better back then. Coldwater was smaller than the other schools it played, and most years it was lucky to field a team.

He approached the stands. He glanced at the scoreboard. Fourth quarter, Coldwater losing by three touchdowns. He dug his hands in his jacket pocket and watched a play.

"Harding!" someone yelled.

Sully froze. The alcohol had dulled his senses, and he'd forgotten the odds of someone recognizing him at his old school — even twenty years later. He turned his head slightly, trying to survey the crowd without being obvious. Maybe he'd imagined it. He turned back toward the field.

"Geronimo!" someone else yelled, laughing.

Sully swallowed. This time he didn't turn around. He stood perfectly still for maybe a minute. Then he walked away.

The Fifth Week

A fire truck came roaring down Cuthbert Road, red lights splashing against the October night sky. Five men of the Coldwater First Engine Volunteer Company began their systematic attack on the flames coming from the upper floor of the Rafferty home, a three-bedroom butter-colored colonial with red wooden shutters. By the time Jack pulled up in his squad car, they had everything under control.

Except the screaming woman.

She had long, wavy blond hair, wore a lime green sweater, and was being restrained on the lawn by two of Jack's guys, Ray and Dyson, who, considering the way they ducked her flailing arms, were losing the battle. They screamed at her over the spraying water.

"It's not safe, lady!"

"I have to get back in!"

"You can't!"

Jack stepped up. The woman was lithe and attractive, probably in her midthirties. And she was furious.

"Let me go!"

"Miss, I'm the police chief. What's the—"

"Please!" She whipped her face toward him, her eyes wild. "There's no time! It could be *burning right now!*"

Her voice was so shrill, even Jack was taken aback, and he honestly thought he'd seen every kind of reaction to flames: people sobbing in the wet grass, people howling like animals, people cursing the firemen for destroying their home with water, as if the fire were just going to put itself out.

"Havetogetinside, havetogetinside," the woman chanted hysterically as she strained against Dyson's grip.

"What's your name, Miss?" Jack said.

"Tess! Let me go!"

"Tess, is this worth risking your—"

"*Yes!*"

"What's in there?"

"You won't *believe me!*"

"Try me!"

She exhaled and dropped her head.

"My phone," she finally said. "I need it. I get calls . . ."

Her voice trailed off. Ray and Dyson looked at each other, rolling their eyes. Jack was silent. For a moment he didn't move. Finally, he waved at the two men — "I got this," he said — and they were only too happy to leave the crazy lady in Jack's authority.

Once they'd gone, he put his hands on her shoulders and looked straight into her pale blue eyes, trying to ignore, even in distress, how beautiful she looked.

"Where's the phone?" he asked.

★ ★ ★

Jack, by that point, had experienced four conversations with his dead son. They all came on Fridays, in his office at the police station, and he spoke with his body hunched over, receiver pressed to his ear.

The shock of hearing Robbie had given way to joy, even anticipation, and each conversation made Jack more curious about his son's surroundings.

"It's awesome, Dad."

"What does it look like?"

"You don't see things . . . You're inside them."

"What do you mean?"

"Like my childhood . . . I see it . . . So cool!"

Robbie laughed and Jack nearly broke down. The sound of his son's laughter. It had been so long.

"I don't understand, son. Tell me more."

"Love, Dad. Everything around me . . . love —"

The call had ended that abruptly — all the calls had been short — and Jack stayed at his desk for an hour, just in case the phone rang again. Finally, he drove home, feeling waves of euphoria, followed by fatigue. He knew he should be sharing this with Doreen — maybe with others too. But how would that look? The police chief in a small town, telling people he's speaking with the afterlife? Besides, a glimpse of heaven is often held close for fear of losing it, like a butterfly cupped in a child's hands. Jack, to that point, had figured he was the only one being contacted.

But now, approaching a house on fire, he thought about this screaming woman and her attachment to her phone, and wondered if he were not alone.

33

★　★　★

Joy and sorrow share the water. It was a song lyric that played in Sully's head as he pushed bubbles in the tub toward his son. The bathroom was as dated as the rest of the apartment, with penny-round tile and avocado green walls. A mirror sat on the floor, waiting for Sully to hang it.

"I don't wanna wash my hair, Dad."

"Why?"

"The stuff gets in my eyes."

"You've got to wash it eventually."

"Mommy let me skip it."

"Always?"

"Sometimes."

"We'll skip it tonight."

"Yes!"

Sully nudged the bubbles. He thought about Giselle, the way she bathed Jules as an infant, how she toweled him dry and wrapped him up in a hooded terry robe. Every movement in every muscle felt attached to how much Sully missed her.

"Dad?"

"Mmm?"

"Did you say good-bye to the plane?"

"To the plane?"

"When you jumped out."

"I didn't jump. I ejected."

"What's the difference?"

"It's just different, that's all."

He caught his reflection in the mirror — mussed hair, bloodshot eyes, jawline coated with stubble. He had spent another week searching for work in the nearby towns of Moss Hill and Dunmore. People were not encouraging. Bad economy, they said. *And with the lumberyard closed . . .*

He had to find a job. He'd been eleven years in the navy, one year in the reserves, and ten months in prison. Every job application had a question about criminal convictions. How could he hide that? How many people around here knew anyhow?

He thought about that football-field screamer. *Geronimo!* Maybe he'd imagined the whole thing. He'd been drunk, right?

"Do you miss your plane, Dad?"

"Mmm?"

"Do you miss your airplane?"

"You don't miss things, Jules. You miss people."

Jules stared at his knees, protruding from the water.

"So you didn't say good-bye."

"I couldn't."

"How come?"

"It happens too fast. It happens just like that."

Sully removed his hand from the tub and snapped his soapy fingers. He watched the bubbles settle.

Husband loses wife. Son loses mother. *Joy and sorrow share the water.*

Just like that.

Small towns begin with a sign. The words are as simple as the title to a story — WELCOME TO HABERVILLE, NOW ENTERING CLAWSON — but once you cross, you

35

are inside that story, and all that you do will be part of its tale.

Amy Penn drove past the sign VILLAGE OF COLDWATER, ESTABLISHED 1898, never realizing how, in the weeks to come, she would change it. All she knew was that her takeout coffee was long gone, the radio was static, and she had driven nearly two hours from Alpena with a constant sense of things shrinking, four lanes down to one, red lights to blinking yellow, overpass billboards to wooden signs in empty fields.

Amy wondered why, if souls in heaven were making contact with the living, it would happen way out here. Then she thought about haunted houses. They were never in the city, right? Always some creepy, lonely place on a hill.

She lifted her iPhone and took snapshots of Coldwater, scouting where she might set up her camera. There was a cemetery surrounded by a low brick wall. A one-garage fire-house. A library. Some stores on Lake Street were boarded up, while others seemed randomly chosen for survival: a market, a bead shop, a locksmith, a bookstore, a bank, a converted colonial home with a porch sign that read ATTORNEYS AT LAW.

Mostly Amy passed houses, old houses, Cape Cod or ranch style, narrow asphalt driveways, small shrubs leading to front doors. She was searching for the home of a Katherine Yellin, whom she had called on the phone (her number was listed) and who sounded a little too excited as she quickly offered her address, which Amy had entered into her phone's GPS system:

24755 Guningham Road. How ordinary an address for a miracle, Amy thought. But then, it wasn't a miracle. It was a colossal waste of time. *Do your best. Be a professional.* She turned her car — marked NINE ACTION NEWS on the side — and realized that not every house on the street had a number.

"Great," she mumbled. "How am I going to find this place?"

As it turned out, she needn't have worried. When she reached the house, Katherine was on the porch, waving.

Faith, it is said, is better than belief, because belief is when someone else does the thinking. Pastor Warren's faith was intact. Belief was coming harder. True, attendance was up at Harvest of Hope Church, and the congregation had fresh energy. Instead of lowered heads praying for employment, people were increasingly seeking forgiveness and making promises of better behavior. Katherine's claim of heavenly contact had inspired this.

Yet Warren remained troubled. He had spoken to that man from the Alpena TV station (how fast the news spreads!), but when asked to explain the phenomenon, he had no response. Why *would* the good Lord be granting two of his members sacred contact with the hereafter? Why those two? Why now?

He took off his reading glasses, rubbed his temples, and pushed his fingers through his fine white hair. His jowls hung loose, like an old hound dog's. His ears and nose seemed to grow larger each year. The days of existential wrestling were long behind him, something from his time in divinity school. Not now, at eighty-two, when his fingers shook just turning the pages in a prayer book.

Earlier in the week, he had called Katherine to his office. He informed her of the inquiry by the Alpena TV station. He suggested she be very cautious.

"What about Elias Rowe?" she asked.

"I haven't heard from him since that day in services."

Katherine looked almost pleased.

"Harvest of Hope was chosen for a reason, Pastor." She stood up. "And when a church is chosen, it should lead the march of faith, not block it, don't you think?"

He watched her pull on her gloves. It seemed more a threat than a question.

That night Elias stopped by Frieda's Diner — the only Cold-water eatery open past nine in the evening. He took the corner booth and ordered a cup of beef barley soup. The place was nearly empty. He was glad. He didn't want anyone asking him questions.

From the moment he'd stood up in church and made his simple declaration — "I got a call, too" — he'd felt like a man on the run. At the time, he'd only wanted to say that Katherine wasn't crazy. After all, he too had received a phone call from the other side — five of them now — and to deny it by silence seemed a sin.

But he was not happy about his calls. They came not from a departed loved one but from an embittered former worker named Nick Joseph, a roofer who'd been with Elias for ten years. Nick liked to drink and carouse, and he would call Elias with one excuse after another for his lateness or shoddy production. He often came to job sites drunk, and Elias would send him home without pay.

One day, Nick arrived clearly intoxicated. While on the roof, he got into a heated argument, spun wildly, and fell off, breaking an arm and injuring his back.

When Elias was notified, he was more angry than sympathetic. He gave instructions to have Nick drug-tested — despite Nick screaming at his coworkers not to call anybody. The ambulance came. The test was given. Nick failed. As a result, he lost his workers' compensation benefits.

Nick never worked again. He was in and out of the hospital, constantly fighting costs due to his insurance limitations.

A year after the accident, Nick was found dead in his basement, an apparent heart failure.

That was eighteen months ago.

Now, suddenly, Elias was getting phone calls.

"Why did you do it?" the first call began.

"Who is this?" Elias asked.

"It's Nick. Remember me?"

Elias hung up, shaking. He looked at the caller ID, but there was nothing there, just the word UNKNOWN.

A week later, in front of Josie, his customer, the phone had rung again.

"I needed help. Why didn't you help me? . . . God . . . forgives me. Why didn't you?"

"Stop. Whoever this is, don't ever call me again!" Elias had yelled, flicking off the phone and dropping it.

Why was this happening? Why him? Why now? A waitress brought his soup, and he swallowed a few spoonfuls, forcing an appetite he hadn't had in weeks. Tomorrow he would change his number. Make it unlisted. If these calls were truly a sign from God, he had done his part. He had confirmed it.

He wanted no more of this miracle.

The Sixth Week

Two years before he invented the telephone, Alexander Bell yelled into a dead man's ear.

The ear, eardrum, and related bones had been carved off a cadaver by Bell's associate, a surgeon, so that Bell, then a young elocution teacher, could study how the eardrum carried sound. He attached a piece of straw to it, put a piece of smoked glass on the other end, and placed a funnel on the outside.

When Bell yelled down the funnel, the eardrum vibrated, moving the straw, which marked the glass. Bell had originally hoped these markings could help his deaf students learn to speak — including his future wife, a young woman named Mabel Hubbard. But he quickly realized an even larger implication.

If sound could vibrate an electrical current the way it did straw, then words could travel as far as electricity. All you'd need is one sort of mechanical eardrum on each end.

A cadaver's skull had sparked that insight. Thus the dead were already part of the telephone, two years before anyone saw one.

The autumn leaves fall early in northern Michigan, and by mid-October the trees were bare. This gave an eerie, empty feeling to the streets of Coldwater, as if a powerful force had vacuumed through them, leaving the town vacant.

It would not last.

A few days before the rest of the world learned of Coldwater's miracle, Jack Sellers, freshly shaved, in a crisp blue shirt, his hair combed straight back, stood inside Tess Rafferty's charred kitchen. He watched her dump a spoonful of instant coffee into her already full cup.

"More caffeine this way," she said. "I try to stay awake, in case a call comes late."

Jack nodded. He looked around. The fire hadn't affected the lower level so much, although smoke damage made the tan walls look like half-toasted bread. He saw an old answering machine on the counter, salvaged from the fire, and of course, Tess's precious telephone, a beige Cortelco wall unit, returned to its place, hanging just to the left of the cabinets.

"So you only have that one phone?"

"It's my mom's old house. She liked it that way."

"And your calls are always on Friday, too?"

Tess paused. "This isn't a police investigation, is it?"

"No, no. I'm as confused as you are."

Jack sipped his coffee and tried to limit how often he looked at Tess's face. He had stopped by, he'd explained, to inspect the fire damage — in a small town like Coldwater, police and fire departments worked together — but they both knew it was a ruse. After all, he'd had her telephone retrieved from the blaze. Why would he do that unless he knew there was something special about it?

Within fifteen minutes, they had confessed to each other. It was like sharing the world's most impatient secret.

"Yes," Tess said, "my calls are only on Fridays."

"Always here? Never at work?"

"I haven't been to work. I run a day care center. The staff has been covering for me. I've been making up excuses. To be honest, I've haven't even left the house. It's silly. But I don't want to miss her."

"Can I ask you something?"

"Uh-huh."

"What did she say the first time? Your mother?"

Tess smiled. "The first time was a message. The next time she wanted to tell me about heaven. The third time, I asked her what it was like, and she just kept saying, 'It's beautiful.' She said the pain we suffer is a way to make us appreciate what comes next."

Tess paused. "She also said this wouldn't last."

"What?"

"This connection."

"Did she say how long?"

Tess shook her head.

"So you haven't told anyone else?" Jack asked.

"No. Have you?"

"No."

"Not even your wife?"

"We're divorced."

"She's still his mother."

"I know. But what would I tell her?"

Tess lowered her eyes. She looked at her bare feet. It had been two months since her last pedicure.

"When did you lose him? Your son?"

"Two years ago. Afghanistan. Came out of a building he was inspecting, and a car exploded six feet in front of him."

"That's awful."

"Yeah."

"But you buried him. There was a funeral?"

"I saw the body, if that's what you mean."

Tess winced. "Sorry."

Jack stared into his cup. They teach you, as children, that you might go to heaven. They never teach you that heaven might come to you.

"Do you think it's just the two of us?" Tess asked.

Jack looked away, embarrassed by the sudden connection he felt to this beautiful woman at least ten years his junior. The way she said "the two of us."

"Maybe," he said, feeling compelled to add, "maybe not."

Amy steered her *Nine Action News* car up the highway ramp. She stepped on the gas, and when the road broadened to three lanes, she exhaled.

After three days in Coldwater, she felt as if she were returning to the real world. Her camera was in the trunk. Next to it was a canvas bag with her tapes. She thought back to her conversations with Katherine Yellin, the redheaded, blue-eye-shadowed woman whose beauty had probably peaked in high school. Despite the old Ford she drove and the homemade coffee cake she served, she was a bit too intense for Amy. They were not so far apart in age — Katherine was in her midforties; Amy was thirty-one — but Amy doubted she could ever seize on anything as fervently as Katherine had seized on the afterlife.

"Heaven awaits us," Katherine had said.

"Let me get the camera set up."

"My sister says it's glorious."

"That's amazing."

"Are you a believer, Amy?"

"This isn't about me."

"But you are, aren't you, Amy?"

"Yes. Sure. I am."

Amy tapped the steering wheel. It was a small lie. So what? She had gotten the interview. She wasn't coming back. She would edit what she had, see if Phil even aired it, and resume her hunt for a better job.

She lifted her iPhone and checked it for messages. In her mind, Coldwater was already a speck in her rearview mirror.

But nothing changes a small town more than an outsider.

The tapes in her trunk would prove it.

Four Days Later

NEWS REPORT
Channel 9, Alpena

(Images of Coldwater telephone poles.)
AMY: It seems, at first, like any other small town, with telephone poles and wires. But according to one citizen of Coldwater, those wires may be connected to a higher power than the phone company!
(Katherine on camera, holding phone.)
KATHERINE: I received a call from my older sister, Diane.
(Photograph of Diane.)
AMY: Here's the twist. Diane died nearly two years ago from an aneurysm. Katherine Yellin got her first call last month, and says she's been getting calls every Friday since.
(Katherine on camera.)
KATHERINE: Oh, yes, I am sure it is her. She tells me she is happy in heaven. She says that she's . . .
(Camera closer; Katherine cries.)
. . . she's waiting for me, that they are waiting for all of us.
AMY: Do you believe this is a miracle?

KATHERINE: Of course.

(Amy, in front of Harvest of Hope Baptist Church.)
AMY: Katherine announced her call at this church last Sunday. The reaction was a mix of shock and hope. Of course, not everyone is convinced.

(Image of Father Carroll.)
FATHER CARROLL: We must be very cautious when speaking about eternity. These are matters best left to — if you pardon the way it sounds — higher authorities.

(Amy, walking under phone line.)
AMY: At least one other person claims to have received a call from the other side, although that person chose not to speak with us. Still, here in Coldwater, people are wondering if they might be the next to get a phone call from heaven.

(Amy stops walking.)
I'm Amy Penn, *Nine Action News*.

Pastor Warren flipped off the TV set. His face was drawn in thought. Perhaps not many people had seen the report, he told himself. It was very short, no? And people forget about the news as quickly as they view it.

He was glad he had not spoken to the reporter, despite several dogged attempts on her part. He had explained, patiently, that it was not for a pastor to comment on such events, as the church had not taken an official position on it. He was happy to let Father Carroll make a general statement, something the other clergymen had agreed upon.

Warren locked his office and walked into the empty sanctuary. He knelt, his knees aching, shut his eyes, and

47

said a prayer. At moments like these, he felt closest to the Lord. Alone in His house. He allowed himself the idea that the Almighty had taken control of this situation, and that would be the end of it — one outburst by a congregant, one curious TV reporter, and nothing more.

On his way out, he took his scarf off the hook and wrapped it tightly around his neck. It was well after five, so the phones had been turned off. Warren left without noticing that every line on Mrs. Pulte's desk was now blinking.

In the dream — which Sully had several times a week — he was back in the cockpit, helmet on, visor down, oxygen mask in place. He felt a terrible thud. The plane wobbled. The gauges froze. He pulled a handle, and a canopy blew away. A rocket exploded beneath him. His skeleton screamed in pain. Then everything went silent. He saw a small fire, far below him, the wreckage of his aircraft. He saw another fire. Even smaller.

As he floated toward earth, a voice whispered, *Don't go down there. Stay in the sky. It's safe up here.*

Giselle's voice.

He jolted awake, sweating. His eyes darted. He was on the couch in his apartment, having fallen asleep after two vodka and cranberry juices. The TV was on. Channel 9, the Alpena station. He blinked at the image of a female reporter standing in front of a familiar-looking church. It was Harvest of Hope, a mile from where Sully was now.

"Still, here in Coldwater, people are wondering if they might be the next to get a phone call from heaven."

"You gotta be kidding me," Sully mumbled.

"Can we eat now, Dad?"

He lifted his head to see Jules leaning against the side of the couch.

"Sure, buddy. Daddy was just sleeping."

"You always sleep."

Sully found his glass and swigged the now-warm alcohol. He groaned and sat up. "I'll make some spaghetti."

Jules pulled a loose piece of rubber on his sneakers. Sully realized he had to buy the kid new shoes.

"Dad?"

"Yeah?"

"When is Mommy going to call us?"

Enough was enough. Although Tess had been sending e-mails to work, saying she needed time to herself and please not to call her, when news of the house fire reached her coworkers, two of them — Lulu and Samantha — drove out to her place. They banged on the door. Tess opened it, shielding her eyes against the sun.

"Oh my God," Lulu gasped. Their friend looked thinner and paler than the last time they'd seen her. Her long blond hair was pulled back in a thick ponytail, which made her face seem even more gaunt.

"Tess, are you OK?"

"I'm all right."

"Can we come in?"

"Sure." She stepped back. "Sorry."

Once inside, Tess's friends looked around. The lower level seemed as tidy as ever, except for smoke stains that speckled the walls. But the upstairs was dark with burn marks. A bedroom door was charred. The stairs were blocked off by two pieces of wood, crossed in a box frame.

"Did you build that?" Samantha asked.

"No. This guy did."

"What guy?"

"A guy from the police department."

Samantha flashed Tess a look. They had been friends for years, and had jointly opened the day care center. They ate together, covered each other's shifts, shared every delight and every distress. A guy? A fire? And she didn't know about it? Samantha stepped forward, grabbed Tess's hands, and said, "Hey. It's me. What's going on?"

Over the next two hours, Tess told her coworkers what had seemed unimaginable just a few weeks earlier. She detailed the calls. Her mother's voice. She explained the fire, how the furnace in the basement had gone out, how she'd put space heaters around the house and one of them shorted out while she was sleeping and with one spark — *whoosh!* — the second level was toast.

She told them about Jack Sellers saving the phone and answering machine from the fire. She confessed how she'd feared she'd lost her mother again, how she'd prayed and fasted, and how, when a call came three days later and she heard the words — *Tess, it's me* — she'd fallen to her knees.

When she finished talking, they were all crying.

"I don't know what to do," Tess whispered.

"Are you one hundred percent sure?"

"It's her, Lulu. I swear it."

Samantha shook her head in amazement. "The whole town is talking about those two people from Harvest of Hope. And all this time, you were getting calls too."

"Wait," Tess said, swallowing. "There are *others*?"

"It was on the news," Lulu confirmed.

The three friends exchanged glances.

"Makes you wonder," Samantha said, "how many more people this is happening to."

Two days after the TV report, Katherine Yellin was awakened at 6:00 a.m. by a noise on her porch.

She had been dreaming of the night Diane died. They'd had plans to go to a classical music concert. Instead, Katherine found her sister collapsed on the living room floor, between the glass coffee table and the tufted leather ottoman. She dialed 911 and screamed the address, then cradled Diane's body, holding her cooling hand until the ambulance arrived. An aneurysm is a swelling of the aorta; a rupture can kill you in seconds. Katherine would later reason that if anything were going to take away her beautiful, funny, precious older sister, it would be that her heart was so big, it exploded.

In the dream, Diane miraculously opened her eyes and said she needed to use the phone.

Where is it, Kath?

Then Katherine was jolted awake by the sound of . . . what was that? Humming?

She slipped on her robe and walked nervously downstairs. She pulled the curtain from her living room window.

She put a hand to her chest.

On her lawn, in the early-morning light, she saw five people in their overcoats, on their knees and holding hands, their eyes closed.

The noise that had woken Katherine was clear now.

It was the sound of people praying.

Amy had once again selected her finest suit and taken care with her makeup, but she had no expectations as she sat down with Phil Boyd. He didn't think much of her talent, she knew that. Yet from the start of this conversation, she detected a new tone.

"So, what did you think of Coldwater?"

"Um . . . it's a small town. Pretty typical."

"And the people?"

"Nice enough."

"How's your relationship with this" — he glanced at a note-pad — "Katherine Yellin?"

"Fine. I mean, she told me the whole thing. What happened. What she thinks happened, anyhow."

"Does she trust you?"

"I think so."

"You went to her house?"

"Yeah."

"Did the phone ring while you were there?"

"No."

"But you saw the phone?"

"It's a cell. Pink. She carries it everywhere."

"And the other guy?"

"He didn't want to talk. I asked. I went to where he works, and—"

Phil held up a palm as if to say, *Don't worry, it happens*. Amy was surprised he was this understanding — or this interested in what she considered a nothing story. Weren't people always claiming to get signs from the "other side"? They saw Mother Mary on a garden wall or Jesus's face in an English muffin. Nothing ever came of it.

"How would you feel about going back?"

"To Coldwater?"

"Yes."

"To do another story?"

"To *stay* on the story."

She lifted her eyebrows. "You mean, wait until they hear from another dead person? Report on it like it's *news*?"

Phil drummed his fingers on the desktop. "Let me show you something." He rolled his chair to his computer screen, banged a few keys, then spun the monitor.

"Did you check the Internet post of your story?"

"Not yet," Amy said, leaving out the reason — that her fiancé, Rick, had confronted her the minute she got home last night, another one of their arguments over how much she valued her career versus how much she valued him.

"Take a look at the comments," Phil said. He was almost smiling.

Amy swept her bangs back with one hand and leaned forward. Beneath the story headlined COLDWATER RESIDENTS CLAIM HEAVENLY CONTACT was a list of e-mailed responses. She saw enough to fill the screen — which was odd, since stories she did usually drew zero.

"That's good, huh?" Amy asked. "What's that . . . five, six . . . eight responses?"

"Look closer," Phil said.

She did. Atop the list she saw something she'd missed, something that sent a shiver down the back of her neck:

Comments: 8 of 14,706.

Sully scooped potatoes onto his son's plate. It was Thursday night. Dinner with his parents. They invited him often, trying to save him money. He still hadn't found a job. Still hadn't unpacked the boxes. He couldn't rouse himself to do much of anything except drink, smoke, take Jules to school — and think.

He wished he could stop thinking.

"Can I have more?" Jules asked.

"That's plenty," Sully said.

"Sully, let him have more—"

"Mom."

"What?"

"He can't waste food. I'm trying to teach him."

"We can afford it."

54

"Well, not everyone can."

Sully's father coughed, which halted the conversation. He put down his fork.

"I saw that news car from Alpena today," he said. "It was parked at the bank."

"Everyone is talking about that story," his mother said. "It's spooky. Dead people making phone calls."

"Please," Sully mumbled.

"You think they're making it up?"

"Don't you?"

"Well, I'm not sure." She cut a piece of chicken. "Myra knows that man from the church. Elias Rowe. He built her house."

"And?"

"She says he found a mistake once in her billing and brought her a check for the difference. Drove all the way over. At night."

"And that means?"

"That he's honest."

Sully poked at his potatoes. "One has nothing to do with the other."

"What do you think, Fred?"

Sully's father exhaled. "I think people believe what they want to believe."

Sully silently wondered how that sentence applied to him.

"Well, if it makes that poor woman feel better about losing her sister, what harm does it do?" his mother said. "My aunt used to talk to ghosts all the time."

"Mom," Sully snapped. He nodded toward Jules and whispered, "Do you mind?"

"Oh," she said, softly.

"Hell, the Bible says God spoke through a burning bush," Fred said. "Is that any stranger than a telephone?"

"Can we drop it?" Sully asked.

They clanked their silverware and chewed silently.

"Can I have more potatoes now?" Jules asked.

"Finish what you have," Sully said.

"He's hungry," his mother said.

"He eats when he's with me, Mom."

"I didn't mean—"

"I can provide for my son!"

"Easy, Sully," his father said.

More silence. It seemed to lie on the table between them. Finally, Jules put his fork down and asked, "What does 'provide' mean?"

Sully stared at his plate. "It means to give to someone."

"Grandma?"

"Yes, sweetie?"

"Can you provide me a phone?"

"Why?"

"I want to call Mommy in heaven."

"You coming to Pickles, Jack?"

The day shift was over. The guys were going for a beer. Coldwater did not have a nighttime police force. Emergencies were handled by 911.

"I'll meet you there," Jack said. He waited until they left. Only Dyson was in the building now, in the break room with the microwave. Jack smelled popcorn. He shut his office door.

"*Dad, it's me . . .*"

"Where are you, Robbie?"

"*You know where. Don't keep it secret. You can tell them the truth now.*"

"What truth?"

"*The end is not the end.*"

Jack had had that exchange less than an hour earlier. That made six Fridays in a row. Six calls from a boy he had buried. He punched up the list of received numbers on his phone. The most recent, Robbie's call, was marked UNKNOWN. Once again — as he had done countless times already — he pressed redial and listened to a series of short, high-pitched beeps. Then nothing. No connection. No voice mail. Not even a recording. Just silence. He wondered again — now that, according to TV, there were others besides Tess and Jack receiving these calls — whether he should start some kind of investigation. But how could he investigate something without admitting he was a part of it? He hadn't even told Doreen yet. Besides, this was Coldwater. They had one squad car, a couple of computers, old metal file cabinets, and a budget that allowed them to operate six days a week.

He grabbed his coat, slipped it on, and caught his reflection in a glass-framed map, the strong chin that he'd once shared with his son. They had both been tall, with loud voices and hearty laughs. "My lumberjacks," Doreen used to call them. Jack thought back to the day Robbie asked him about joining the marines.

"Are you sure about this, son?"

"*You* fought, Dad."

"It's not for everyone."

"But I want to make a difference."

"Could you see yourself *not* doing it?"

"No, I can't."

"Then I guess you have your answer."

Doreen was livid. She insisted Jack could have talked Robbie out of going, instead of being so stupidly proud of his son's courage.

In the end, Robbie enlisted — and Jack and Doreen split up. Four years later, when two soldiers came to Coldwater to deliver the bad news, they had to choose between houses. They went to Jack's house first. Doreen never forgave him, as if that were also his fault, along with Robbie dying ten thousand miles away.

The end is not the end.

Jack leaned forward, still wearing his coat, and once again pressed the redial button on the phone. The same beeps. The same silence. He dialed a different number.

"Hello?" he heard Tess Rafferty say.

"It's Jack Sellers. Did you get a call today?

"Yes."

"Could I stop by?"

"Yes."

She hung up.

In the early 1870s, Alexander Bell showed Mabel's father — his future father-in-law — a list of his proposed inventions. Gardiner G. Hubbard was impressed with several of them. But when Bell mentioned a wire that could transmit the human voice, Hubbard scoffed.

"Now you're talking nonsense," he said.

On Saturday morning, Sully, fed up with the nonsense of heavenly phone calls, parked his father's car outside a trailer marked ROWE CONSTRUCTION, which he'd located on the outskirts of town. It was important to confront this thing, shoot it down before it did more damage. Grief was hard enough. Why should he have to explain hocus-pocus lies to his child? *I want to call Mommy in heaven.* Sully was angry, wound up, and he hadn't done anything besides mourn in so long, this actually felt like a purpose. In the navy he had investigated cases within his squadron — accidents, equipment failures. He was good at it. His commanding officer told him to try for the JAG corps, be a full-time legal guy. But Sully preferred flying.

Still, it hadn't taken much to track down Elias Rowe's place of business. Sully approached the trailer, which sat at the front of a dirt lot. Two skiffs, a backhoe, and a Ford pickup truck were parked out back.

He stepped inside.

"Hi, is Mr. Rowe in?"

The heavyset woman behind a desk had her hair pulled up in a bandana. She studied Sully before answering.

"No, I'm sorry. He's not."

"When does he get back?"

"He's out on jobs. Is this about a new project?"

"Not exactly."

Sully looked around. The trailer was cramped, crowded with blueprints and file cabinets.

"Do you want to leave a name and number?"

"I'll come by later."

He returned to his car, got in, and cursed. As he began to pull away, he heard an engine start. He looked in his rearview and saw a man behind the wheel of the Ford pickup. Had he been there the whole time? Sully stopped his car, jumped out, and raced to the truck, waving his arms until it stopped. He approached the window.

"Sorry," he said, panting. "Are you Elias Rowe?"

"Do I know you?" Elias asked.

"My mother knows somebody you know. Look." He exhaled. How was he going to put this? "I'm a dad, OK? A single dad. My wife . . . died."

"I'm sorry," Elias said. "I have to—"

"My son, he's still dealing with it. But this stuff about phone calls from heaven. You're one of those . . . you say you got a call?"

Elias bit his lip. "I don't know what I got."

"See? That's the thing. You don't *know*! But come on! You have to believe it wasn't someone calling from the *dead*, right?"

Elias stared at the dashboard.

"My son. He thinks . . ." Sully's heart was racing. "He thinks his mother is going to call him now. Because of your story."

Elias set his jaw. "I'm sorry. I don't know how to help you."

"It would help me — it would help *him* — if you told everybody it's *not true*."

Elias squeezed the wheel and said, "I'm sorry," again, this time as he pressed the accelerator. The truck lurched forward and turned onto the street, leaving Sully standing, with his palms up, alone in the lot.

That evening, Elias drove to a public pier on Lake Michigan and waited for the last light to fade from the sky. He thought about the guy who'd stopped him earlier. He thought about the son he'd mentioned. He thought about Nick and Katherine and Pastor Warren and the sanctuary.

Finally, when darkness was complete, he stepped out of his truck, walked to the end of the pier, and took his phone from his coat pocket. He remembered when he was a boy and his mother would give away their leftovers to a soup kitchen. One time he asked, Why couldn't they just throw their food out the way most people did?

"What the Lord gives you," his mother had said, "you do not squander."

Elias looked at his phone and mumbled, "Forgive me, Lord, if I am squandering your gift." Then he threw the phone high and far toward the water. He lost sight of it in the darkness, but heard a tiny *plop* as it broke the lake's surface.

He stood there for a minute. Then he got back in the truck. He had decided to leave Coldwater for a while, let his chief foreman oversee the jobs. He didn't want any more strangers running up to him, seeking help. He had canceled the number, canceled the account, and rid himself of the actual unit.

He drove out of town feeling relieved and exhausted, as if he'd just slammed a door against a rainstorm.

The Seventh Week

As the days passed in Coldwater, Katherine noticed people staring at her. In the bank. At Sunday-morning service. Even here in the market, where she'd been shopping for years. Daniel, the stock boy, glanced away when she caught him looking, and Teddy, the bearded man behind the meat counter, caught her gaze and too quickly said, "Hey, Katherine, how's it going?" At the end of the aisle were two older women in long coats, who didn't even bother to hide their pointing.

"You're the one, aren't you?" they asked.

Katherine nodded, unsure of how to respond. She quickly pushed her cart away.

"May God bless you," one of them said.

Katherine turned. "May God bless you too."

Katherine wrestled with her desire to be humble, as the Bible said, and her desire to shout in glory, as the Bible also said. It made every encounter a challenge. All these eyes on her! She'd had no idea how one TV interview could make you so *visible*.

At the checkout counter, she lined up behind an overweight, balding man in a Detroit Lions sweatshirt.

He unloaded his basket. When he looked at her, his expression changed.

"I know you," he said.

She forced a smile.

"You showed us a house once. Me and the missus."

"I did?"

"It was too expensive."

"Oh."

"I ain't been working."

"I'm sorry."

"It is what it is."

The woman behind the cash register eyed the two of them as she rang up the man's few items, a large bag of potato chips, butter, two cans of tuna, and a six-pack of beer.

"Do they let you talk to anyone else?" the man asked.

"I'm sorry?"

"When they call you. The spirits from heaven. Could you talk to someone else if you wanted to?"

"I don't understand."

"My father. He died last year. I was wondering . . ."

Katherine bit her lip. The man looked down. "It's all right," he said. He handed the cashier a wad of one-dollar bills, took his bag, and left.

Three Days Later

NEWS REPORT
Channel 9, Alpena

(Amy stands in front of Harvest of Hope Baptist Church.)

AMY: As we told you first here on *Nine Action News*, it all started in this small town, when a woman named Katherine Yellin informed her church of a phone call from a most unlikely source — her sister, Diane, who died two years ago.

(Close-up of Katherine and Amy.)

KATHERINE: She's called me six times now.

AMY: Six times?

KATHERINE: Yes. Always on a Friday.

AMY: Why Friday?

KATHERINE: I don't know.

AMY: Does she explain how she's doing this?

KATHERINE: No. She just tells me she loves me. She tells me about heaven.

AMY: What does she say?

KATHERINE: She says everyone you lose here, you find again there. Our family is all together. Her. My parents.

(People on lawn of Katherine's house.)

AMY: Since *Nine Action News* first reported the strange calls, dozens of people have flocked into Coldwater to meet Katherine. They wait for hours to talk to her.

(Katherine speaks to them in a circle.)

OLDER WOMAN: I believe she has been chosen by God. I lost my sister too.

AMY: Are you hoping for a similar miracle?

OLDER WOMAN: Yes. *(She starts crying.)* I would give anything to speak to my sister again.

(Amy, standing in front of house.)

AMY: We should note that so far no one has been able to verify these calls. But one thing is certain.

(She points to crowd.)

Lots of people believe that miracles *do* happen.

(She looks at camera.)

In Coldwater, I'm Amy Penn, *Nine Action News*.

Pastor Warren tugged on his hat and headed out, giving a small wave to Mrs. Pulte, who was on the phone. She lowered the handset and whispered, "When will you be back?" but was interrupted by the other line ringing. "Harvest of Hope . . . Yes . . . Can you hold a minute, please?"

Warren exited, shaking his head. For years, the church could go all morning without a phone call. Now poor Mrs. Pulte barely had time to use the bathroom. They were getting calls from around the country. People asked if their Sunday services were available over the Internet. They asked if there were special prayer books the congregants used — especially the ones who heard the blessed voices from above.

Warren hobbled down the street, leaning into a whipping autumn wind. He noticed three unfamiliar cars in his church parking lot, and saw unfamiliar faces staring out through the windows. Coldwater was not a place where strangers went unnoticed. Families lived here for generations. Houses and businesses were passed on to children. Longtime residents were buried in the local cemetery, which dated to the early 1900s. A few of the tombstones were so worn and faded you could no longer read them.

Warren recalled the days when he knew every congregant in town, and was healthy enough to visit most of them on foot, hearing the occasional "Morning, Pastor!" yelled from a porch. The familiarity had always comforted him, like a low, steady hum. But lately that hum had turned to a screech. He felt disquieted — not only by strange cars in his parking lot or a news reporter in his sanctuary.

For the first time in his life, Warren felt less belief than others around him.

"Pastor, please, have a seat."

The mayor, Jeff Jacoby, pointed to a chair. Warren sat down. The mayor's office was just two blocks from the church, in the rear of the First National Bank. Jeff was also the bank president.

"Exciting times, huh, Pastor?"

"Hmm?" Warren said.

"Your church. Two TV reports! When was the last time that happened in Coldwater?"

"Mmm."

"I know Katherine from the mortgage world. She took her sister's death real hard. To get her back that way . . . wow."

"Do you think she's gotten her back?"

Jeff chuckled. "Hey. You're the expert."

Warren studied the mayor's face, his thick eyebrows, bulbous nose, a smile that shot up quickly, revealing capped teeth.

"Listen, Pastor, we've gotten a lot of calls." As if on cue, he checked his cell phone for messages. "There are rumors that it's not just Katherine or the other fellow — what's his name?"

"Elias."

"Yeah. Where did he disappear to?"

"I don't know."

"Well, anyhow, I was thinking it would help to have a town hall meeting, you know? Just for Coldwater folks. Answer some questions. See what to do next. I mean, this thing is getting pretty big. I'm told the hotel in Moss Hill is filled."

Warren shook his head. The hotel was filled? In October? What did all those people want? Jeff was typing something on his phone. Warren glanced at the man's shoes, supple brown leather with perfectly tied laces.

"I think you should lead the meeting, Pastor."

"Me?"

"It happened in your church."

"That wasn't my doing."

Jeff put down his phone. He lifted a pen and clicked it twice.

"I noticed you haven't been in those TV reports. Are you not speaking to the media?"

"Katherine is speaking enough."

Jeff chuckled. "The woman *can* talk. Anyhow, we should have a plan, Pastor. I don't have to tell you our town's been hurting. This little miracle could mean real opportunities."

"Opportunities?"

"Yeah. Maybe tourist stuff? And visitors gotta eat."

Warren folded his hands in his lap.

"Do you believe this is a miracle, Jeffrey?"

"Ha! You're asking *me*?"

Warren said nothing. Jeff lowered the pen. He flashed those capped teeth again.

"OK, honestly, Pastor? I have no idea what's happening with Katherine. I don't know if it's real or made-up. But have you noticed the traffic out there? I'm a businessman. And I can tell you this much—"

He pointed to the window.

"That is good for business."

Their most recent conversation had only been a minute long, but Tess could not forget it.

"Do you still feel things in heaven, Mom?"

"*Love.*"

"Anything else?"

"*A waste of time, Tess.*"

"What is?"

"*Anything else.*"

"I don't understand."

"*Anger, regret, worry . . . They disappear once you are here . . . Don't lose yourself . . . inside yourself . . .*"

"Mom. I'm so sorry."

"*What for?*"

"For everything. Fighting with you. Doubting you."

"*Tess . . . these things are all forgiven . . . Please, now . . .*"

"What?"

"*Forgive yourself.*"

"Oh, Mom."

"*Tess.*"

"I really miss you."

A long pause.

"*Do you remember making cookies?*"

The line went dead.

Tess burst into tears.

Cookies — and other desserts — had brought Tess and Ruth together. Ruth ran a small catering business and, unable to afford any help, she used Tess as her assistant. Ruth had been supporting herself since divorcing her husband, Edwin, when Tess was five. Edwin bolted to Iowa without the slightest custody effort and was never seen in Coldwater again. People in town rolled their eyes and whispered, "Now *there's* a story and a half." But over the years, when Tess would ask about her father, Ruth would only say, "Why speak about unpleasant things?" After a while, Tess stopped asking.

70

Like most children from broken homes, however, Tess yearned for the party that was missing and battled with the one that remained. A single mom was not common in Coldwater, and it bothered Tess that wherever she went, people asked, "How's your mother?" as if divorce were some kind of lingering illness that required regular checkups. Tess often felt like a caregiver for her mother's solitude. At weddings, she and Ruth silently organized desserts in the kitchen and, when the music played outside, they glanced at each other like fellow wall-flowers. With most everyone at these affairs attached to a spouse, Ruth and Tess were viewed as a couple; it made people more comfortable that Mrs. Rafferty had *somebody*.

The Catholic church was another story. Divorce was still frowned upon there, and Ruth endured the disapproving stares of other women, which grew more intense as Tess blossomed into a stunning teenager, whom the men always seemed to pat on the shoulder when they said hello. Tess grew weary of the hypocrisy and stopped attending services once she graduated from high school. Ruth implored her to return, but she said, "It's a joke, Mom. They don't even *like* you there."

Right up to the end, when Ruth was in a wheelchair, Tess refused to take her to Catholic Mass. But now she sat in her living room, Samantha sitting across from her, and wondered if she should call her old priest.

Part of her wanted to keep these talks with her mother small, private, the way a dream can always be private, as long as you don't share it.

On the other hand, something supernatural was happening in Coldwater. Jack Sellers. The woman on TV. The other man they mentioned from Harvest of Hope. She was not alone. Maybe the church could provide an answer.

These things are all forgiven, Ruth had said.

She looked at Samantha.

"Call Father Carroll," she said.

Jack pulled his car into the driveway. His heart was pounding.

He had made up his mind to tell Doreen about the calls, today, no delaying. He had phoned to say there was something they needed to discuss, and he planned to get right to it when he walked in, no waiting until something distracted her and he lost his nerve. He didn't care if her new husband, Mel, was there. This was Doreen's son. She had the right to know. Jack figured she'd be mad that he hadn't told her thus far. But he was used to her being mad. And every day he waited made it worse.

Coldwater was changing. Strangers were flocking in. People were even praying on a woman's lawn! Jack and Ray drove somewhere every day to address a new complaint, a parking problem, a disturbance of the peace. Everybody carried a cell phone. Every ring made people anxious. There was now a town meeting being scheduled to discuss the phenomenon. The least Jack could do was tell Doreen they were part of it.

He walked to the porch, took a deep breath, and gripped the doorknob. It was open. He let himself in.

"Hey, it's me," he announced.

No response. He went to the kitchen. He walked down the hall.

"Doreen?"

He heard a sniffle. He stepped into the living room area.

"Doreen?"

She was sitting on the couch, holding a photo of Robbie. Tears fell down her cheeks. Jack swallowed. It was one of those times. He would have to wait.

"You OK?" he asked softly.

She blinked back tears. She pressed her lips together.

"Jack," she said, "I just spoke to our son."

"Mr. Harding to see Ron Jennings."

The receptionist picked up the phone and Sully quickly took a seat, hoping nobody noticed him.

The *Northern Michigan Gazette* was a modest operation. An open floor plan revealed the inexorable geography of journalism, editorial to one side, business to the other. On the left, the desks were messy, papers were stacked in chaotic corners, a white-haired reporter had a phone to his ear. To the right the desktops were tidier, the neckties tighter, and one office was noticeably larger than all others. Now emerging from that office was the publisher, Ron Jennings, pear-shaped, balding, tinted eyeglasses. He waved at Sully, motioning him to come back. Sully rose and made his feet move one in front of the other, just as he had done upon emerging from prison.

"Mark told me you were coming by," Jennings said, offering his hand. "We went to college together."

"Yeah, thanks for seeing" — Sully's voice suddenly choked dry, and he swallowed — "me."

Jennings looked hard at Sully, and Sully hated what he must have looked like; a man loathing the job he was about to ask for. What choice did he have? He needed work. There was nothing else out there. He forced a smile and stepped inside the office, feeling about as far from a fighter pilot as a man can get.

Sales, he thought glumly. *A newspaper.*

He wondered if they'd written about him.

"So, as you can guess, we're pretty busy around here," Jennings said, grinning from behind his desk. "This heavenly-phone-calls story has us hopping."

He held up the latest edition and read the headline. "'Ghosts from the Other Side?' Who the heck knows, right? Good for the paper, though. We've had to reprint our last two editions."

"Wow," Sully said politely.

"See that guy?" Jennings nodded toward the white-haired man on the editorial side, shirt and tie, phone to his ear. "Elwood Jupes. Was the only reporter here for thirty-four years. Wrote about snowstorms, the Halloween parade, high school football. All of a sudden, he's on the biggest story ever.

"He just did an interview with some paranormal expert. The guy says people have been picking up dead people's voices for years — over the radio! I never knew that, did you? Over the radio? Can you believe it?"

74

Sully shook his head. He hated this conversation. "Anyhow . . ."

Jennings opened a drawer. He took out a folder. "Mark says you're interested in our account job?"

"Yes."

"I'm a little surprised."

Sully didn't respond.

"It's not glamorous."

"I know."

"Just ad pickups. Commission."

"That's what Mark said."

"We're a small outfit. We publish once a week."

"I know."

"It's not flying jets or anything."

"I'm not looking for—"

"I know you don't want to talk about that whole incident. I understand. I believe in second chances. I told Mark that."

"Thank you."

"I'm sorry about your wife."

"Yeah."

"It was such a freak thing."

"Yeah."

"Did they ever find those air traffic recordings?"

I thought we weren't going to talk about it. "No, they never found them."

Jennings nodded. He looked at the drawer.

"Anyhow, this isn't that big of a job—"

"It's fine."

"It's doesn't pay a whol—"

"It's OK, really."

The two men looked at each other uncomfortably.

"I need work," Sully said. "I have a son, you know?"

He tried to think of something else to say. Giselle's face came to his mind.

"I have a son," he repeated.

Jules had been born a few years into their marriage, and Sully picked his name after a singer named Jules Shear, who wrote one of Giselle's favorite songs, "If She Knew What She Wants."

Once their son was born, he knew this was exactly what she wanted: a family. Giselle and the boy were like clay from the same soul. Sully could see her natural curiosity in the way Jules explored his toys, her gentle nature in how Jules hugged other children or patted a dog.

"Happy?" Sully had asked Giselle one night, the three of them on the couch, little Jules asleep on her chest.

"Oh, God, yes," she said.

They'd talked about having more kids. Instead, here he was, a single father of a single child, having just accepted a job he didn't want. He left the *Gazette*, lit a cigarette, got in his car, and sped to the liquor store. Once, when Giselle was alive, he thought about the future. Now he only thought about the past.

For as long as there has been religion, there have been amulets: pendants, rings, coins, crucifixes, each thought to be imbued with blessed power. And just as ancient believers held those amulets close, so did Katherine

Yellin now hold on to the salmon-pink cell phone that once belonged to her sister.

She gripped it during the day. She slept with it at night. When she went to work, she set it for the loudest ring and put it in her bag, which she secured over her shoulder and cradled like a football. She charged the phone constantly, purchasing a backup to the backup in case one charger went bad. She instructed everyone no longer to call that number but instead to use a second one that she'd acquired from a different provider. Her old phone — Diane's old phone — was reserved for Diane only.

Wherever Katherine went, that phone went too. And now, wherever Katherine went, Amy Penn from *Nine Action News* followed. Amy had taken Katherine for a nice dinner (Phil's suggestion; he even paid for it) and listened to seemingly endless stories about her beloved sister, promising that she and everyone at the station wanted only to spread word of the miracle. Katherine agreed that such a blessed event should not be confined to the borders of tiny Coldwater, and that Amy's TV camera, which she carried like luggage wherever she went, was actually, in this modern world, an instrument of God.

Which is how they came to arrive together, on a Tuesday morning, at the Coldwater Collection real estate offices, next to the Coldwater Post Office, across the street from the Coldwater Market. When they came through the door, there were four people in the waiting area, and each had told the young receptionist, "We want to meet with Katherine Yellin." When asked if someone else could help them, they said no.

This did not sit well with the three other realtors in the office, Lew, Jerry, and Geraldine, who had no new customers and few new prospects. Before Katherine's arrival that Tuesday, the three of them had been huddled around a desk, grumbling about the fuss over their colleague's heavenly claims.

"How do we even know it's true?" Lew said.

"She's never gotten over Diane," Geraldine said.

"People hallucinate," said Jerry.

"They're praying on her lawn, for God's sake!"

"She's bringing in more leads than ever."

"So what? If they're all for her, what good is it?"

The conversation continued this way, with added complaints: Lew needed to support his grandchildren, who were now living with him; Geraldine had never really cared for Katherine's preachy attitude; Jerry wondered if it wasn't too late for him, being only thirty-eight, to switch professions.

Then Katherine entered, with Amy behind her. The conversation stopped and the false smiles came out.

You might think a person who brings proof of heaven would be embraced. But even in the presence of a miracle, the human heart will say, *Why not me?*

"Morning, Katherine," Geraldine said.

"Morning."

"Heard from your sister?"

Katherine smiled. "Not today."

78

"When was the last call?"

"Friday."

"Four days ago."

"Um-hmm."

"Interesting."

Geraldine looked at Amy, as if to say, *You might be here for nothing.* Katherine glanced at her coworkers, exhaled, then unpacked a Bible from her bag.

And, of course, her phone.

"I should get started with the clients," she said.

The first was a middle-aged man who said he wanted to get a home near Katherine's, a place where he might get "calls" too. Then came a retired couple from Flint, who spoke about their daughter, killed in a car crash six years earlier, and how they hoped to reconnect with her in Coldwater. The third client was a Greek woman in a dark blue shawl who didn't even mention real estate. She simply asked Katherine if she could pray with her.

"Of course," Katherine answered, almost apologetically. Amy moved to the back to give them privacy, taking her large TV camera with her. It was ridiculously heavy; she always felt as if she were heaving a lead suitcase. One day, she promised herself, she would work for a station that would send an actual cameraman with her. One day, as in her next job.

"Heavy load, huh?" Lew observed as Amy thudded it on the desk.

"Yeah."

"You'd think they'd make them smaller by now."

"They do. But we don't have those models."

"They save 'em for New York and LA, huh?"

"Something like —"

She stopped. Lew's face had changed. His head turned. So did Geraldine's and Jerry's. When Amy realized why, a jolt of adrenaline shot through her veins.

Katherine's phone was ringing.

Every story has a tipping point. What happened next in the Coldwater Collection real estate offices was quick, chaotic, and captured in its entirety by Amy's sporadic and shaky camera-work. It took less than a minute, yet would soon be seen by millions across the planet.

Katherine grabbed her ringing phone. Everyone turned. The Greek woman started praying in her native tongue, swaying back and forth, her hands over her nose and mouth.

"Pater hêmôn ho en toes ouranoes—"

Katherine inhaled and pushed back in her chair. Lew swallowed. Geraldine whispered, "Now what?" Amy, who had frantically grabbed her camera and flipped it on, was trying, at the same time, to balance it on her shoulder, look through the viewfinder, and move in closer when — *whomp!* — she banged into a desk, causing the camera to fall, the film still rolling, as Amy sprawled over a chair, smacking her chin.

The phone rang again.

"Hagíasthêtô to onoma sou," mumbled the Greek woman.

"Wait! Not yet!" Amy yelled. But Katherine pressed a button and whispered, "Hello? . . . Oh, God . . . Diane . . ."

"Hagíasthêtô to onoma sou—"

Katherine's face was illuminated.

"Is it her?" Lew asked.

"Jesus," Geraldine whispered.

Amy scrambled to an upright position, her thigh pounding from the impact, her chin starting to bleed. She caught Katherine in the lens just as she said, "Yes, oh, yes, Diane, yes, I will . . ."

"*Genêthêtô to thelêma sou, hôs en ouranô—*"

"It's really her?"

"*Kae epí tês gês. Ton arton hêmôn ton epíousíon—*"

"Diane — when will you call me again . . . Diane? . . . Hello? . . ."

Katherine lowered the phone, then dropped back slowly, as if pushed with an invisible pillow. Her eyes were glazed.

"*Dos hêmín sêmeron; kae aphes hêmín ta opheílêmata—*"

"What happened?" Amy asked, playing the reporter, camera on her shoulder. "What did she say to you, Katherine?"

Katherine looked straight ahead, her hands on the desk. "She said, 'The time has come. Don't keep it a secret. Tell everyone. The good will be welcome in heaven.'"

The Greek woman covered her face with her hands and wept. Amy zoomed in on her, then zoomed in on the phone, which Katherine had dropped on the desk.

"Tell everyone," Katherine repeated dreamily, not realizing that, thanks to the blinking red light on Amy's camera, she was.

The Eighth Week

History suggests that Alexander Bell's telephone was, quite literally, an overnight sensation.

One that almost didn't happen.

In 1876, America was celebrating its hundredth birthday. A centennial exhibition was held in Philadelphia. New inventions were being displayed, things that would mark greatness in the next hundred years, including a forty-foot-high steam engine and a primitive typewriter. At the last minute, Bell's crude communication device was granted a small table in a narrow spot between a stairway and a wall, in a hall called the Department of Education. It sat for weeks with no real attention.

Bell was living in Boston. He had no plans — or money — to attend the exhibition. But on a Friday afternoon he went to the train station to see off his fiancée, Mabel, who was heading there to visit her father. She cried at the idea of leaving him. She insisted he come too. As the train pulled away, Bell, to comfort her, jumped aboard — without a ticket.

By acting on that impulse, Bell found himself at the exhibition two days later, on a hot Sunday afternoon, when a tired and sweaty delegation of judges walked by. Most of them just wanted to go home. But one, the esteemed emperor of Brazil, Dom Pedro de Alcantara, recognized the dark-haired inventor from his work with deaf students.

"Professor Bell!" Dom Pedro said, greeting him with open arms. "What are you doing here?"

After Bell explained, Dom Pedro agreed to witness his invention. The weary judges resigned themselves to staying a few more minutes.

A wire had been strung across the room. Bell went to the transmitter end while the emperor went to the receiver. Just as he had done with Thomas Watson months earlier (*Come here. I want to see you*), Bell spoke into his device as the emperor lifted the receiver to his ear. His expression suddenly brightened.

With the crowd looking on, the emperor declared in astonishment, "My God! It talks!"

The next day, the invention was moved to a featured position. Thousands mobbed to view it. It won first prize and a gold medal, and the world ignited with a previously unimaginable idea: speaking to someone you could not see.

Had it not been for a man's love for a woman, making him jump aboard a train, Bell's phone might never have found an audience. Once it did, life on earth was altered forever.

Eggs. There were not enough eggs. Frieda Padapalous shoved a fifty-dollar bill into her nephew's hands and said, "Get all they have at the market. Hurry."

Frieda had never been one for miracles, but she wasn't going to turn down this sudden boost in business. Monday had been busy. Tuesday had been busier. Today her diner was so noisy, people were yelling to be heard. The parking area was jammed. The booths were filled with strange faces. And for the first time ever on a Wednesday morning, there was a line outside her door. It wasn't even eight o'clock!

"More coffee, Jack?" Frieda said. She poured before he could answer, then sped off to someone else.

Jack sipped from his cup and lowered his head like a man with a secret. He deliberately hadn't worn his uniform today. He wanted to observe the growing pilgrimage — now that an Internet video had turned the whole town upside down. He spotted three people with TV cameras and at least four others whom he pegged for reporters — in addition to the flock of strange new faces, old and young, that kept asking where they could find Katherine Yellin, or the church, or the real estate office. He saw two Indian couples, and a table full of young people in religious clothing that he couldn't identify.

"Excuse me, hi, are you from here?" a fellow in a blue ski parka asked, sliding alongside Jack's stool.

"Why?"

"I'm with Channel Four from Detroit. We're talking to people about the miracles. You know. The phone calls? Could we get you on camera for a quick minute? It won't take long."

Jack glanced at the door. More people were streaming in. Morning coffee at Frieda's had been his daily routine for so long, he could walk from home to the counter and never open his eyes. But this was uncomfortable. He still hadn't told Doreen about his calls from Robbie — not after she told him. For some reason, he felt he needed to listen first. To gather information. Doreen said Robbie told her he was in heaven, he was safe, and that "the end was not the end." When she asked Jack what he thought, he said, "Doreen, does it make you happy?" and she started crying and said, "I don't know, yes, oh my God, I don't understand any of this."

He didn't want these reporters knowing about his ex-wife. He didn't want them knowing about him. He thought about Tess. He didn't want them knowing about her, either.

"You'd be on TV," the man in the ski parka urged, as if trying to close a deal.

"I'm just passing through," Jack said, dropping two dollars on the counter and moving toward the door.

Jason Turk unlocked the employee entrance of the Dial-Tek Phone Center. He yawned loudly. A rangy twenty-seven-year-old with a Felix the Cat tattoo on his bicep, he was exhausted from another late night playing online video games. He grabbed a can of Coke from a small refrigerator, took a few gulps, then belched, reminding himself of something his girlfriend often said: "Jason, your habits are disgusting."

He entered the office, pulled off his sweater, and pulled on a short-sleeved blue-and-silver work shirt that read DIAL-TEK. He leafed through yesterday's mail. An envelope from the corporate office. Another envelope from the corporate office. A brochure for cleaning services.

The buzzer sounded. He glanced at his watch. It was 8:10a.m. He expected one of the delivery truck drivers. But when he opened the back door, he saw a tall guy in an old suede jacket.

"Hi. I'm Sully. With the *Gazette*."

"Oh, right. I'm Jason."

"Hey."

"You're new."

"Yeah. Started last week."

Didn't look too happy about it, Jason thought.

"Come on in."

"I guess we're hoping you want to re-up for another three months —"

"Save the pitch," Jason said, waving his hand. "My boss already gave me the check." He rummaged through a drawer. "What happened to the girl they sent the last couple of times? Victoria?"

"Dunno," Sully said.

Too bad, Jason thought. She was cute.

"Anyhow, here you go." He handed Sully an envelope, marked GAZETTE: OCTOBER – DECEMBER.

"Thanks," Sully said.

"No problem." Jason swigged his Coke, then held out the can. "Mmm. You want one?"

"I'm good. I'll get going—"

Bnnnpp!

They turned.

"What was that?" Jason asked.

"I don't know," Sully said.

Bnnnpp!

It sounded as if a bird had flown into a glass pane. But wait. There it was again. *Bnnnp!* Then again. *Bnnnp!* Then continuous, growing louder, like a drumbeat.

Bnnnpbnnnpbnnnpbnnnpbnnnp!

"What the hell?" Jason mumbled. Sully followed him out to the showroom. What they saw froze them both in place: outside the store, pressed against the windows, were at least two dozen people, bundled in their coats. At the sight of Jason and Sully, they surged forward, like fish to the surface when food is tossed.

Bnnnpbnnnpbnnnpbnnnpbnnnp!

The two men ducked back into the office.

"What is *that* about?" Sully yelled.

"Who the hell knows?" Jason said, looking for his keys. It was still an hour before he was scheduled to open, and it wasn't like they were having a sale or something.

"Are you gonna let them in?"

"I guess . . . right?"

"You want me to stick around?"

"No. I mean. Maybe. Yeah. Just wait in here, OK? This is so freaking *weird*."

Jason exited, keys in hand. He approached the front entrance. He hesitated. The crowd pushed in closer.

He unlocked the door.

"Sorry, we're not open until—"

The people rushed inside, bumping past him, dashing to the displays.

"Hey, hang on!" Jason yelled.

"Do you have this model?" shouted a man in a leather coat and gray sweatshirt. He held a printed page to Jason's face. Jason saw the image of a woman holding up a pink phone.

"That's a Samsung, I think," he said.

"You have it? That exact one?"

"Probably—"

"I want all you have!"

"No!"

"Share them!"

"I want one!"

"I want three!"

Instantly, Jason was surrounded. He felt a hand on his back, then one on his shoulder, then someone grabbing his arm and someone waving paper in his face. He was being banged from person to person, tossed in a choppy sea of bodies, and someone yelled "Wait!" and someone yelled "Give him room!" and then—

"EVERYBODY BACK OFF!"

It was Sully, now in front of Jason in a protective stance, his arms out as a shield. His screaming made the people quiet and they slid back a few inches, allowing Jason to catch his breath.

"What's the matter with all of you?" Sully yelled.

"Yeah, what's the deal?" Jason gasped, feeling braver with Sully next to him. "We're not even *open* yet. What do you *want*?"

A thin old woman pushed forward. Dark circles shadowed her eyes, and her head was wrapped in a scarf. She appeared to be quite ill.

"The phone," she said, her voice scratchy. "The one that calls heaven."

What happened with Amy's video was what happens with many snippets of news in the modern world. It was tossed onto the Internet and whisked into cyberspace. There was no filtering, no editing, no vetting or verifying; someone watched it, passed it on, and the process was repeated not once or twice but in tens of thousands of occurrences, in less time than it takes water to boil. The tag on the video — "Phone Call from Heaven" — accelerated its rapid spread. The shaky camera-work — including the moment when Amy stumbled and the lens went dizzy — created an aura of bizarre authenticity.

It aired first on the Alpena news station and immediately became the most watched video in the history of the *Nine Action News* website, which brought Amy a congratulatory call from Phil. "Keep it coming," he'd told her. Religious groups tagged the video, and soon images of Katherine's face, the praying Greek woman, and the phone on the desk were being replayed countless times the world over. It was the modern-day version of the moment when Bell's invention took the Centennial by storm — except that things moved at warp speed now.

Within a week, Coldwater, Michigan, was the most-searched-for location on the Internet.

Pastor Warren peeked into the sanctuary. It was nearly full with worshippers — on a Wednesday afternoon.

Some had their heads in their hands, others were down on their knees. Warren noticed two men in fisherman caps swaying in prayer, but holding in their outstretched hands not a Bible or a hymnal but . . . their cell phones.

Warren let the door close quietly. He moved back to his office, where the four other Coldwater clerics were waiting.

"I'm sorry," Warren said, sitting down. "I was looking at all the people."

"Your flock," said Father Carroll.

"It's not my flock. They're here because of a congregant's story."

"They are here because of God," Father Carroll said.

Yes, yes, came a chorus of agreement.

"Believers are finally coming to us, Warren, not the other way around."

"Yes, but—"

"At the town meeting next week, we should emphasize this point. Use it to inspire others. Haven't we all grown tired of chasing people to ignite their faith?"

The other clergymen nodded their heads in agreement: "That's right." "He's right." "Amen."

"This resurgence, Warren, is a gift beyond whatever voices may be speaking to us from heaven—"

"Or not," Warren interrupted.

"Or perhaps," the priest responded.

Warren studied Father Carroll's expression. He seemed different. Calmer. Almost smiling.

"Do you *believe* in this miracle, Father?"

The clerics leaned forward. St. Vincent's was the largest church in town. What Father Carroll thought was critical.

"I remain . . . skeptical," he said, his words measured. "But I have called my bishop to arrange a visit."

Eyes darted back and forth. This was important news.

"With due respect, Father," Warren said, "the two congregants . . . they've been in our church for a long time. Baptist. You know this."

"I do."

"So the bishop — to be coming here — he wouldn't be speaking with them, not as non-Catholics."

"That's right."

Father Carroll lowered his chin. He crossed his hands in his lap. It was understood.

There was another.

What Father Carroll had not revealed was that two days earlier, he'd received a message on behalf of a former congregant, Tess Rafferty. Would he come to her house? It was terribly important.

Until that point, he had dismissed these "otherworldly" claims as foolery. Fakes. The opposite would be too much to accept; that the Lord, in his infinite wisdom, had forsaken the Catholic church in revealing his eternal paradise to the living world — and had chosen the bumbling Pastor Warren over him.

Tess Rafferty changed all that. In the kitchen of her home, which had survived a recent trial by fire, this thin woman of lapsed faith revealed that she too had been contacted from the other side — by her deceased mother, Ruth, whom Father Carroll remembered. More important, according to the calculations, her initial phone call had come around 8:20 a.m., several hours before Katherine Yellin's.

This was pleasing news indeed, news that Father Carroll intended to share with the anxious world.

If earthly mortals were being contacted by souls in heaven, Tess, a Catholic, had been the first.

On Thursday afternoon, Sully picked up Jules at school. He met him as he came out the door.

"Hi, buddy."

"Hi."

"How was everything today?"

"OK. Peter played with me."

"Peter, the kid with no front teeth?"

"Yeah."

They walked to the car. Sully looked down and saw something light blue protruding from his son's jacket pocket.

"What you got there?"

His son didn't answer.

"Jules, what's in your pocket?"

"Nothing."

Sully opened the car door. "It's not nothing."

"The teacher gave it to me. Can we go home?"

Jules crawled into the backseat and covered the pocket with his arm. Sully sighed and moved the arm out of the way.

It was a plastic phone receiver.

"Aw, Jules."

The boy grabbed for it, but Sully pulled it back.

"It's not yours!" Jules yelled, loud enough to draw looks from nearby parents.

"OK, OK," Sully said, handing it over. Jules shoved it inside his pocket.

"Is this about Mom?"

"No."

"Is that why you asked for it?"

"No."

"What did your teacher tell you?"

"She said I could talk to Mommy if I wanted to."

"How?"

"I can close my eyes and use the phone."

"And?"

"And maybe Mommy will call me like those other people."

Sully was stunned. Why would a teacher say that? Bad enough the boy was grieving. To fill him with false hope? Had this whole town gone insane? The mob at the phone store, that Internet video, the nutcases praying on Katherine Yellin's lawn, as if she were some kind of prophet. Now this?

"Jules, I don't want you keeping that thing, OK?"

"Why not?"

"It's a toy."

"So?"

"It won't work the way you want it to."

"How do *you* know?"

"I just do."

"No, you don't!"

Sully started the car and exhaled so hard he felt his chest sink. When they arrived at his parents' house, Jules pulled the handle and raced out the door without looking back.

Fifteen minutes later, Sully drove alone along Route 8, the two-lane road that connected Coldwater to the outside world. He was still steaming. He wanted to speed back to the school, grab the teacher, and holler, "Do you have *any idea* what you're doing?" Tomorrow. He'd do it tomorrow. He had to work now, collect a check from a furniture store in Moss Hill. The roads were wet after a light sleet, and he flipped on the wipers to clear the crud kicked up from passing vehicles.

As he came around the bend to the open expanse known as Lankers Field, he saw the old sign, NOW LEAVING COLD-WATER — THANK YOU FOR VISITING.

He blinked.

The sign had a sticker across the bottom: HAVE YOU BEEN SAVED? In the field behind it were at least a dozen RVs and trailers. There were large white tents, and thirty or forty people in winter coats milling about, some reading from books, some digging a fire pit, one playing a guitar. It looked to Sully like a religious pilgrimage — except that those were in places like the Ganges River in India, or Our Lady of Guadalupe in Mexico City. Not in Lankers Field, where he used to ride his bike to set off firecrackers with his schoolmates.

This has got to stop, Sully told himself as he slowed the car. Cult worshippers? Paranormal experts? What was next?

He pulled the car over and rolled down the window. A middle-aged man with a hooked nose and long silver hair tied back in a ponytail took a few steps in his direction.

"What's going on?" Sully yelled.

"Hello, brother," the man said.

"What's all this?"

"This is a holy place. God is speaking to his children here."

Sully fumed at the word *children*.

"Who told you that?"

The man took the measure of Sully's expression, then grinned. "We can feel it. Would you like to pray with us, brother? You might feel it too."

"I actually live here. And you're wrong. Nobody is speaking to anyone."

The man put his hands together, as if in prayer, and smiled again.

"Jesus," Sully mumbled.

"Now you're talking, brother," the man said.

Sully hit the accelerator and screeched away. He wanted to yell at every one of those foolish believers, the pit diggers, the guitar player, Jules's schoolteachers, the phone customers. *Wake up!* he wanted to say. *The living can't speak to the dead! If they could, don't you think I would? Wouldn't I trade my next hundred breaths for one word from my wife? It's not possible. There is no God who does such things. There is no miracle in Coldwater. It's a trick of some kind, a con, a deceit, a massive hoax!*

He'd had enough. He would confront Jules's teacher. He'd confront the whole damn school board if he had to. And something else. He would attack this phony heaven thing. Expose it as the fraud it had to be. He may have been imprisoned, he may have been disgraced, he may have been scraping by in a new, lousy life, but he still had his brain. He still knew the difference between the truth and a lie. He would do for his son — and for others dealing with real loss — what had never been done for him.

Get to the bottom of the story.

The Ninth Week

"Say that again."

"Three thousand and fourteen."

"From one store?"

"One store."

"How many do they usually carry?"

"Four."

"I'll get back to you."

Terry Ulrich, a regional vice president for Samsung, hung up and jotted down some numbers. The Dial-Tek outlet in Coldwater, Michigan, had placed an insane order for a single model phone, the Samsung 5GH. It was not a particularly special unit. It flipped open, made calls, and, with the right plan, could connect to the Internet. But that was it. Phones today did so much more — took video, ran games. Why would one store be selling thousands of an older, lesser model?

The answer, Terry had just been informed, was that the Samsung 5GH was the phone being used by a woman claiming to speak to heaven.

And she'd purchased it in the Coldwater store.

Terry ran two fingers along his chin. He looked out the window at the Chicago skyline. The profit on this order alone would be close to six figures. He spun back to his computer, searched the Internet, and found a series of stories about this Coldwater phenomenon. He watched a video from *Nine Action News* in Alpena, which he found rather hokey.

But when he saw how many hits the videos had received, he grabbed the phone.

"Get the guys from marketing down here. Fast."

Alexander Bell's mother was deaf. When people spoke to her, they did so through a rubber ear tube. But Alexander did not. Early on, he sensed that she could better understand him if he put his mouth near her forehead and spoke in low, sonorous tones. The vibrations of his voice could be better absorbed that way — a principle that would one day be integral to his development of the telephone.

When Giselle was in the hospital, Sully spoke to her like that, his lips close to her forehead, his lowered voice vibrating with every memory he could think of.

Remember our first apartment? Remember the yellow sink? Remember Italy? Remember pistachio ice cream? Remember when Jules was born?

He would go on like this, sometimes for an hour, hoping the vibrations would get through. He had always been able to make her laugh. He dreamed of finding a memory so uncontrollably funny that it stirred her from the coma and she said, "Oh, God, I *remember* that."

She never did. Sully never stopped trying. Even in prison, he would sit alone, eyes closed, reciting memories as if his thoughts could somehow fly to her hospital bed. From the day of the crash until the day she died, all he really wanted was to hear her voice.

To hear her voice.

It never happened.

Which is why these Coldwater claims had irked him so much. And why, on Monday morning, he took notepads and file folders from the *Gazette* supply closet and purchased a small tape recorder to begin his own investigation.

What these people were claiming, he had already tried. He had called out for Giselle. Nothing came back. There was no heaven. Dead was dead.

It was time everyone accepted that.

The largest indoor gathering place in Coldwater was the high school gymnasium. With the bleachers pulled out and the floor lined with folding chairs, it could seat almost two thousand people.

By 6:00 p.m. Tuesday, every one of those seats was filled.

A small podium had been erected against the back wall, beneath an American flag and a scarlet-and-white banner that read COLDWATER BASKETBALL — DISTRICT CHAMPIONS, 1973, 1998, 2004. Sitting on the podium were Father Carroll, Pastor Warren, and a legislator from the district, whose belly hung heavy over his belt and who wiped his forehead periodically with a handkerchief. Jack Sellers sat up there as well, wearing his police blues, a reminder that decorum would be maintained.

Mayor Jeff Jacoby, in an open-collared shirt and navy sports coat, stepped to the podium and put his hands on the microphone. His first words — "Good evening" — squeaked with feedback. People covered their ears.

"Hello? . . . test, test . . . is that better?"

The meeting was limited to Coldwater residents only. Driver's licenses were presented at the door. The media was excluded, but reporters waited outside, sitting in their cars, engines running. People who'd been camping out were on-site as well, gathered under a streetlight in the parking lot, warming their hands by a fire in a metal trash bin. Ray and Dyson, from the police department, took turns walking the perimeter, although each of them wondered what they would do if the crowd got unruly, two officers against all these people.

Inside, the mayor had solved the microphone problem. "So," he began, "I think we all know why we're here. What's happened in Coldwater — and with you, Katherine — has been remarkable."

Katherine, sitting in the front row, nodded modestly, and the crowd mumbled agreement.

"But it has also brought many challenges."

More mumbling.

"We now have to deal with visitors, traffic congestion, public safety, and the news media."

Louder mumbling. Jack shifted in his seat.

"That's some of what we'll address tonight. First, Father Carroll, do you want to get us started?"

Father Carroll stepped to the microphone and adjusted its height. Pastor Warren watched and waited. He had told the mayor he did not feel comfortable addressing a secular crowd. Father Carroll was much better at that sort of thing. Even the way he moved. Almost regal. Warren thought.

"First, let us pray," Father Carroll began. "May the good Lord bring us strength this evening . . ."

As people lowered their heads, Sully, sitting in an aisle seat, reached into his jacket pocket and felt the spine of the reporter's notebook. Reaching in the other pocket, he pressed the record button of the small tape recorder.

"My friends, we do not always know God's plan," Father Carroll continued. "The Bible is full of unlikely heroes, reluctant to hear the call.

"Moses did not want to speak to Pharaoh. Jonah hid from the Lord. Young John Mark abandoned Paul and Barnabas. Fear is part of our makeup. God knows this . . ."

People nodded. A few yelled, "Amen."

"What I ask here tonight is this: do not be afraid. You are among friends. You are among neighbors. Scripture teaches us that we are bound to spread the good news. And it *is* good news."

Pastor Warren looked to his fellow clergymen, confused. Wasn't Father Carroll only going to offer a benediction?

"And so, to begin, I ask . . . who among us has received a word from heaven? Or believes he has? Tell us who you are and how you have been blessed."

A rumble went through the room. This was unexpected. A public roll call for miracles? People turned their heads left and right.

Katherine Yellin, sitting in the front row, stood up proudly, hands crossed.

"My sister," she declared. "Diane Yellin. Praise God!"

The crowd nodded. Katherine, they knew. Heads turned, checking for others. *Where's Elias Rowe?* Tess, sitting five rows back, looked to the podium. Father Carroll nodded. She closed her eyes, saw her mother's face, inhaled, and stood up.

"My mother, Ruth Rafferty!" she announced.

People gasped. Katherine's jaw fell open.

Then, from the left side, another voice.

"My son!"

Heads turned. Jack's eyes widened.

"Robbie Sellers. He died in Afghanistan," Doreen said.

She was standing, her hands clasped together. She looked to Jack on the podium, and he suddenly felt as if the whole auditorium were looking at him too. He glanced at Tess, who, upon meeting his gaze, looked away. The crowd whispered. *Three? Now it's three?*

An Indian man rose near the front.

"My daughter called me! Praise God!"

A few rows back, an older man followed his lead.

"My ex-wife!"

Then a teenage girl.

"My best friend!"

A man in a suit.

"My former business partner!"

Each announcement drew louder reactions, like an organ in those old movie houses as the tension rises.

102

Sully had the notebook out and was scribbling fast, trying to make mental images of the faces.

When the gasping stopped, there were seven of them, seven Coldwater residents, standing like high weeds in a field of low grass, each claiming to have done what was previously unimaginable: spoken with heaven.

The gymnasium fell silent. Jeff tugged Father Carroll to the side.

"My God, Father," he whispered. "What do we do now?"

Four Days Later

NEWS REPORT
ABC News

ANCHOR: Finally, tonight we go to a small town in Michigan, where citizens are claiming to be reunited with loved ones in a most unusual way. Alan Jeremy reports.

(Images of Coldwater.)

ALAN: The population is less than four thousand. The most notable landmark is a cider mill. Coldwater, Michigan, is no different from thousands of small-town American communities — or at least it wasn't, until people began getting phone calls that they claim are heaven-sent.

(Short sound bites.)

TESS: My mother has called me many times.

DOREEN: My son has been in regular contact.

TEENAGER: My friend died in a car accident last year. Three weeks ago, she called and said I should stop crying.

(Photos of the deceased.)

ALAN: The common denominator is that all the people calling are dead, some for years. The seemingly impossible has local clergy wrestling with the question.

FATHER CARROLL: We must be open to God's miracles. Many people are returning to the church after learning of these calls. Perhaps that is God's will.

(Scenes of crowds praying.)

ALAN: Coldwater is fast becoming a mecca for believers, with impromptu services being held in parking lots and open fields. Local police are taxed.

(Face of police chief Jack Sellers.)

JACK: We're a small department. We can't be everywhere. We just ask folks to respect privacy and to hold their prayers at decent hours, you know? None of the midnight stuff.

(Archival footage.)

ALAN: From clairvoyants to Ouija boards, people have long claimed to converse with the dead. Researchers into electronic voice phenomena believe Coldwater is not the first time voices have been heard from the other side.

(Face of Leonard Koplet, paranormal expert.)

LEONARD: We've seen a history of tape recordings that capture a dead person's voice, machines that sweep radio signals and pick up the strangest things. But this is the first time the telephone has been used so regularly. It's just another step in our connection to the other side.

(Image of Samsung billboard.)

ALAN: Even Samsung has gotten on the bandwagon. This billboard — a rendering of clouds, the phone used by one of the lucky recipients, and the word DIVINE — now hangs on Route 8.

(Face of Samsung executive Terry Ulrich.)

TERRY: We didn't design the phone for this purpose, but we're glad it has been "chosen." We're honored and humbled. And we've made the model widely available.

(Image of scientist at his desk.)

ALAN: As you might expect, critics have been quick to dismiss the Coldwater claims. Daniel Fromman is with Responsible Scientists International in Washington, D.C.

(Close-up of scientist, talking to Alan.)

FROMMAN: Phone service is a man-made activity. The satellites are man-made. The routing devices are man-made. The contact these people are suggesting is not only impossible, it's laughable. This just isn't something people should take seriously.

ALAN: Then how do you explain the calls?

FROMMAN: You mean the calls people claim to get?

ALAN: Are you saying they're lying?

FROMMAN: I'm saying people in grief can imagine many things. It makes them feel better. It doesn't make it real.

(Alan, standing by large tent.)

ALAN: Nonetheless, believers are flocking to Coldwater.

(Face of silver-haired man.)

SILVER-HAIRED MAN: This is a sign. Eternity exists, heaven exists, salvation exists — but folks had better get right with the Lord! Judgment Day is coming!

(Close-up on Alan.)

ALAN: Real or imagined, something is happening as winter approaches in this small midwestern town. But what exactly is it? Many here said . . . they need to pray on it. In Coldwater, I'm Alan Jeremy.

(Back to studio.)

ANCHOR: From all of us here at *ABC News*, good night.

106

The Tenth Week

By the first of November, Coldwater was overrun. Cars clogged the streets. There was no place to park. Long lines were common in the market, the bank, the gas station, and any place to eat or drink.

On Tuesday night, Sully hurried by crowds on Lake Street with his hands dug into his pockets, passing a group of young people sitting on a car hood, singing spirituals. He was heading to the Coldwater Public Library, a single-story white brick building with an American flag by the front entrance and a swinging sign that featured a different message each week. This week it read: GIVE THANKS! DONATE A USED BOOK FOR T'GIVING!

It was nearly 8:00p.m., and Sully was glad to see the lights still on. With no Internet service of his own, and the computers at the *Gazette* being out of the question (he didn't want anyone to know what he was doing, least of all reporters), this was his best and only option for doing research; a place where he once wrote grade-school book reports.

He stepped inside. It seemed deserted.

"Hello?"

He heard shuffling from a corner desk. A young woman — maybe twenty years old? — leaned into view.

"Cold out there?"

"Freezing," Sully said. "Are you the librarian? Do they still call them librarians?"

"Depends. Do they still call them readers?"

"I think so."

"Then I'm the librarian."

She smiled. Her hair was dyed an eggplant shade with a streak of shocking red, cut in a short pixie style. She wore light pink glasses. Her skin was creamy and flawless.

"You seem kind of young," Sully said.

"My grandma had the job before me. She was more the old librarian type."

"Ah."

"Eleanor Udell."

"That's your name?"

"My grandmother's."

"I had a teacher growing up here, Mrs. Udell."

"Coldwater Elementary?"

"Yeah."

"Third grade?"

"Yeah . . ."

"That was her."

"Oh, God." Sully closed his eyes. "You're Mrs. Udell's *granddaughter*."

"Guess I'm really young now, huh?"

Sully shook his head.

"You guys have a computer, right?"

"Um-hmm. Over there."

He looked to the corner. A beige tower model. It looked ancient.

"Is it OK to—"

"Sure. Go ahead."

He took off his coat.

"Liz, by the way."

"Hmm?"

"My name is Liz."

"Oh. Hey."

Sully moved the mouse on the desk — a wired mouse, he noted — but nothing happened on the screen.

"Is there a trick to this?"

"Hang on. You have to log in."

Liz rose. Sully did a double take. Although her face was the picture of young, attractive health, her left leg was bent and she walked with a severe wobble that came down hard on her right foot. Her arms seemed slightly short for her body.

"Here," she said, edging past, "let me get it."

Sully moved out of the way, too quickly.

"I have MS," she said, smiling again. "In case you thought this was a new dance move."

"No . . . I know . . . I . . ."

Sully felt like an idiot. She typed in a password, and the screen came up full.

"You researching the afterlife?"

"Why do you ask that?"

"Come on. Coldwater is like 1-800-HEAVEN now."

"I'm not here for that."

He reached for his cigarettes.

"Can't smoke in a library."

"Right."

He pushed them back in his pocket.

"You go to that meeting?" Liz said.

"What meeting?"

"The one at the high school. It was insane. All these people getting calls from dead relatives."

"You believe it?"

"Nah. Too weird. Something's up."

"Like what?"

"I dunno."

She moved the mouse, watching the cursor dart across the screen. "It would be nice though, huh? If you could just talk to everyone you lost?"

"I guess."

He pictured Giselle. She'd been about this girl's age when they met, a Thursday night, at Giuseppe's Pizza, just off campus. Giselle worked there as a waitress. She wore a tight, purple uniform blouse with a black wraparound skirt. She had such beautiful life in her eyes that Sully asked for her number in front of all his friends. She laughed and cracked, "I don't date college boys." But when she handed him the bill, he saw a phone number on the back, with the words "unless they're cute."

"Anyhow . . ." Liz tapped her hands twice on her thighs.

"Thanks."

"No problem."

"What time do you close?"

"Nine tonight and Thursday. Six the other nights."

"OK."

"Holler if you need something. Although officially, you're supposed to" — she dropped her voice — "*whisper.*"

Sully smiled. She returned to her desk. He watched her painful limp, the awkward twist of her young body.

"Sully," he said. "My name is Sully Harding."

"I know," she said, not turning around.

Hours later, alone in her bedroom, Katherine pulled back the covers and slid beneath them. She stared at the ceiling.

She began to cry.

She hadn't gone to work in days. She hadn't addressed the worshippers on her lawn. She felt violated. Betrayed. What had been a private blessing was now a circus. She could still see the crowd at the gymnasium, moving past her, swarming around others who claimed to receive heavenly contact. It was loud and confusing, and the mayor kept yelling over the microphone, *"Another meeting will be scheduled! Please check with the village office!"*

The scene outside was even worse. The bright glare of TV camera lights; the cacophony of yelling, praying, excited conversations; people pointing, nodding, grabbing one another to share some new detail they just heard.

Six other people? Impossible. They were clearly envious of her contact with Diane and had concocted their own stories in desperation. Look at Elias Rowe. He made a claim, then disappeared, probably from embarrassment at his lie. A teenage friend? A business partner? These were not the blood bonds that heaven would honor. Katherine wondered if any of these people even *went* to church.

She listened to the sound of her accelerated breathing. *Calm down. Dry your tears. Think of Diane. Think of the Lord.*

She closed her eyes. Her chest rose and fell.

And her phone rang.

The next morning, Tess stood by the mirror, pulling her hair into a plastic clip. She buttoned the highest button. She skipped the lipstick. Meeting a Catholic bishop required modesty.

"Does this look OK?" she asked, entering the kitchen.

"Fine," Samantha said.

Samantha stayed with Tess much of the time now. She listened for the phone if Tess was drawn away. Since the calls no longer only came on Fridays, Tess worried about missing even a single ring. She felt silly, being consumed by a telephone. But when she heard her mother's voice, the most blessed sensation would wash over her, the bad of life rinsed away.

"*Don't be burdened by this, Tess,*" her mother had said.

"Mom, I need to tell somebody."

"*What's stopping you, honey? . . . Tell everyone.*"

"I called Father Carroll."

"*That's a start.*"

"I haven't gone to church in so long."

"*But . . . you've gone to God. Every night.*"

Tess was startled. She said private prayers before going to sleep — but only began after her mother died.

"Mom, how did you know that?"

The line had gone dead.

Tess looked at Samantha now. They heard a car door slam.

Moments later, the doorbell rang.

Father Carroll entered behind his companion, Bishop Bernard Hibbing from the Roman Catholic Diocese of Gaylord, a broad-faced man with ruddy skin, wire-rimmed glasses, and a pectoral cross. As she let them in, Tess noticed a crowd across the street. She quickly closed the door.

"Would you like coffee or tea?" she asked.

"Thank you, no."

"We can sit here."

"Very good."

"So." Tess looked at them. "How does this work?"

"Well, the simplest way," Bishop Hibbing began, "is to tell me what happened. From the beginning."

He sat back. It was the bishop's duty to investigate alleged miraculous events — and to be skeptical, as most proved to be coincidences or exaggerations. If he believed something divine had truly taken place, he was to promptly report it to the Vatican, which would turn the investigation over to the Congregation for the Causes of the Saints.

Tess began with her mother's sad demise from Alzheimer's. Next, she detailed the phone calls. Bishop

Hibbing listened for clues. Did the woman see herself as "chosen"? Did she believe she had initiated this phenomenon? Both were red flags. The few true miracles seemed to choose their witnesses, not the other way around.

"Tell me about your childhood. Did you ever hear voices?"

"No."

"Any visions or revelations?"

"I never felt that connected."

"And your occupation?"

"I run a day care center."

"For the poor?"

"Some are. We take in kids whose parents can't pay. It's not smart business, but, you know . . ."

She shrugged. Bishop Hibbing made his notes. He'd been skeptical of Coldwater as a church matter. There was a difference between the miraculous and the paranormal. Blood on a statue of the Virgin Mary? Saint Teresa of Avila encountering a spear-wielding angel? These at least involved sacred contact. Hearing from ghosts did not.

On the other hand, there was one very serious concern with these phone calls. It was the biggest reason Bishop Hibbing had come, and why his superiors in the Catholic Church privately awaited a swift report.

If people truly believed they were talking with heaven, how soon before they expected to hear from the Lord?

114

"In these conversations," the bishop continued, "does your mother talk of Jesus?"

"Yes."

"And of the Holy Father?"

"Many times."

"God's grace?"

"She said we are all forgiven. The calls are very short."

"What has she told you to do with your messages?"

Tess looked at Samantha. "Tell everyone."

"Tell everyone?"

"Yes."

He exchanged glances with Father Carroll.

"May I see the phone?"

Tess showed him. She played the old answering machine with the first message and her mother's voice. They listened to it many times. At the clergyman's request, Tess gathered several family photos, and the obituary that had been written in the *Gazette* upon her mother's passing.

After that, Father Carroll and Bishop Hibbing collected their things.

"Thank you for your time," the bishop said.

"What happens next?" Tess asked.

"Let us pray about that?" Father Carroll suggested.

"Indeed," said Bishop Hibbing.

The two men smiled. They said good-bye.

When they opened the door, a pack of TV reporters was waiting for them on the sidewalk.

★ ★ ★

Life at the police station had changed dramatically. Ever since the town meeting, the phones had not stopped ringing. If it wasn't crowd problems, noise complaints, cars parked on lawns, or out-of-towners calling for directions, then it was radio stations or newspapers asking Jack Sellers to comment on his ex-wife's claims, or to ask her to speak at a church or a conference on the afterlife. Doreen's number was unlisted, but "Coldwater Police" was easy to find.

Jack had lied the first time they asked, "Have *you* been contacted, Chief?" After that, he'd had no choice but to continue the deceit. His days were a mix of personal and professional denials — telling people to scatter, to move, to calm down, all the while knowing that what they suspected was real. By the end of each day, he felt as wrung out as a washrag.

What made it endurable — the only thing that made it endurable — was the sound of Robbie's voice. The calls had continued, regularly, and Jack realized how much he'd missed talking to his son, how hard he'd tried to cover that pain since the funeral. Hearing him again was like patching a hole in his heart, covering it with fresh veins and tissue.

"Son, your mother told everyone," Jack said in their most recent call.

"*I know, Dad.*"

"The whole town was there."

"*That's so cool.*"

"Did she do the right thing?"

"*God wants people to know . . .*"

116

"To know what?"

"*Not to be afraid . . . Dad, I was so scared when I was fighting . . . Every day, afraid for my life, afraid I might lose my life . . . But now I know.*"

"What do you know?"

"*Fear is how you lose your life . . . a little bit at a time . . . What we give to fear, we take away from . . . faith.*"

The words gave Jack goose bumps. Where was *his* faith? Why was he afraid to do what Doreen had done — to come forward? Did his reputation matter so much to him?

"Robbie?"

"*Yeah?*"

"You won't stop calling me, will you?"

"*Don't be afraid, Dad . . . The end is not the end.*"

The line went dead. *The end is not the end.* Jack felt tears falling, but he did not wipe them away. The tears were part of the miracle too, and he wanted to keep both around as long as he could.

Sully clicked the mouse. He rubbed his eyes. It was midmorning in the library, and he'd been here since dropping Jules at school. He was amazed at what he'd found just researching "contact with the afterlife." There were so many claims! From voices that came through dreams to clairvoyants who professed to see the dead to "channelers" who wrote down messages from the spirit world. Many people insisted they had received phone calls from loved ones hours after they'd died, before the bodies had been discovered. There was also a great deal of research into this "EVP" — electronic voice phenomena — that *ABC News* had mentioned, in which the sounds of dead people are somehow captured through tape recordings or so-called ghost boxes. Sully read about a Swedish painter who was recording the sounds of birds half a century ago. Upon playback, he heard the voice of his dead wife.

Sully clicked to something else.

An hour later, he pushed back from the screen and sighed, staring again at the notes on his yellow pad. Seven people had stood in the gym — and he couldn't get a foothold on any of them. All he had was a suspicion that these calls were not real. But if not, then what were they? And if heaven was not sending them, who was?

As he had done in his military days, he collected information and analyzed it for a pattern. *Be methodical and systematic*, the navy had taught him. Back then it was maps, weather, aircraft failure, intelligence data. Here he gathered the seven names, searched their addresses through county records, found most of their phone numbers using the library's Internet, and, through a casual lunchtime conversation with Ron Jennings at the *Gazette*, collected a good deal of personal information. He jotted all this on the left side of his pad, then made a category on the right labeled CONNECTIONS?

Were they related to each other? No. Did they live on the same street? No. Did they all attend the same church? No. Were they all in the same business? Hardly.

Same sex? No. Same age? No. Did their last names start with the same letter? Did they all have children?

No. No. No. No.

Sully ran his pen aimlessly across the paper. He glanced over at Liz behind the desk, earbuds stuck in her ears. She caught him looking and smiled, giving an exaggerated head nod to the rhythm of whatever music she was listening to.

Buddeladeep! . . . Buddeladeep! . . .

It was Sully's cell phone. The *Gazette* had given him one and told him to stay in touch, most likely to ensure he wasn't goofing off on their time — as he was right now.

"Uh . . . hello?" he said, keeping his voice low.

"It's Ron Jennings. Where are you at?"

"Just paying for some gas. What's up?"

"I forgot to put one client on the sheet. Can you get to them this afternoon?"

Sully hadn't even gone to the three he was supposed to visit this morning.

"Who is it?"

"Davidson and Sons."

Sully paused. "The funeral home?"

"You know it?"

"I was there once."

"Oh, God, right . . . I'm sorry, Sully."

An awkward silence.

"It's OK," Sully said. "I didn't realize they advertised."

"One of our oldest clients. Ask for Horace."

"Is he the tall guy? Kinda pale?"

"That's him."

Sully shivered. He had hoped not to see that man again.

"Tell him about the 'Heaven Calling' special edition. See if he's up for a full page."

"OK, Ron."

"You know the rate sheet?"

"Got it with me."

"A full page would be good."

"I'll try, Ron."

"Gotta go," Jennings said. "Got a TV reporter waiting outside the office. Crazy, huh?"

He hung up. Sully rubbed his forehead. Another TV reporter? A special edition? The funeral home?

"Hey. No cell phones."

Sully looked up. Liz was standing by the table.

"It's a library, remember?"

"Sorry."

"Do I have to confiscate it?"

"No, ma'am. I'll shut it off."

"Promise?"

"Promise."

"We'll forgive you this time."

"Thank you."

"Under one condition."

"What?"

She sat down, resting her small hands on the table. She looked at her fingertips.

"What?" Sully said again.

"Tell me what happened to you."

Sully looked away.

"What do you mean?"

"Come on, I work in a *library*. I read stuff all day long. You're *from* here. Your parents still *live* here. People talked about it when it happened. When your plane hit that other plane. You having to go to jail."

"Yeah? What did people say?"

She hooked her hands. She shrugged. "They felt sorry for you, mostly. Your wife and all." She looked straight at him. "What really happened?"

Sully took a deep breath.

"Come on. I won't tell anyone," she said.

He rapped his knuckles on the table.

"I'll just shut the phone off, OK?"

What really happened? People had asked him that from the day of the crash to the day they put him behind bars.

Lynton Airfield was a small Ohio facility, used for both civilian and military airplanes. It was Saturday morning. Sully was coming in for a landing. He had grabbed Blake Pearson's assignment to fly the Hornet F/A-18 jet across the country because it gave him a chance, during his two weeks of mandatory reserve duty, to stop and see Giselle for a few hours. Then he'd fly on to the West Coast, where the plane was expected by nightfall.

Clouds enveloped the aircraft. Sully checked his gauges, tucked inside the cramped single-seat cockpit — like sitting in a high, tight canoe. A thunderstorm was approaching, but not close enough to threaten his flight pattern. He radioed in, speaking through his oxygen mask and the small snoutlike tube that hung from it.

"Firebird 304 checking in for a full stop," he said, transmitting his landing clearance request.

There were only a few people on duty that Saturday morning, and most were finishing a midnight shift, getting ready to go home. Elliot Gray, the air traffic controller, had just come in. He had a reedy, nasal, high-pitched voice, the kind of voice you would not want to hear singing.

Sully would never forget that voice.

It cost him everything.

"*Firebird 304, roger*," it said quickly. "*You are established for twenty-seven right.*"

"Firebird 304, copy," Sully answered.

It was routine stuff, Sully being cleared for the right runway. He lowered his landing gear and heard the rumble of the wheels extending. He thought about seeing Giselle in a few minutes.

I want to see you.

I want to see you, too.

Maybe they could go to that pancake house near Zanesville. Jules loved waffles with ice cream.

"Lynton Tower, Firebird 304 on final five miles twenty-seven right," Sully said.

"*Firebird 304, roger. Cleared to land on twenty-seven right . . . Traffic in the pattern for twenty-seven left.*"

Sully slowed his speed. With the landing gear locked, the ride changed, from a smooth rocket to a flying tank. He adjusted the trim, adjusted the throttle, and established himself on the glide slope for the landing approach. Nothing outside but soupy clouds.

He heard a crackle on his radio, a few garbled words. Maybe the traffic from 27 left, the other runway. He waited for more, but there wasn't any.

Three miles from the airfield, Sully brought the Hornet out of the mist. He saw the earth below him, cut into huge squares of crop fields, trees, and farm properties. He caught sight of the runway. He was right on course. Ten more minutes, and he'd be talking pancakes with his wife.

And then.

Currrromph!

A jolting thud from below. A huge shake. The plane bumped wildly.

"What the *hell?*" Sully said.

It was as if he'd run something over — eight hundred feet above the ground.

Aviate. Navigate. Communicate.

That's that they teach you when you learn to fly. It is drilled into your head by every instructor, the time-tested blueprint for trouble in the air.

Aviate. When a problem occurs, first keep flying the plane.

Navigate. Next, figure out where you need to go.

Communicate. Finally, tell the ground what's going on.

Do any of these out of order, you're in deep. So before he could even make sense of the thudding impact. Sully increased power and tried to level out.

Aviate. Fly the damn plane! Within seconds he realized that was impossible. The warning panel was flashing red. The gauges were winding down. The steady bleat of *beep-beep-beep* was in his ears. *Seven hundred feet.* He was losing power. The air-frame began to shudder. *Six hundred feet.* Even through his helmet, Sully could hear the engine noise weakening, the pitch beginning to lower and die.

Navigate. Could he still reach the airfield? He checked his glide slope, looked out the windshield, and realized he could not make the runway, and with the plane's damage, another pass was out of the question. *Five hundred feet.* He was dropping too fast. With no safe place to land, the choice was clear: point the plane away from population and kiss it good-bye. *Four hundred feet.* He spotted an empty clearing maybe half a mile from the airfield and steered that way.

Communicate. "Firebird 304 declaring emergency!" he yelled. "Aircraft uncontrollable. Initiating ejection."

He had practiced this once a year in a simulator on a naval base and, like every pilot, prayed that was as close as he would ever get. His heart pounded; every nerve was electrically charged. He was suddenly sweating. He set the controls for the plane to dive, then let go of the stick and slammed his back against the seat, lest he snap his neck from the force of the ejection. He reached both hands over his head for the handle.

Pull!

A rocket exploded beneath him. In an instant he was through the glass and into the heavens.

Aviate. Navigate. Communicate.

Evacuate.

There was snow on the porch of Davidson & Sons Funeral Home. Sully removed his ski cap, stomped on the mat, and let himself inside. He was hoping maybe Horace would not be there, but of course he was, stepping quickly out of his office, with his wispy straw-colored hair, his long chin, his dour, sickly expression.

"Hello again," Sully said, offering his hand.

"Hello."

"Do you remember me?"

"Mr. Harding."

"Call me Sully."

"All right."

"Ron Jennings says hello."

"Tell him the same."

"I'm in a different capacity this time."

"Yes."

"I'm working with the *Gazette*."

"Ah. You like newspapers?"

Sully inhaled. *Actually*, he wanted to say, *I hate them*.

"Your advertising contract is up at the end of the month—"

He paused, hoping Horace would say, "Oh, yes, here's the check." But the man stood straight as an upright knife.

"Ron mentioned you're one of the longest advertising customers the *Gazette* has, so . . ."

Still nothing.

"So . . . would you like to renew?"

"Yes, of course," Horace said. "Come with me."

Finally. Sully followed Horace back to his office, where he produced an envelope typed and ready.

"There you are," Horace said.

Sully put it in his bag. "Oh, also, Ron wanted me to mention they're doing a special section on . . ." He paused. "On what's been going on in town."

"In town?"

"The phone calls? People talking to the . . ."

He swallowed before saying "dead."

"Ah," Horace said. "Yes."

" 'Heaven Calling.' That's the name of the section."

" 'Heaven Calling.' "

"Maybe you'd like to take an ad?"

Horace touched his chin.

"Does Ron think it's a good idea?"

"He does. Yes. He thinks a lot of people will read it."

"What do *you* think?"

Sully hated this. He wanted to say the whole thing was a crock. He couldn't even look Horace in the eye.

"I think Ron's right. A lot of people will read it."

Horace stared at him.

"Probably a lot of people," Sully mumbled.

"How big an ad?"

"Ron suggested a full page."

"Very well," Horace said. "Have him bill me for it."

As they walked out, Horace remembered something. "Can you wait here a moment?"

He came back with another envelope. "Could you also bring Ron this check for the obituaries? I was going to mail it, but since you're here—"

"Sure, no problem."

Sully took the envelope. "If you don't mind my asking, what do you mean by 'the obituaries'?"

"It's a service we provide."

"Really?"

"Yes. Most people who come to us are understandably upset. They don't want to talk to just anyone. We have a wonderful woman, Maria, who gathers all their information and puts it together for an obituary. The *Gazette* runs them every week."

"Oh."

"They often run nice photos."

"Right."

"We provide those, too."

"OK."

"We collect money on behalf of the *Gazette* and pay them at the end of each month. One less bill for the family."

Sully nodded. His gaze drifted.

"Is something wrong?" Horace asked.

"No, I just — I figured it was a reporter who wrote the obituaries."

Horace offered a weak smile. "We're a small town. The *Gazette* is a small paper. Anyhow, no reporter could gather information better than Maria. She's very gentle and very thorough. A real people person."

An odd phrase, Sully thought, coming from this guy.

"OK, well, I'll get it to Ron and we're all set."

127

"Very good," Horace said.

He walked Sully to the door. Then, out of the blue, he placed a hand on his shoulder.

"How are you doing, Mr. Harding?"

Sully was so taken aback, all he could do was swallow. He looked into the man's eyes, which seemed suddenly sympathetic. He remembered walking out of here the last time, with Giselle's ashes held close to his chest.

"Not so great," he whispered.

Horace gave his shoulder a squeeze.

"I understand."

Ejecting from an airplane compresses your spine. Sully had been six foot two when he'd pulled that handle. He'd be a half inch shorter by the time he reached the ground.

As he floated toward earth, the chair gone, the parachute open, his body ached and he felt stunned into dull observation, as if the whole world were dipped in slowly poured honey. He watched his plane impact the ground. He saw it burst into flames. His hands gripped the risers. His feet swung below him. The oxygen hose, still attached to his mask, flopped beneath his nose. Off in the distance were thick gray clouds. Everything was dreamily silent.

Then, in an instant — *whoomph* — his mind rushed back, like a boxer snapping back from a blow. He yanked off the mask so he could breathe easier. His senses were on fire, his thoughts clashing like atoms.

First, thinking like a pilot: he was alive, *good*; his chute had functioned, *good*; his plane had gone down in an unpopulated clearing, *good*.

Next thinking like an officer: he had just destroyed a multimillion-dollar aircraft, *bad*; he would be subject to an investigation, *bad*; he'd be months in paperwork and reports, *bad*; and he still had no idea what he'd hit or the damage his own plane had done, *bad*.

Simultaneously, thinking like a husband — Giselle, poor Giselle, he had to let her know he was OK, he was not burning in that fiery metal, its plume of black smoke rising. He was here, floating, a speck in the air. Had she seen him? Did anybody see him?

What he could not know, hanging above earth, were the actions being taken by those on the ground. What he could not know was that, in the minutes that would follow, Elliot Gray, the air traffic controller, the man behind the reedy, nasal voice, would flee the tower, leaving the scene.

What he could not know was that minutes later, Giselle, arriving late, would be in her car, on a single-lane road, and she would see the rising black smoke in the distance. And, being the wife of a pilot, she would jam down on the accelerator with the worst thoughts flashing through her mind.

What he could not know was that the last thing his wife would say as she flew around a curve was a prayer.

Oh, God, please, let him be safe.

He gripped the ropes and descended toward earth.

The radio played, a gospel station. Amy glanced out the car window as they drove by Frieda's Diner. It was jammed, with cars parked up and down the street.

"Good for Frieda," Katherine said, eyes on the road, both hands on the wheel. "Before all this started, she talked to me about having to sell her house."

"Oh yeah?" Amy replied. Amy said "Oh yeah?" to almost anything Katherine said now.

"And they have three kids. It would be hard to find something in her price range."

Katherine smiled. Her mood had improved since the last call from Diane. It came just as she prayed it would.

"*Kath . . . don't be sad.*"

"Diane, what about these other people?"

"*They have their blessings . . . But God has blessed us, too. We are together so you can heal . . . Knowing heaven . . . is what heals us on earth.*"

Katherine repeated the words to herself. *Knowing heaven is what heals us on earth.*

"Am I the one? Have I been chosen to spread the message?"

"*Yes, sister.*"

The words left Katherine serene.

Amy, on the other hand, grew more agitated by the day.

She had hoped to keep a lid on this story, perhaps win an award, pique the interest of a larger market. But after the town hall meeting, that was a pipe dream.

There were now at least five TV stations camped in town. Network news had been there. *Network news!* Amy had stood ten feet from Alan Jeremy, the famous ABC reporter, who wore jeans, a blue dress shirt, and a tie, under an expensive-looking *ABC News* ski parka. Any other time, she'd have gone right up to him, maybe flirted a bit. You never know how someone can help your career.

But under these circumstances, Alan Jeremy was the competition. He had wanted to speak to Katherine, but when Katherine asked what Amy thought about that, Amy quickly suggested he might not be trustworthy. He came from New York. What was his motivation?

"Well, then, we won't speak to him," Katherine said.

"Right," Amy said. She felt a pang of guilt. But Phil had told her, "Stay one step ahead of them. You were there first. Remember, this is our biggest story of the year."

Our biggest story of the year. How Amy had longed for such a chance. But it was a feeding frenzy. *Network news?* And here she was, still lugging around her own camera. She felt so amateurish. How insulting to get trampled by the very organizations she hoped to join.

So she did what they could not. She glued herself to Katherine and made herself indispensable. She offered to shop for her, to make deliveries, to intercept the countless messages in her mailbox and manage the visitors on her front lawn. She acted like her friend and referred to herself as such. The last few nights, Katherine had even allowed Amy to sleep in her guest bedroom, where Amy's suitcase was now stored.

Today, they were going to a nearby hospital to visit a patient with advanced leukemia. He had written to Katherine asking if she would share her understanding of heaven with him. At first, Katherine wanted Pastor Warren to come, but something inside her said no, she could handle this.

"Don't you agree?" Katherine had asked.

"Oh, yeah," Amy had answered.

At the hospital, Katherine held hands with a seventy-four-year-old retired autoworker named Ben Wilkes. Withered from months of chemotherapy, his hair had thinned to strands, his cheeks were sucked in, and the lines around his mouth seemed to crack when he spoke. He was delighted that Katherine had come to see him and showed great interest in her story.

"Your sister," Ben asked. "Does she describe the world around her?"

"She says it's beautiful," Katherine said.

"Does she explain the rules?"

"The rules?"

"About who gets in."

Katherine smiled gently. "All who accept the Lord get in." Diane had never actually used those words, but Katherine knew it was the right thing to say.

"Are you sure she's in heaven?" Ben asked, squeezing her hand tightly. "I mean no disrespect. But I so want to believe it's true."

"It's true," Katherine said. She smiled, closed her eyes, and placed her other palm over their joined hands. "There is life after this life."

132

Ben's mouth fell slightly open, and he inhaled weakly. Then he smiled.

Amy, standing behind her camera, smiled too. She'd been filming the whole thing. No other station had this angle. *There is life after this life.*

And a better job after this job.

The next day, Ben passed away.

Doctors were puzzled. His vital signs had been fine. His medications were the same. There was no reason to suspect a sudden demise.

The best they could conclude was that, following Katherine's visit, his system had "voluntarily" shut down.

Simply put, Ben had given up.

The Eleventh Week

On the morning of February 14, 1876, Alexander Graham Bell applied for a patent on his telephone invention. On that same day, Elisha Gray, the Illinois engineer, applied for a caveat on his own version. Many believe Gray filed first, but that improper actions between Bell's lawyer and the patent examiner, an alcoholic who owed the lawyer money, led to Bell's ultimate victory. His entry was listed as the fifth of the day. Gray's was listed as thirty-ninth. Had Gray acted sooner, even by a day, his place in history might be quite different.

Instead, centuries later, Bell still receives the credit and prestige that come with being first.

In Coldwater, a similar jockeying had begun. According to the archdiocese, Tess Rafferty's message from her mother, the one that caused her to drop her phone in shock, came on a Friday at 8:17 a.m., as marked by the computerized voice on her answering machine. This was nearly two hours earlier than what was previously thought to be the first call, the one claimed by Katherine Yellin, of Harvest of Hope Baptist.

Time lines were important, the archdiocese said. While the Catholic Church was still deliberating the status of this "miracle," it could safely say that whatever was happening to the populace of this tiny Michigan town, Tess Rafferty had been the first.

"So what does that mean?" Samantha asked Tess when they heard about the church's statement.

"Nothing," Tess said. "What difference does it make?"

But that afternoon, when Tess pulled back the curtains, she saw the difference it made.

Her front lawn was covered with worshippers.

Sully held Jules's hand as they walked to the car. The light blue plastic phone remained in the boy's pocket.

Sully had confronted Jules's teacher and principal, his voice so loud he even startled himself.

Since when, he demanded to know, was it a teacher's place to advise a child on the afterlife? To give him a toy phone and tell him he could speak to his dead mother?

"He just seemed so sad," pleaded the teacher, Ramona, a short, heavyset woman in her twenties. "From the first day of school, he was so introverted. I could never get him to answer a question, not even simple math.

"Then one day he raised his hand. Out of the blue. He said he saw on TV that people could talk to heaven. He said his Mommy was in heaven, so that meant she was alive.

"All the other kids were just staring at him. Then one of them started laughing, and you know how kids are

— they all did. And Jules just shrank in his chair and cried."

Sully clenched his fists. He wanted to smash something.

"During recess, I found a toy phone in the kindergarten room. To be honest, Mr. Harding, I had planned to show him how phones were *not* magical. But when I called him in, he saw the phone and he smiled so fast and he asked for it so quickly and . . . I'm sorry. I didn't mean anything. I just told him whatever he believed he could believe."

She began to cry.

"I'm a churchgoing person," she said.

"Well, I'm not," Sully said. "That's still allowed in this town, isn't it?"

The principal, a serious woman in a navy wool blazer, asked if Sully wanted to file a complaint. "It is not our policy to advise on religious matters, and Miss Ramona knows that. We're a public school."

Sully dropped his head. He tried to hold on to his anger, but he felt it withering. If Giselle were here, she'd touch his shoulder, her way of saying, *Calm down, forgive, be nice.* What was the point? A formal complaint? Then what?

He left with a promise it would never happen again.

In the car now, he turned to his son, his beautiful son, his soon-to-be-seven-year-old son with the wavy locks and the skinny chest and the joyful eyes of the mother he hadn't spoken to since the day of the crash, nearly two years now. Sully wished he believed in God again, just to ask Him how He could be so cruel.

136

"Can I talk to you about Mommy, kiddo?"

"OK."

"You know I loved her very much."

"Yeah."

"And you know she loved you more than anything in the world."

Jules nodded.

"But Jule-i-o," he said, using the nickname Giselle playfully called him, "we can't talk to her. I wish we could but we can't. That's what happens when someone dies. They go away."

"You went away."

"I know."

"And you came back."

"It's different."

"Why?"

"Because I didn't die."

"Maybe Mommy didn't, either."

Sully felt his eyes water.

"She did, Jules. We don't like it, but she did."

"How do you know?"

"What do you mean, how do I know?"

"You weren't there."

Sully swallowed. He rubbed a palm over his face. He kept his gaze straight ahead because it was suddenly too hard to look at his child, who with three simple words had repeated the torture Sully put himself through every day.

You weren't there.

With the black smoke of his destroyed airplane spreading in the sky above him, Sully touched the earth, keeping his legs bent and rolling to his side. The parachute, its duty done, lost its gut and flattened into the ground. The grass was damp. The sky was gunmetal gray.

Sully unhooked his fittings, released himself from the chute, and pulled the emergency radio from his vest. He was aching, disoriented, and he wanted more than anything to speak to Giselle. But he knew military protocol. Follow procedure. Radio in. No names. The people on duty would inform her.

"Lynton Tower, this is Firebird 304. I have ejected safely. Location is half mile southwest of airfield. Plane impacted in a clearing. Wreckage location maybe half mile farther south-west. Standing by for pickup."

He waited. Nothing.

"Lynton Tower. Copy my last?"

Nothing.

"Lynton Tower? Nothing heard."

Still no response.

"Lynton Tower?"

Quiet.

"Firebird 304 . . . Out."

What was going on? Where was the tower? He collected his chute, first trying to fold it compactly. But something stirred inside him, and as the image of a worried Giselle grew stronger, he became anxious and gathered the chute haphazardly, pulling it to his chest as if collecting large pillows. He saw a white car in the distance, heading toward the wreckage.

Aviate. He waved his arms.

Navigate. He ran to the road.

Communicate. "I'm OK, I'm OK," he yelled, as if, in some way, his wife might hear him.

One Day Later

NEWS REPORT
Channel 9, Alpena

(Amy, standing in front of Harvest of Hope Baptist Church.)
AMY: They're calling it the Coldwater miracle. After Katherine Yellin started receiving what she says are phone calls from her deceased sister, people wanted to know more. One man in particular is Ben Wilkes. He suffers from advanced leukemia.
(Footage from the hospital.)
BEN: Your sister? Does she describe the world around her?
KATHERINE: She says it's beautiful.
(Images of Ben.)
AMY: Doctors have told Ben he doesn't have much hope. But Katherine's phone calls have heightened his spirits.
(Footage from the hospital.)
BEN: Are you sure she's in heaven? I mean no disrespect. But I so want to believe it's true.
KATHERINE: It's true . . . There is life after this life.
(Amy in front of the church.)

AMY: While there are reports of others receiving heavenly phone calls, Katherine remains the focus of attention.

KATHERINE: If the Lord has chosen me to spread the message, then I have to do it. I'm happy we were able to give Ben some hope today. That made me feel good.

AMY: In Coldwater, I'm Amy Penn, *Nine Action News*.

Phil stopped the tape. He looked at Anton, the station's lawyer.

"I don't see how we're liable," Phil said.

"We're not," Anton replied. "But the Yellin woman might be. She is clearly telling the patient he has nothing to fear. That footage could be used in a lawsuit."

Amy shifted her gaze from one man to the other — Phil with his Viking beard, Anton with his shaved head and charcoal suit. She had been summoned back to Alpena that morning. There could be a problem, she was told. Her report — hurriedly assembled, as Channel 9 could not get enough of the Coldwater story — had run the night of the hospital visit. As usual, it spread rapidly on the Internet.

The next day, Ben died.

Now the cyber world was on fire with finger-pointing.

"There are protests planned," Phil said.

"What kind of protests?" Amy asked.

"People who don't believe in a heaven — or don't want to. They claim this Ben guy killed himself over a lie."

"He didn't *kill* himself," Anton interjected.

"They're blaming Katherine?" Amy said.

"She told him there's life after this life—"

"As does every religion in the world," Anton noted.

Phil thought about that. "So they don't have a leg to stand on?"

"Who knows? You can bring anything to court."

"Wait," Amy said. "These protests—"

"What is the family saying?" Anton asked.

"Nothing yet," Phil answered.

"Be careful there."

"The *protests*?" Amy repeated.

"I don't know," Phil said, turning back to her. "I think tomorrow. Depends on what blog you read."

"You're just reporting the news," Anton said. "Remember that."

"That's right." Phil nodded. "You're right." He turned again to Amy. "Go back."

"What about the protests?" she said.

He looked at her as if the answer were insanely obvious.

"Cover them," he said.

"Be ready at 10:00 a.m.," Samantha had e-mailed. "I've got a surprise for you."

Tess put on makeup for the first time in weeks. She had endured enough surprises recently. But she was going stir-crazy in the house, and quite honestly, any change to the routine would be welcome.

She walked through the kitchen and, as was her pattern now, glanced at the phone to ensure it was on the hook. Thanks-giving was two weeks away. She'd made no plans. She had an aversion to the holiday, anyhow. After the divorce, her mother would hold open-house Thanksgivings and invite half the neighborhood, anyone who didn't have family or was recently widowed or old or alone. It was like that Woody Allen movie where he collects misfit entertainers — a stuttering ventriloquist, a woman who plays drinking glasses — and has a Thanksgiving meal of frozen turkey dinners and Tab. Ruth always made a fuss over who got to pull the turkey wishbone. "Make a wish! Make a wish!" Tess imagined every person in the house wishing one thing: that they wouldn't have to come back next year.

But now she realized what a kindness her mother had offered to people at a vulnerable time. And how it had given Ruth a way to fight her own loneliness. Tess used to wish her father would drive by, honk the horn, and whisk her away.

"God, Tess," she whispered now, angry with herself for being so naive.

A ray of sun dropped through the kitchen skylight. She thought about those people on her lawn. Weren't they freezing?

She grabbed paper cups and the full pot from the coffee machine.

When she opened her front door, a rumbling went through the crowd. Many of them rose. A few yelled "Good morning!" and "Bless you, Tess!" Then suddenly everyone was yelling something. There had to be two hundred people.

Tess held up the cups and squinted into the morning sun.

"Does anyone want coffee?" she yelled. She realized her pot would only serve a fraction of this crowd. She felt like a fool. *Coffee? They want miracles, and you're offering them coffee?*

"I can make more," she mumbled.

"Did your mother speak to you today, Tess?"

Tess swallowed. She shook her head.

"Has she told you why you were chosen?"

"You were the first!"

"Will you pray with us?"

"Bless you, Tess!"

The hubbub was suddenly interrupted by three quick blasts of a car horn. The yellow van from Bright Beginnings, her day care center, was pulling into the driveway. As the crowd backed away, Samantha got out and pulled open the side of the van. A dozen kids in their winter coats jumped to the ground and looked at the crowd.

Tess put a hand to her mouth. Because she could not come to work, her friend had brought work to her.

Tess had never been so happy to see those children in her life.

Doreen carried two Cokes over to the table. She sat at one end, Jack at the other, their guests in between. She still felt uneasy around her ex-husband. The divorce. The papers. The house keys he'd left on the front hall counter. Every snapshot of their disassembled marriage came flipping back in his presence.

144

Had it really been six years already? She was married to a different man. Had a different life. But here was Jack, sitting at their old table in their old house, the house she'd gotten in the breakup, the house Mel, her new husband, had objected to Jack even setting foot inside of, until Doreen told him, "Robbie's friends want to talk to us." Mel grumbled fine, whatever, he was going for a beer.

"Thanks, Mrs. Sellers," said the young man named Henry.

"Thanks, Mrs. Sellers," echoed the one named Zeke.

"It's Mrs. Franklin now," Doreen said.

They looked at each other.

"It's all right," she added.

They were handsome young men, fit, square-shouldered, childhood friends of Robbie's from the old neighborhood. They used to ring the bell, and Robbie would come bounding down the steps clutching a football and brush past Doreen with a "See ya, Mom" and she'd say, "Zip up your jacket," the words chasing after him like the breeze of a fan.

All three boys had enlisted out of high school. They did basic training together and, thanks to somebody who knew somebody, were stationed together in Afghanistan. Neither Henry nor Zeke was with Robbie the day he was killed. Doreen was glad about that.

"When did you boys get back?" Jack asked.

"September," Zeke said.

"Yeah, September," Henry said.

"Good to be done?"

"Oh, yeah."

"Yes, Sir."

Everyone nodded. Zeke sipped his Coke.

"So, like, we were talking . . . ," Henry said.

"Yeah," Zeke picked up, "We were asking each other . . ." He glanced at Henry. "You wanna go?"

"No, it's OK, you can—"

"Nah."

"I mean . . ."

They both stopped.

"It's all right," Jack said. "You can talk to us."

"Yes," Doreen said, squirming at the word *us*. "Of course, boys, talk about anything."

Finally, Zeke said, "We were just wondering, like . . . what does Robbie tell you? When he calls?"

Jack leaned back. He felt a shiver.

"He only calls his mother. Doreen?"

She told them. Her conversations had been reassurances mostly, that Robbie was OK, that he was safe, that he was in a beautiful place.

"He usually says something that I like," she added. "He says . . . 'The end is not the end.'"

Zeke and Henry exchanged sheepish grins.

"That's funny," Henry said.

"What is?" Jack said.

Henry fingered the Coke bottle.

"No, it's just . . . it's this rock band. He was totally into them. House of Heroes."

"They have this CD," Zeke said, "*The End Is Not the End*. He kept asking for someone to send it to him."

"Yeah, for, like, months. *The End Is Not the End*. Send me *The End Is Not the End*. It's kinda punk music."

"Yeah, but, like, a Christian band, I think."

"Right."

"House of Heroes."

"His favorite CD."

"*The End Is Not the End*."

Jack looked at his ex-wife. *A band?*

"So, like, besides that," Henry continued, "does he ever talk about the guys in his squadron?"

Jason Turk, the phone store clerk, rubbed his hands briskly as he slammed the door on the snowstorm. Again, he'd forgotten his gloves. Again, his girlfriend was right. *Your brain works part-time, Jason.*

He opened the closet marked DIAL-TEK EMPLOYEES ONLY. His cheeks were wet and his nose dripping. He grabbed a box of Kleenex off the shelf and heard a rapping on the back door.

"Aw, come on," he mumbled. "It's not even eight o'clock." When he opened the door, there was Sully, bundled up in his suede jacket and ski cap.

"Hey, it's Iron Man," Jason said, grinning.

"How ya doing?"

"Come on in."

"Thanks."

"I don't have any money for you, bro."

"I know."

"You want a Coke?"

"I'm good."

They entered the office.

"So what's up?"

Sully exhaled. He pulled a yellow pad from his bag. "I need a favor."

An hour later Sully returned to his car, wondering what he'd stumbled into.

Following a hunch, he'd shown Jason the names, numbers, and addresses of the seven Coldwater residents who claimed contact with heaven. He knew Katherine Yellin had purchased her phone at that store — the whole country seemed to know that — but Sully wondered if the others had as well.

Jason punched the information into his computer. What came back was curious. Four of the seven showed as customers — not unusual, given the paucity of phone stores around Coldwater — but six of the seven, all but Kelly Podesto, the teenage girl, had the same phone provider.

And the same type of service.

"What is it?" Sully asked Jason.

"It's this web-based storage thing, kind of like the cloud, you know? Keep your e-mail, your pictures, save it in one account."

Sully looked at his pad. He ran a finger down several categories he'd drawn up. One of them was "DOD" — date of death.

"Can you pull up how long they each had that service?"

"Probably. It might take a few minutes." Jason started to type, then stopped and leaned back. "I can get in major crap for showing you this."

148

"I kinda figured," Sully said.

Jason drummed his fingers on his knees.

"Ah, what the hell. Let's do it." He grinned. "I hate this job anyhow. My girlfriend says I should be a professional photographer."

"Maybe she's right."

"She's a pain. You got a girlfriend?"

"No."

"Married?"

"I was."

"She dump you, or you dump her?"

"She died."

"Whoa. Sorry, bro."

Sully sighed. "Me too."

Alexander Bell met the love of his life, Mabel, when she came to him as a deaf student. She was ten years his junior, but Bell fell for her hard, and over the years, her encouragement spurred him on in his work. Had her tears not drawn him onto that train car to Philadelphia, his greatest invention might never have blossomed. Yet the telephone remained something that Mabel, who'd lost her hearing from scarlet fever, would never be able to share with her husband.

Sometimes, love brings you together even as life keeps you apart.

In the ambulance after the plane crash, Sully demanded a cell phone (his own phone, like the rest of his possessions, was burning in the wreckage), and he called Giselle a dozen times. No answer. He called her parents. Nothing there, either. He tried the airfield again on his emergency radio. Nothing. Something was seriously wrong. Where was everybody?

His head was pounding, and his lower back was now screaming with pain. At the hospital — a small regional facility in Lynton — they ran through standard tests, checked all of Sully's vital signs, took blood, cleaned up several cuts, and did X-rays of his spinal column. They gave him pain medication that left him woozy. Someone told him the plane that he'd collided with, a small twin-engine Cessna, had landed safely. He didn't ask why the two planes were on the same landing path. The entire time, he kept asking about his wife.

"Give me her number," a nurse said. "We'll have someone keep calling it until we get her."

"Airfield, too," Sully croaked.

As he skimmed the surface between consciousness and sleep, he saw the nurse talking and giving instructions, saw someone come in and pull her outside, saw her come back in and talk to someone else, then saw them all disappear.

His eyes closed. His mind quieted. These would be the last blissful minutes that he did not know what he could not know:

That Giselle had seen the rising smoke and accelerated toward the airfield in her Chevy Blazer.

That Elliot Gray, the air traffic controller, had fled the facility and jumped into a blue Toyota Camry.

That Giselle had chanted a prayer — *Please God, let him be safe* — as her hands gripped the wheel so tightly they shook.

150

That Elliot Gray's Camry reached sixty-three miles per hour on the narrow access road.

That Giselle's Chevy came flying around a bend and, in a blinding instant, smashed full-speed into the Camry.

That Elliot Gray was hurled twenty feet in the air.

That Giselle, strapped in by a seat belt, did three rotations as the Chevy flipped over. That her vehicle landed in a ditch. That she was wearing a lavender sweater. That the Beatles' "Hey, Jude" was playing on the radio.

That she'd need to be cut loose from the twisted metal. That she'd be medevaced to a hospital in Columbus.

That she'd be unconscious by the time she arrived.

That she would never wake up.

That Elliot Gray was dead.

The Twelfth Week

"Here now, not hereafter! Here now, not hereafter! Here now, not—"

Katherine put her hands to her ears. "Good Lord, why don't they stop?"

"Maybe we should go downstairs," Amy said. "It's quieter."

"No!" Katherine snapped. "This is my home. I won't hide in a basement."

Outside, the protesters continued.

"HERE NOW, NOT HEREAFTER! HERE—"

They had gathered in the street just before noon. There were at least fifty people, many with signs like HEAVEN CAN WAIT! and some harsher: BELIEF KILLS! or DEATH BY HOAX!

The Ben Wilkes video had spread even faster than the original Phone Call from Heaven video, once news of Ben's death became widespread. It was followed by reports of six other patients around the world with terminal illnesses who had reportedly seen the Coldwater videos and then died unexpectedly — as if deliberately letting themselves go.

152

Although these people would have passed away eventually, the mystery of death is why it chooses a particular moment. With no earthly answer, coincidence can become conspiracy. And given the media's insatiable appetite for Coldwater, stories that heaven might be *killing* people were irresistible.

"These religious nuts should stay away from sick patients," one angry man told a TV camera.

"They're no better than those terrorists who promise a reward if you blow yourself up," added a young woman.

"I knew Ben Wilkes years ago," an older factory worker claimed. "He was a fighter. He wouldn't have let go if these people hadn't hypnotized him — or whatever they do."

Before long, a group called Hang Up On Heaven had formed, and protests were organized — like the one outside Katherine's house right now.

"HERE NOW, NOT HEREAFTER! HERE NOW—"

Inside, Amy boiled water and made peppermint tea. She brought the cup over, but Katherine was so lost in thought, she didn't even see it.

"Have some," Amy coaxed.

"Oh." Katherine blinked. "Thank you."

Amy felt torn. She knew Phil wanted a story on these protesters — but how could she talk to them and not lose Katherine's trust, the one thing that kept her a notch ahead of the other reporters?

"You're a friend," Katherine said.

"Of course," Amy mumbled.

"This all started once those other people got involved, didn't it? Tess Rafferty? Honestly. She stopped going to church years ago. She admitted it!"

Katherine waved her hands, as if trying to convince an invisible witness. She squeezed her pink phone. She rolled it over in her palm. She stared at it for several seconds. Then her tone changed.

"Amy?"

"Yeah?"

"Do you believe me?"

"I do."

The truth was, Amy believed that Katherine believed. That was close enough, wasn't it?

"I called my kids," Katherine said. "They're down in Detroit. You know what they told me?"

"What?"

"They said I spend too much time on religion." She almost laughed. "I was hoping they might come up. Stay with me. But John says he's buried at work. And Charlie says . . ."

She gulped back a word.

"What?"

"I . . . *embarrass* him. That's what Diane's daughters told me, too. That's why they haven't come to see me."

She started to cry. Amy looked away. How could you not feel sympathy for this woman — deluded as she might be?

The chanting of the protesters grew louder. Amy glanced through the bay window and saw a squad car parked by the curb. Jack Sellers, the police chief, was holding up his hands as he spoke. A TV crew held boom microphones overhead. The news would be everywhere. Phil would be furious.

"I didn't kill anyone," Katherine whispered.

"Of course not," Amy said.

Katherine buried her face in her hands.

"How can they say such things? My sister is in heaven. God is watching all of us. Why would I kill anyone?"

Amy looked at her camera, sitting on the kitchen table.

"You know what?" she said. "Let's tell them that."

Pastor Warren read from Scripture every afternoon, sitting in his office on the brown leather couch. Today he focused on the book of Isaiah. He came upon a verse in chapter 60:

Look and see, for everyone is coming home. Your sons are coming from distant lands; your little daughters will be carried on the hip. Your eyes will shine and your hearts will thrill with joy.

He loved those words. In another time, he might have marked the passage, saved it for his Sunday sermon. But now he wondered if it wouldn't be used as validation for these phone calls from the dead. *Look and see, for everyone is coming home.* He hated having to filter his messages this way. He felt like a piece of paper being constantly ripped in half, getting smaller and smaller. Serve God. Serve the people. God. The people.

155

Colleagues told him he should be happy. All the churches in Coldwater were filled, and Sunday services were standing room only. St. Vincent's, Father's Carroll's congregation, had grown the most, quadrupling since Tess Rafferty and her visit from the bishop.

Brrrnnnng!

"Yes?"

"It's me, Pastor."

"Come in, Mrs. Pulte."

She entered without her message pad. He could tell by her expression that something was wrong.

"Pastor, I have to tell you something. It's hard for me to say."

"Feel free to tell me anything."

"I need to leave."

"Leave early?"

"Leave the job. It's too . . ." She began to tear up. "I've been here seven years."

"You've been wonderful—"

"I wanted to help the church . . ."

Her breathing accelerated.

"Sit down, please. It's all right, Mrs. Pulte."

She remained standing but spoke rapidly, the words spilling out. "All these calls from around the world — I can't handle it anymore. They ask me things — I tell them I don't know, but they keep going, some of them crying, some of them yelling, and I . . . I don't know what to do. Some tell me about a loved one, they beg to speak with them again. And others are so angry! They say we're spreading false gospel. In all my years, I never thought . . . Well. I go home every night and just

156

collapse, Pastor. My blood pressure, the doctor checked it last week, it's very high, and Norman is concerned. I'm sorry. I'm so sorry. I don't want to let you down. I just can't . . ."

She cried so hard she could no longer speak. Warren offered a sympathetic smile.

"I understand, Mrs. Pulte."

He went to her and put a hand on her shoulder. Outside the office he could hear the never-ending ringing of the phones.

"Will God forgive me?" she whispered.

Long before He forgives me, Warren thought.

Jack Sellers spun the flashing light atop the police cruiser and gave the siren a short blast. The worshippers on Tess's lawn stirred and shifted. He stepped out of the car.

"Morning," he said, stiffly.

"Morning," a few of them responded.

"What are you all doing here?"

He kept eyeing the door. What he really wanted was the same thing they wanted — for Tess to come out.

"We're praying," a skinny woman answered.

"For what?"

"To hear from heaven. Do you want to pray with us?"

Jack pushed Robbie from his mind. "You can't just congregate on someone's lawn."

"Are you a believer, officer?"

"What I believe isn't important."

"What you believe is *most* important."

Jack kicked his shoe into the ground. First, those protesters at Katherine Yellin's house. Now this. Of all the things he never expected to handle in tiny Coldwater. Crowd control.

"You're gonna have to go," he said.

A young man in a green parka stepped forward.

"Please. We're not causing any trouble."

"We only want to pray," added a girl kneeling on the lawn.

"Wait, I've read about you," the young man said. "The policeman. Your wife — she's heard from your son. She's a chosen one. How can you tell us to leave?"

Jack looked away.

"My ex-wife. And that's none of your business."

Tess appeared in the doorway, a red tartan blanket around her shoulders, frayed jeans and blue boots, her hair pulled back in a long ponytail. Jack tried not to stare.

"Do you need help?" he yelled.

Tess looked over the worshippers.

"No, I'm fine," she yelled back.

Jack motioned with his hands, *Is it OK if I come in?* She nodded, and he eased through the crowd, which fell silent as he passed, something he was used to whenever he wore the uniform.

Jack looked like a cop — flat line of a mouth, strong chin, probing, deep-set eyes — but he had never been crazy about police work. His father was on the force, and his father's father before him. After the army, Jack was expected to follow suit. He started in Grand

Rapids. Did six years of patrol work. Then Robbie was born, and he and Doreen moved to Coldwater. A small-town life. That's what they wanted. He put away his badge and opened a lawn and garden supply store.

"It's better to work for yourself," he told his father.

"A cop's a cop, Jack," his father said.

Three years later, the store went under. With no other skills, Jack returned to his bloodline. He joined the Coldwater police.

By his thirty-seventh birthday, he was the chief.

In the eight years since, he'd never had to fire his gun. He'd only pulled it six times; one of those turned out to be a fox (not a burglar) rooting around in a woman's cellar.

"You didn't speak up at the meeting," Tess said, handing him a cup of coffee.

"No."

"Why?"

"I don't know. Fear? My job?"

She pursed her lips. "At least you're honest."

"My son says I should tell everyone. About heaven. When he calls."

"My mother does too."

"Am I letting him down?"

Tess shrugged. "I don't know. At times I feel like nothing matters anymore. I think, this life is just a waiting room. My mother is up there — and I'll see her again.

"But then I realize I always believed that. Or I said I did."

Jack slid his cup back and forth on the counter. "Maybe you just wanted proof."

"Is that what I have now?"

Jack thought about his discussions with Robbie's army buddies. *The end is not the end.* Something bothered him about that.

"I don't know what we have."

Tess looked at him.

"Were you a good father?"

No one had ever asked him that. He thought about the time he encouraged Robbie to enlist. The trouble with Doreen.

"Not always."

"Honest again."

"Were you a good daughter?"

She smiled. "Not always."

The truth was, Tess and Ruth also had their stormy years. When she went off to college, Tess's beauty was quickly noticed. A string of boyfriends followed. Ruth never approved. The spirit of an absent father haunted their conversations.

"What would you know about keeping a man?" Tess once screamed.

"These aren't men, they're boys!"

"Stay out of it!"

"I'm trying to protect you!"

"I don't need your protection!"

And on and on. After graduation, Tess lived with three different men. She stayed away from Coldwater. One day, when she was twenty-nine, she got a strange

160

call from Ruth, who was looking for a phone number. A woman named Anna Kahn.

"What do you need Anna's number for?"

"We have her wedding this weekend."

"Mom, she got married when I was, like, fifteen."

"What are you talking about?"

"She lives in New Jersey."

A confused pause. "I don't understand."

"Mom? Are you all right?"

It was diagnosed as early-onset Alzheimer's. It advanced rapidly. The doctors warned that Ruth should not be left alone, that women in her condition could sometimes wander off, cross busy streets, forget basic safety. They recommended home health aides, or assisted living. But Tess knew the one thing her mother cherished most was the one thing this affliction would inevitably take away — her independence.

So Tess came home. And they were independent together.

Sully and his mother had a different sort of relationship. She asked. He answered. She deduced. He denied.

"What are you doing?" she'd inquired the night before. Jules was eating and Sully was on the couch, studying his notes.

"Just checking some stuff."

"For work?"

"Sort of."

"Sales calls?"

"Kind of."

"Why does this matter to you?"

He looked up. She was standing over him, her arms crossed.

"If people want to talk to ghosts, let them."

"How do you know I'm—"

"Sully."

One word was all it took.

"OK," he said, his voice lowered. "I don't like it. Jules carries a phone. He lives in a fantasy. Someone has to expose this."

"So you're a detective?"

"No."

"You've got notes."

"No."

Deduce. Deny.

"You think they're all lying?"

"I don't know."

"You don't think God works miracles?"

"Are you done?"

"Almost."

"What else?"

She looked at Jules, who was watching TV. Her voice lowered.

"Are you doing this for him or for you?"

He thought about that now as he sipped his coffee and slouched inside the Buick, which was parked down the street from Davidson & Sons. Maybe some of this *was* for him, to make him feel like he was doing something with his life; maybe some of it was to make the rest of the world feel the pain that he was feeling, that dead is dead, that Giselle was never making contact again and neither were their mothers or sisters or sons.

He shifted in his seat. He had been here over an hour, waiting, watching. Finally, just after noon, he saw Horace come out, wearing a long overcoat. He got in his car and drove away. Sully hoped he was going for lunch. He needed to check on something.

He hurried to the door and let himself in.

Inside, as always, was quiet and warm. Sully went to the main office. No one there. He walked down the hall, poking his head into different rooms. Soft music played. Still nobody. He came around a corner and heard the tapping of computer keys. Inside a narrow, carpeted office sat a small woman, cherub-cheeked, with an upturned nose and a pageboy haircut, doughy arms, and a silver cross around her neck.

"I'm looking for Horace," Sully said.

"Ooh, I'm so sorry, he just left for lunch."

"I can wait."

"You sure? He might be an hour or so."

"That's OK."

"Would you like some coffee?"

"Coffee would be nice. Thank you." He held out his hand. "My name's Sully."

"I'm Maria," she said.

I know, he thought.

Maria Nicolini was indeed, as Horace had claimed, a people person. She chatted. And chatted. Any one of your sentences elicited three from her. She was endlessly interested, and on your mentioning a

163

particular event or destination, she would lift her gaze and say, "Ooh, tell me about that." It didn't hurt that she was in the Rotary Club and on the Coldwater Historical Commission and that she worked weekends at Zeda's bakery, from which half the town bought its bread. Maria either knew you or knew someone who did.

Thus, when grieving families met with her at the funeral home, they were not reluctant to talk about their departed loved ones — in fact, they were happy to share memories. It made them feel better. Small stories. Funny details. They trusted Maria to write the obituary. Her *Gazette* pieces were always long and complimentary.

"Account sales, tell me about that," she asked Sully.

"It's pretty simple. You go to businesses, ask if they want to advertise, sell them the space."

"Is Ron Jennings a good boss?"

"He's fine. By the way, your obituaries are really well done. I read a few."

"Goodness, thank you." She seemed touched. "I used to want to be a real writer — when I was younger. But this is a good way to help others. The families keep them, so it's important to be accurate and thorough. I'm up to one hundred and forty-nine, you know."

"One hundred and forty-nine obituaries?"

"Yes. I have them all here."

She pulled open a file drawer, which fairly glowed with organization. Each obituary was arranged by year and by name. There were additional files marked by plastic tabs, the tabs lined up perfectly with the files behind them.

"What are all those?" Sully asked.

"My notes. I transcribe our conversations, just so that I don't miss anything." She lowered her voice. "Sometimes when people talk to me, they're crying so badly, it's hard to understand them the first time. So I use a little tape recorder."

Sully was impressed. "You're more thorough than any big-city reporter I ever met."

"You know real reporters?" she asked. "Ooh, tell me about that."

The first time Sully ever made a newspaper was for the worst thing that ever happened to him.

PILOT CRASHES PLANE AFTER MIDAIR COLLISION, read the top headline. And underneath, in smaller letters: WIFE AND CONTROLLER IN FATAL ACCIDENT.

Sully saw the paper in the cafeteria of the Ohio hospital where Giselle lay in a bed, hooked to tubes and intravenous drips, bruised to purplish, orangish colors that didn't look human. He had been there two sleepless days already. Everything was a blur.

The nurse in Lynton, where he'd been brought after the crash, had told him the news. He remembered hearing *accident* and *wife* and *Columbus*, and then he was in a cab, screaming at the driver to go faster, his brain wafting in and out of focus, and then somehow he was running crooked through an emergency room, yelling at doctors, *Where is she? Where is she?* and then breaking down at her bedside when he saw her — *Oh my God, oh my God, oh my God* — feeling arms on

165

him, medical staff, then security, then his in-laws, then his own hands, holding himself as his body shook.

Two days. Two nights. His back was in awful pain, he couldn't sleep, he was dizzy and disheveled. Just to make his body move, he'd gone to get a coffee from the first-floor cafeteria. There, on a side table, was a discarded newspaper. He glanced at it once, then glanced again. He recognized his younger face in an old navy photo. Alongside it were photos of the damaged Cessna, which had landed safely, and Sully's wrecked F/A-18, scraps of the fuselage scattered across a field, a tip of the wing, a burned-out engine. He stared as if studying a painting. He wondered how newspapers decided headlines. Why was PILOT CRASHES PLANE above WIFE AND CONTROLLER IN FATAL ACCIDENT? To him, "wife" was infinitely more important. Giselle, poor, innocent, beautiful Giselle, who did nothing wrong but drive to get her husband — her husband, who did nothing wrong but listen to an air traffic controller, an air traffic controller who made a grievous mistake and was too gutless to face it and who ran like a coward, killing himself and nearly killing the best person Sully would ever know. That was the headline. They had it all wrong.

He crumpled up the newspaper. He threw it in the trash. There are two stories for every life; the one you live, and the one others tell.

A week before Thanksgiving, there was not a hotel room available within ten miles of Coldwater. The gathering of pilgrims at Lankers Field was now

166

estimated at five thousand people, and the protesters outside Katherine Yellin's house were at least three hundred strong — half in support, half against. Jack's Coldwater police force, totally overwhelmed, had borrowed officers from Moss Hill and other neighboring towns, but it still wasn't enough. They could spend all day just writing parking tickets. The Coldwater Market had delivery trucks several times a day now, as opposed to once a week. The gas station had to close periodically when it ran out of fuel. Frieda's hired extra staff and became the first twenty-four-hour business in Coldwater's history. The local hardware store ran low on plywood and paint, in part due to people making signs that sprang up on lawns everywhere: PARKING $5, then PARKING [dolla]10, then PARKING $20.

There seemed to be no end to the hysteria. Everyone in town carried a phone, sometimes two or three. Jeff Jacoby, the mayor, received dozens of license requests for new businesses, from T-shirt companies to religious merchandisers, all willing to quickly move into the boarded-up shops on Lake Street.

Meanwhile, a national daytime talk show, the most popular in the country, was sending a crew from Los Angeles — including the famous host! — to do a special broadcast. Many residents complained about the intrusion, but Jeff had no shortage of locations quietly asking to be a part of the program.

The seven phone call recipients had become familiar names to everyone in town — as had their story lines. In addition to Katherine, Tess, and Doreen, there were Eddie Doukens and his deceased ex-wife, Jay James

167

and his former business partner, Anesh Barua and his departed daughter, and Kelly Podesto and her teenage best friend, killed last year by a drunk driver.

All but Katherine had agreed to participate in the talk show.

She was planning something of her own.

Two Days Later

NEWS REPORT
Channel 9, Alpena

(Close-up of Katherine.)
KATHERINE: I didn't kill anyone. I would never kill anyone. I spread the words given to me from heaven.

(Amy in front of protesters.)
AMY: It's a message Katherine Yellin wants these protesters to understand. What happened with Ben Wilkes, the terminally ill former autoworker, was what he wanted.

(Footage of Ben at hospital.)
BEN: I so want to believe it's true.

(Amy in front of protesters.)
AMY: Ben Wilkes died of a terminal cancer. Yet these angry protesters claim Katherine Yellin was in some way responsible. The burden of being a so-called chosen one has been difficult for Yellin, as she shared in an exclusive conversation with *Nine Action News*.

(Close-up of Katherine, crying.)
KATHERINE: I didn't ask for this blessing. God sent my sister back for a reason.
AMY: What's been the hardest part?

169

KATHERINE: That people don't believe me.

AMY: Like the people protesting out there?

KATHERINE: Yes, exactly. They scream all day. They say horrible things. Some of their signs . . .

(She breaks down.)

AMY: It's all right.

KATHERINE: I'm sorry.

AMY: It's all right.

KATHERINE: You see, they're the ones missing out. They're the ones not hearing God's message — that heaven is real, and that none of us should be afraid anymore.

(Footage of protesters.)

PROTESTERS: HERE NOW, NOT HEREAFTER!

(Amy in front of house.)

AMY: Katherine Yellin said she is so certain of the messages, she is willing to do something no one else has.

(Close-up of Katherine.)

KATHERINE: I will share a call with everyone out there.

AMY: With these protesters?

KATHERINE: With anyone. I am not afraid. I will ask my sister to speak to these people, to tell them the truth. When they hear her words, they'll know.

(Amy on the street.)

AMY: The details of this shocking new development are still to come, but soon the whole town may get a chance to hear what heaven sounds like. We at *Nine Action News* will keep you posted — first and always. In Coldwater, I'm Amy Penn.

In his office in Alpena, Phil watched the final frame of her report and smiled.

Brilliant, he said to himself.

This Amy Penn might make it after all.

Jules sat at the library table, leafing through a Curious George book. Liz stood over him.

"Do you like monkeys?"

"They're OK," Jules mumbled.

"Just OK?"

"I like tigers better."

"Maybe I can find you a tiger book."

Jules looked up.

"Come on," Liz said.

He jumped from the chair and put his palm in hers. Sully watched with mixed emotions. He loved that his son had taken a woman's hand. He still wished it were Giselle's.

Before him, spread out, were the *Gazette* obituaries of each of the people who had supposedly called from heaven. Thanks to Maria, they were bursting with details — family history, job history, favorite vacation spots, pet expressions. Sully had been hesitant to ask for these at the *Gazette* offices (what reason could he give that didn't seem like snooping?), but when he mentioned something to Liz, she went to a cabinet, pulled open two drawers, and said, "What do you need? We keep every issue here."

Of course, Sully realized — local paper, local library, why wouldn't they? He entered details now on his yellow pad. The more he wrote, the more his mind drifted to the other files in Maria's office — the transcriptions of conversations she'd had with the families. The details in those would be even greater, enough to paint a truly complete portrait of the people who died and perhaps reveal a link that Sully had been missing.

The real mystery, of course, remained the voices themselves. Every person contacted swore those voices were real. It couldn't be an impersonator. No one could pull that off. Was there a machine that could change the tonality of a voice? Something someone could speak through and sound like someone else?

Sully's cell phone vibrated. He looked at the display. Ron Jennings. He ignored it. A minute later, a text message appeared on the screen

Where are you?

Sully shut off the phone.

"Dad, look."

Jules was holding a picture book. Its cover was a tiger.

"That was fast," Sully said.

Liz grinned. "I spend a lot of time looking at these shelves."

Jules climbed into his chair and began leafing through the pages.

"He's a doll," Liz said.

"He is," Sully said. "That a good book, Jule-i-o?"

"Yeah." He flipped the pages. "I'm gonna tell Mommy I read the whole thing."

Liz looked away. Sully went back to the obituaries, searching for clues to prove that death is silent.

Bad news has no limit. We often feel it should, like a rainstorm that can't possibly get any heavier. But a storm can always worsen, and the burdens of life can, too.

Sully's plane had been destroyed, his wife had been in a catastrophic accident, the recordings from the air traffic tower were indecipherable, and the man whose voice was on them — the only man who could vindicate Sully's actions — was dead and buried, his body too mangled, they said, to even have the coffin open at his funeral.

This was more than any one man should handle. But eight days after the crash, with Giselle's condition still unchanged, Sully looked up to see two naval officers entering her hospital room.

"We need you to come with us," one of them said.

Bad news getting worse.

The blood report had come back from the hospital. It showed traces of alcohol in Sully's system. Although they never mentioned this, when the investigators in the small naval office in Columbus began to ask him questions — "Take us through the events of the night before" — Sully immediately sensed it, and he felt as if a giant hammer had just come down on his stomach. In the rush of events that had spiraled him downward, he never thought about the night before the flight. He hadn't planned on flying. He hadn't worried about drinking. *Think, think!* He'd had a vodka tonic with two of his squadron mates in the hotel restaurant before going to his room, but what time was that? Was

173

it one vodka or two? What time had he flown? The rule was, "Twelve hours from bottle to throttle" . . .

Oh God, he thought.

He felt his future collapsing in front of him.

"I want a lawyer," he said, his voice shaking.

The Thirteenth Week

A heavy snow descended on Coldwater and by sunrise on Thanksgiving morning, the streets were coated in a thick white layer. All around town, people stepped outside to grab a newspaper or shovel the front walk. They breathed in the cold, silent air, a balm to the hysteria of the last few weeks.

Inside her house on Cuthbert Road, Tess tightened her robe and came into the kitchen. She hoped the snow would send the people on her lawn someplace else, and in fact, many had left for the shelter of Coldwater's churches.

Still, when Tess opened her front door — the sunlight bouncing brightly off the fresh white powder — at least thirty people remained, covered in blankets or cramped inside tents. She saw a baby's crib, empty, its bottom covered in snow, the mother and child peeking out from a tent flap.

"Good morning, Tess."

"God bless you, Tess."

"Pray with us, Tess."

She felt her chest well up as if she were going to cry, all these people in the cold, all these people who *weren't* getting calls, who held their phones in hopes of having happen to them what was happening to her, as if miracles were contagious. She thought about her mother. The open-house Thanksgivings.

"Come inside," she said suddenly. Then louder, "Please! All of you! Come inside and get warm!"

At Harvest of Hope Baptist Church, the smell of fried potatoes laid claim to the kitchen. Turkeys were being cut and distributed. Gravy was ladled from a stainless steel pot.

Pastor Warren moved among the strangers, pouring them iced tea, offering them encouragement. Most of the volunteers were his regular congregants, who had delayed their own Thanksgiving meals to serve others. The snow had brought in more outsiders than they'd expected. Folding chairs were carried from the storeroom.

Earlier, Warren had a phone call from Katherine Yellin. They hadn't spoken in weeks.

"Happy Thanksgiving, Pastor."

"Yes, Katherine. To you, too."

"Are you well, Pastor?"

"The Lord got me up this morning — against all odds."

It was an old line, but he heard her chuckle. He'd almost forgotten how, before all this started, Katherine had frequently visited him — to grieve for her sister, yes, but to also seek his counsel, to study Scripture. She'd been a loyal churchgoer, and she doted on him like a family member, even drove him to the doctor once when he stubbornly fought a head cold.

"Pastor, I'd like to help with the meal today."

"I see."

"Do you think that's OK?"

Warren hesitated. He'd witnessed the commotion Katherine now caused. The protesters. The TV crews.

"Of course, my dear, we'd welcome your help normally. But I think . . ."

A pause.

"Never mind, I understand," she said.

"It's difficult—"

"No, no, I—"

"Maybe we—"

"It's all right. I just wanted to wish you a good holiday."

Warren swallowed.

"God be with you, Katherine."

He heard her breathe out deeply.

"Yes, Pastor. God be with you, too."

All blessings do not bless the same. While the other so-called chosen ones felt a healing glow each time their loved ones spoke from heaven, Doreen, regrettably, no longer did. Her initial elation had given way to something unexpected: a heightened sadness. Even depression.

She realized this on Thanksgiving morning, when she stood in her kitchen, doing the math for the evening's meal. In counting the names — *Lucy, Randy, the two kids, me and Mel* — she'd actually counted Robbie as if he were coming. But he wasn't coming. Nothing had changed. Before he'd made contact, she had started to close the wound on his death. She had finally reached level ground with Mel, who so often in the last two years had grumbled, "Enough. Life is for the living. We gotta move on."

Now she'd been hurtled backward. Robbie was part of her life again. But what kind of part? The initial joy of hearing his voice had turned to an unsettling dissatisfaction. Instead of feeling reconnected with her only son, she felt his loss as palpably as she did when the news of his death arrived. An unexpected phone call here or there? A clipped conversation? A phenomenon that might disappear as quickly as it came? The awful part would still not change. Robbie was never coming home. He would never again be hunkered at the kitchen table, his hooded sweatshirt loose on his muscular young frame; he would never again stuff his mouth with milk-soaked Frosted Flakes; he would never again be sprawled across the couch, barefoot, flipping the remote from one cartoon to the next, or pull up in his old Camaro with Jessica, his pixie-haired girl-friend, their music blasting; he would never grab Doreen from behind in a mighty bear hug and rub his nose in the back of her head and say, "MommyMommyMommyMommy."

Heaven, everyone told her. *It's proof. Your son is in heaven.* But she'd already believed that, long before she heard his voice. Somehow, heaven was more comforting when it was only in her mind.

She fingered the phone cord and followed it to the wall. Then, abruptly, she unclipped the connector and let it drop.

Circling the house, she disconnected every phone, wrapping the cords around the units themselves. She put them all in a box, got her coat from the closet, and drove through the snow to the Goodwill drop on Main Street.

No more calls. No more defying nature, she told herself. There is a time for hello and a time for good-bye. It's why the act of burying things seems natural, but the act of digging them up does not.

Thanks largely to the navy, Sully and Giselle had lived in five different states. There was Illinois — where they met in college — Virginia, California, Florida (where Jules was born), and Michigan, suburban Detroit, where they settled after Sully joined the reserves, a good midway spot between their families.

No matter where they were, every Thanksgiving, Sully's parents came to visit. Now, for the first time since high school, the visit was reversed; Sully was back at the family holiday table, alongside his Uncle Theo and Aunt Martha, both in their eighties; Bill and Shirley Castle, the longtime next-door neighbors; Jules, his face covered in mashed potatoes — and Liz, from the library, whom Jules had invited last week while she was reading him *Tilly the Tiger* and who had accepted on the spot.

"Is it OK?" Jules had later asked his grandmother at Sully's insistence. "Liz is my friend."

"Certainly, sweetheart. How old is she?"

"Twenty."

She turned, eyebrows raised, to Sully.

"Wait till you see her hair," he added.

Privately, Sully was glad. Liz was like a big sister to Jules. Sully trusted her to watch him while he did his work. Anyhow, there were worse places for a kid to hang out than a library.

Sully's mother entered with the turkey. "Here it is!" she announced.

"Beautiful," said Uncle Theo.

"Wow," said Liz.

"I had to order it a month in advance. You can't count on anything at the market anymore. With all the crazies here, you go in to buy ketchup and they're out of it."

"What market runs out of ketchup?" Aunt Martha said.

"The town has gone bananas," said Bill.

"How about the traffic?" added his wife.

"If it weren't so cold, I'd walk everywhere."

"You said it."

"Bananas."

It went on this way, as it did at nearly every dinner table in town, families reflecting on how much Coldwater had changed since the miracles. There were complaints, head shakes, more complaints.

But there was also talk about heaven. And faith. And God. There were more prayers said than in years past. More requests for forgiveness. The volunteers for soup kitchens far exceeded the need. The mattresses at churches far outnumbered the weary.

Despite the traffic snarls, the long lines, or the port-a-johns now positioned on streets in town, nobody went hungry or homeless in Coldwater this Thanksgiving, a fact not recorded in anyone's journal or reported on by any news service.

"How about a toast?"

The group filled its glasses with wine. Sully took the bottle from Uncle Theo, flashed a look at his parents, then passed it straight along to Aunt Martha.

Sully would no longer drink in front of his father. Fred Harding had been in the air force during the Korean War. Sixty years later, he retained the angular crew cut of a military man and the same no-nonsense point of view. He had been proud when Sully signed up for officer training out of college. The two of them didn't speak so much when Sully was growing up, but as he rose through the ranks of navy fliers, they found common ground in conversing about today's equipment versus that of the Korea days, when fighter jets were something new.

"My boy flies the F/A-18," Fred would tell people proudly. "Nearly twice the speed of sound."

All that changed with Sully's toxicology report. Fred had been furious. Any wet-eared recruit, he chided, understood the cardinal rule of bottle to throttle. It was as simple as telling time.

"What the hell were you thinking?"

"It was a couple of drinks, Dad."

"Twelve hours!"

"I wasn't planning on flying."

"You should have told your CO."

"I know, I know, you think I don't know? It doesn't change anything. I was fine. The controller screwed up!"

That didn't seem to matter — not to his father or, for a while, anyone else. When the crash first happened, people were sympathetic: the other plane had, thankfully, landed safely, Sully had endured a traumatic ejection, Giselle was clearly an innocent victim. Poor couple.

But when the toxicology report leaked out, public perception flipped on Sully, like a wrestler slipping his hold and pinning him down. A newspaper was first to get a copy; it ran the headline WAS PILOT UNDER INFLUENCE DURING CRASH? The TV news stations followed up, changing the question to more of an accusation. Never mind that it was a trace of alcohol, that he was in no way impaired. The military, with a zero-tolerance policy, took such things seriously. And with this being the latest development (and the media always chasing the freshest scent), the backstory faded, and Sully was pushed out front as The Man To Blame. No one talked anymore about the missing flight recordings — something that never happens — or Elliot Gray fleeing the scene and causing a car crash.

Suddenly Sully Harding was a drunken flyboy whose irresponsibility, as one cynical commentator put it, "landed his wife in a coma."

When he read that, Sully stopped reading altogether.

Instead, day after day, he sat by Giselle's bedside in a Grand Rapids hospital, where she'd been transferred to be closer to the family. He held her hand. He stroked her face. He whispered, "Stay with me, baby." In time, her bruises faded and her skin color returned to a more natural shade, but her lithe body shriveled and her eyes remained closed.

Months passed. Sully couldn't work. He was bleeding money for lawyers. At first, at their urging, he'd filed a suit against the Lynton Airfield facility, but with Elliot Gray dead and the few witnesses useless, he was forced to drop that and focus on his defense. The lawyers encouraged him to go to trial; his case was solid, they said, and a jury would be sympathetic. But in truth, his case was not solid at all. In military court, the rules were quite clear. Drinking within twelve hours of flight time was a clear violation of NATOPS, the naval aviation bible. In addition, they could get him for destruction of government property. It didn't matter who'd screwed up in the tower, or whose wife was a tragic victim. There had been two witnesses to Sully's drinking at the hotel restaurant. They'd attest to the hour.

He was in hell. Or worse, purgatory. A blade hung over his head. No job, wife in a hospital, father ashamed of him, in-laws not speaking to him, son who kept asking for his mother, dreams so haunted he hated sleep, real world so haunted he hated to wake up. What mattered to him most was not what mattered to the lawyers. The critical thing was time. If he pleaded guilty, he'd serve faster and be back sooner. Sooner to Jules. Sooner to Giselle.

Against his counsel's wishes, he agreed to a plea deal.

They gave him ten months.

Sully entered prison remembering the last thing he'd said to his wife.

I want to see you.

I want to see you, too.

Those words were his mantra, his meditation, his prayer. They kept him going, kept him believing, right up to the day they told him she was dead.

When all belief died inside him, too.

Thanksgiving night, Sully drove home with Jules already asleep in the backseat. He carried him up the stairs, laid him in bed, and let him sleep in his clothes. He went to the kitchen and poured himself a glass of bourbon.

Flopping on the couch, his stomach still full, he clicked on the TV and found a football game. He set the volume low and sank in. He wanted to forget for the rest of the night.

Just as his eyes were closing, he thought he heard a tap. He blinked.

"Jules?"

Nothing. He shut his eyes — and there it was again. The door? Was there someone at the door?

He got up, went to the keyhole, and felt his heart start to race.

He turned the knob and pulled it open.

Elias Rowe stood before him in a construction jacket and mustard-colored gloves.

"Can I talk to you for a minute?" he said.

The Fourteenth Week

NEWS REPORT
Channel 9, Alpena

(Amy on Main Street.)
AMY: Stunning news from the town of Coldwater today. Kelly Podesto, a teenager who claimed her best friend had contacted her from heaven, now says she made the whole thing up.

(Kelly at press briefing, cameras snapping.)
KELLY: I want to tell everybody I'm sorry. I just really missed my friend.

(Reporters yelling questions.)
REPORTER: Why did you do it?
KELLY: I don't know. It made me feel good, I guess. All those other people were getting calls.

(More yelling.)
REPORTER: Kelly, did you just do this for attention?
KELLY: (crying.) I'm really sorry. And to Brittany's family, I'm really sorry.

(Amy on Main Street.)
AMY: There are still six others who, at a town meeting last month, claimed to have received phone calls from

heaven. So far, none of them have changed their stories. Some, like Eddie Doukens and Jay James, felt sorry for Podesto.

(Faces of Doukens and James.)

DOUKENS: She's just a kid. I'm sure she didn't mean any harm.

JAMES: It doesn't change what happened to us.

(Amy in front of Harvest of Hope Baptist Church.)

AMY: Kelly told her parents the truth yesterday, after she was interviewed in advance of a national talk show. Her parents insisted she tell everyone. Now, some people are saying, "I told you so."

(Faces of protesters.)

PROTESTER ONE: No, we're not surprised. Been saying all along this whole thing is a sham!

PROTESTER TWO: They never had no proof. I'll bet you the other people admit it's a fake by next week.

AMY: But so far, others are holding firm.

(Image of Katherine.)

KATHERINE: There is nothing false about God's love. If we have to show it to everyone, we will.

(Amy walks on Main Street.)

AMY: Katherine Yellin says she still plans to publicly air a phone call with her departed sister. We will continue our exclusive coverage of that story as it happens.

(Amy looks into camera.)

In Coldwater, I'm Amy Penn, *Nine Action News*.

Jeff Jacoby asked his secretary to bring bottled water and snacks for his guests. He needed to reassure them in every way possible.

"So, listen. I know this caught us a bit off guard . . ."

He scanned the faces around the conference table. There were four men from the souvenir kiosks that had opened in town, three producers from the national TV show, two representatives from the sporting goods outfitter that sold tents and shelter gear out of the cider mill, three women from a religious merchandising company, and the guy from Samsung.

"I want to assure you," Jeff continued, "everything is fine—"

"It's *not* fine," snapped Lance, one of the producers, a wavy-haired man in a black turtleneck. "We may have to cancel."

"I'd say it's likely," added his colleague, Clint.

"But Kelly's just a teenager," Jeff said. "Teenagers do stupid things."

"It's become a risk," Lance said.

"You don't want to be duped," Clint said.

"He's right," said Terry, the Samsung executive. "It casts doubt on the whole thing."

"One teenager?" Jeff said. "You still have all the others."

"Just the same, we better put a hold on that billboard order. We want to see how this plays out."

Jeff bit his lower lip. Samsung had leased eight billboards from the town — part of an official "sponsorship" of Coldwater that Jeff had negotiated for a ridiculously high price. Now they were pulling out?

He needed to save this. He took a breath. He was so furious at Kelly Podesto he could scream.

"Let me ask you something," he said, pushing up his most professional smile. "Do you really think all those other people would make this up? They're not kids. They have reputations to protect. Anesh Barua is a dentist, for goodness' sake. He's not going to risk his patients. Tess Rafferty runs a day care program. Doreen Sellers was married to our police chief!

"I really believe this was an isolated incident."

His guests were quiet. Some tapped their fingers on the table.

"It may not be salvageable," Lance said.

"It's gotten a lot of publicity," Clint said.

"Don't they say there's no such thing as bad publicity?" Jeff offered.

"That's for movie stars."

"Not news stories."

"Or selling phones," added Terry.

Jeff ground his teeth together. *Think. Think.*

"Look. I want to put your minds at ease. I'm the mayor. What do you need from me?"

"To be honest?" Lance looked around the room. "They say they're talking to heaven? We could use some *proof.*"

The others nodded. Jeff nodded with them.

His thoughts turned to Katherine Yellin.

The quiet of a small-town room is different from the quiet of a city room, because the quiet of a city room disappears when you open a window. In a small town, passing from inside to outside is often indistinguishable, except maybe for the sound of birds.

189

It was something Pastor Warren always enjoyed about Coldwater. But today he was awakened from a morning nap by something he had never heard in his small-town room before: people screaming outside his window.

Opposing groups were squaring off by the church, apparently incited by Kelly Podesto's confession. At first they stood with signs, glaring at each other, and then chants started, and eventually someone yelled something, and someone answered back, and now the group with signs that read, REPENT: HEAVEN IS REAL! was within spitting distance of the group with signs that read, PEOPLE WHO HEAR VOICES ARE USUALLY CRAZY.

Insults spilled into insults. Threats followed threats.

"Leave us alone!"

"You're all frauds!"

"Praise the Lord!"

"Do it somewhere else!"

"We're trying to help mankind!"

"You're letting people kill themselves!"

"This is America! We have the right to our religion!"

"You don't have the right to force it on us!"

"God is watching!"

"Liars!"

"Save your souls—"

"Frauds!"

"God's angels—"

"Shut up!"

"Going to hell—

"Insane—"

190

"You're insane!"

"Get away from me!"

Someone swung, someone swung back, and the groups engaged like water spilled from two glasses, running messily into each other and forming a new shape. Signs fell. Screams became incomprehensible. People pushed and ran — some into the fray, some away from it.

Pastor Warren hobbled outside with his hands on his head. "Please, stop! All of you!" A police car whirred, and Jack Sellers jumped out, running with Dyson and screaming, "Break it up! Everybody! Right now!" But there were too many of them, at least several hundred.

"Do something!" Jack heard someone scream. Then, "Help us! . . . Over here!"

He looked left and right. The worshippers were mostly hunched over, the protesters more aggressive.

"Call Moss Hill and Dunmore!" Jack yelled to Dyson. They would need way more officers for this. In larger cities, police have shields, vests, helmets, riot gear. But here was Jack in his winter parka, a billy club on his waist, and a holstered gun he would never wave in a crowd like this. Over the blur of people shoving and jostling, he saw TV reporters and cameramen approaching from the street, running with their equipment.

"BACK AWAY!" he screamed as he waded into the mob. "BREAK THIS UP!" It was useless. Jack went for his club, but as his fingers gripped it, he thought about Robbie. He suddenly felt as if his son were watching him, judging his every move.

Pushing through people, trying to determine which side was which, he saw a young man in a tan jacket — he looked to be about Robbie's age — put his elbow in front of his face and chant, "Save me, Father. Save me, Father!" Jack hurried toward him — then felt something hard clomp him on the head. He stumbled to the ground and landed on all fours, his vision blurry, his scalp bleeding, as the screaming noise rose into the air of once-quiet Coldwater, like smoke from a pile of burning leaves.

Samantha pulled bread out of five different toasters and carried a plateful over to the den, where Tess sat on the floor with several dozen worshippers. Ever since Thanksgiving, Tess had been inviting them inside each day for breakfast. They came in shifts, ate something, went back outside, let others take their place. Some of them now shopped at the market for bread and jam and boxes of cereal.

At first it was an awkward dynamic. Although Tess wore old sweaters and jeans, the people saw her as blessed, a chosen one, and she noticed them staring at her when they thought she wasn't looking.

But their real interest was in Tess's phone calls, and when she shared what her mother was telling her, they were rapt.

"*Don't work so long and hard, Tess.*"

"Why, Mom?"

"*Take time . . . to appreciate God's creation.*"

"How does time pass in heaven?"

"*Time was made by man . . . We are above the sun and moon . . .*"

"Is it light there?"

"*Always light . . . but not how you think.*"

"What do you mean?"

"*Remember when you were a girl, Tess? Were you afraid of the dark . . . when I was in the house?*"

"No. I knew if you were there, you would protect me."

"*Heaven . . . is the same feeling . . . No fear. No dark. When you know you are loved . . . that's the light.*"

Worshippers dropped their heads when Tess said that. They smiled and took each others' hands. It was clear that Tess herself was moved when quoting her mother. For the final year of her life Ruth had sat in a wheelchair, a living statue, allowing Tess to brush her hair, button her blouse, occasionally slip on a necklace. Tess fed her. Bathed her. She yearned to hear her speak. So often, we push away the voices closest to us.

But once they're gone, we reach for them.

"Your mother," said a Spanish-accented woman, wearing a small cross around her neck, "she is a *saint.*"

Tess pictured Ruth at this very table, creating finger sandwiches of ham or egg salad.

"No." Tess smiled. "She was a caterer."

Sully left the furniture store with a check in his bag. On his way out the door, a saleswoman said, "Merry Christmas."

The holiday was still three weeks away, but homes and businesses around Coldwater were draped in colored lights. Many had wreaths on their doors. Sully started his car and flipped on the heat, rubbing his hands together. He checked his watch; still two hours before Jules got out of school. He drove toward the Dial-Tek store, where he was scheduled to meet Elias Rowe.

He thought back to last week, the night Elias showed up at his door. Sully had offered him a drink, and they sat at his kitchen table.

"It's my first time back here in weeks," Elias said. He'd been staying at his cabin in the Upper Peninsula, avoiding "all the crazies" who'd been trying to contact him. He'd only come home for Thanksgiving to be with his brother's family. But seeing the town — the cars, the vans, the campers, the crowds — seeing how it had swelled into something almost unrecognizable, he felt compelled to find Sully before he left.

"I keep going back to that day you ran up to my truck. I've been doing a lot of thinking, wondering if I shouldn't have just kept my mouth shut . . . Anyhow, I'm sorry if I caused any trouble with your son."

Sully glanced toward Jules's bedroom. He thought about showing Elias the blue plastic telephone tucked beneath the boy's pillow.

Instead, he asked, "What made you leave?" Elias told him about Nick Joseph, their history, Nick's troubled death. He told him about the phone calls asking "*Why did you do it?*" and about throwing the phone in Lake Michigan.

In turn, Sully told him his belief that this was all a hoax and his discovery that six customers had shared

194

the same phone plan. Not surprisingly, the one who did not was Kelly Podesto.

Elias dropped his head back. "Oh, man. I had that same plan, too. A couple of years ago."

"That can't be a coincidence," Sully said.

Elias shrugged. "Maybe not. But it doesn't explain how I was talking to Nick."

Sully looked down. That was the problem.

"But you've had no contact since, right?"

"I had no phone."

"Would you be willing to try something? To prove this one way or another?"

Elias shook his head. "Sorry. No way. It felt like I was messing with some powerful magic. To be honest, it scared the hell out of me."

Sully ran his hands through his hair. He tried to hide his frustration. People were either hypnotized by speaking to heaven or terrified of it. Why did no one want to expose it?

He noticed Elias looking over his shoulder. He turned around to see Jules, standing in the hallway, rubbing his eyes.

"Daddy?"

The boy leaned into the doorframe and lowered his chin to his chest.

"What's the matter, kiddo?"

"My stomach hurts."

Sully went to him, picked him up, and carried him back to bed. He sat with him for several minutes, stroking his hair until he fell back asleep. When he returned, Elias had his big hands clasped together, his forehead leaning into them.

"He misses his mom?"

"Something fierce."

"You really think this is a hoax?"

"It's gotta be."

Elias sighed. "What do you need me to do?"

Sully almost smiled. "Get a new phone."

Amy pulled into a highway gas station and parked next to an air pump. She left the engine running. Phil got out of the car and stretched like an awakening bear.

"Whoa, it's cold!" he declared, turning his stretch into a rigorous elbow rub. "Do you want a coffee?"

"Thanks."

"Cream?"

"Black."

He darted off.

Amy was bringing Phil — at his insistence — to Coldwater, where she had been rooted for the last two months. This proposed broadcast of a Katherine Yellin phone call was something he felt he should oversee personally. Amy didn't mind. Actually, she was happy Phil was coming. He could see how much she'd been doing for the station, virtually living in this tiny backwater town, ingratiating herself with Katherine. It was only thanks to Amy that Katherine had refused to go on the upcoming national TV show, only thanks to Amy that Katherine had agreed to let *Nine Action News* have the first shot at broadcasting a call from her sister. Phil would see that on this trip. If nothing else, the Coldwater phenomenon would be Amy's ticket out of weekend news. She was already on the Monday-through-Friday broadcasts more than any other reporter at the station. They jokingly referred to her as "Coldwater Amy."

She took her phone and dialed Rick, her fiancé.

"Hello?"

"Hi, it's me," Amy said.

"Yeah, hi," he said, his voice dropping into annoyance.

Alexander Bell may have created the phone, but he never had to endure its peculiar effect on relationships. Because Mabel, the love of his life, was deaf, she never held the other end of the receiver, and Bell never heard her voice go flat, or dull, or distant, never suffered that discomfort when we hear but cannot see our loved ones and must interpret their disappointment with a single question:

What's the matter?

Amy had been saying it for weeks, calling Rick from Coldwater after she'd filed her TV reports. He'd grown withdrawn. Irritated. Last night, in a rare visit to her own apartment, she found out why.

"Is this really what you want to do?" Rick demanded, his voice rising into argument mode.

"What do you mean?"

"Milk people for their weirdo stories?"

"It's called the news, Rick. It's my job."

"It's an obsession. You sleep there. For God's sake, Amy, I know CEOs that put in less time."

"I don't tell you how to do your job!"

"But I come *home* from my job! I'm willing to talk about something else. Every one of your conversations is about Coldwater, what Katherine said, what ABC did, what the newspapers have, how you're going to beat them, how you need your own cameraman. Amy, don't you hear yourself?"

"I'm sorry! This is how it works, OK? Everyone who makes it has one story that puts them on the map!"

Rick shook his head, his mouth half open. "Listen to you. On the map? What *map?* There *is* no freaking map! You haven't once talked about you and me. We're supposed to get married. What about *that* map?"

"What do you want me to *do?*" Amy snapped, her face tight with anger.

It was more of a threat than a question.

The Fifteenth Week

Back when they were married, Doreen used to visit Jack at the police station. It was less than a mile from their house. Sometimes she and young Robbie would bring roast beef sandwiches for the guys, and the junior officers would show Robbie their guns, which fascinated the boy and annoyed his mother.

Since the divorce six years earlier, Doreen had not set foot in the place. So all heads turned when, on Monday morning, she appeared at the front desk and unwrapped her scarf.

"Hello, Ray."

"Hey, Doreen!" Ray said, too enthusiastically. "How have you been!? You look great!"

"Thank you." She was wearing an old red winter coat and not an ounce of makeup. She knew she didn't look great. "Can you tell Jack I'm—"

"Come on back," Jack said, standing in his doorway. It was too small an office not to know your ex-wife was there. Doreen smiled tightly and walked to the back. She nodded at Dyson and two men she didn't recognize. Jack shut the door behind her.

"Mel didn't want me to come here," she began.

199

"Um . . . OK," Jack said.

"I was worried about you. How badly are you hurt?"

"It's nothing." He touched his head. He had a bandage on his temple and a half-inch scar underneath it. During the church skirmish last week, someone had hit him with a sign — unintentionally, it was determined — but it left him on his knees, a sight captured by the TV cameras. The image of the town's ranking police officer down on all fours sent panic through the community, prompting the governor to assign six state troopers to Coldwater for an indefinite period. Two of them — the men Doreen didn't recognize — sat outside the office now.

"What were you doing in that mess?" Doreen asked.

"I was trying to break it up. There was a kid, he reminded me of . . ."

"What?"

"Doesn't matter."

"Robbie?"

"Doesn't matter. I was trying to help him. It was dumb. But I'm fine. My pride is hurt more than my head."

Doreen noticed a framed photo on his desk — the three of them, Robbie, Jack, and Doreen, wearing orange vests on a jet-boat trip when Robbie was a teenager.

"I took the phones out, Jack."

"What?"

"Of the house. I got rid of them. I can't do it anymore."

"You stopped talking to him?"

She nodded.

"I don't get it."

She exhaled deeply.

"It wasn't making me happy. To be honest, it just made me miss him more."

She looked again at the photo. Despite the tears forming, she gasped a laugh.

"What is it?" Jack said.

"That picture. Look at what we're wearing."

"What are we wearing?"

"Life preservers."

Unbeknownst to Doreen, Jack had spoken to Robbie the previous Friday.

"*Dad, are you OK?*"

Jack assumed he meant the injury. He told Robbie about the protests.

"*I know, Dad . . . You were awesome.*"

"People don't know what to do with this, Robbie."

"*It's cool. Everything's cool.*"

Jack winced. It was how Robbie had spoken in life, but Jack somehow expected a different vocabulary now.

"Robbie—"

"*When people don't believe in something, they're lost.*"

"Yeah. I guess."

A pause. "*Everything's cool.*"

"Listen, son, what do you mean when you say, 'The end is not the end'?"

Another pause. Longer than usual.

"*The end is not the end.*"

"Are you saying that about life? Because your friends came by — Zeke and Henry. They said something about a band. Is it a song by a band?"

"*I love you, Dad.*"

"I love you, too."

"*Dad?*"

"Robbie?"

"*Doubt . . . is how you find him.*"

"What do you mean?"

But the connection was gone.

Jack had been troubled by that exchange all weekend. He thought about it now with Doreen sitting across from him, explaining why she no longer wanted conversations with their dead son. She wiped her eyes with a tissue.

"I just thought I should tell you," she said. "Because I don't mean to take away something you want."

Jack studied her face, wrinkled now around the eyes and dotted with a few age spots. So many years had passed since they'd met and married and settled in Coldwater. He almost couldn't remember the feeling between them anymore. When love dries in a marriage, the children become mortar for the bricks. When the children leave, the bricks just sit atop each other.

When the children die, the bricks tumble.

"It's all right," Jack said. "He was calling you, not me."

Sully marked his yellow pad with the heading DETAILS? He reviewed the names on his list: Tess Rafferty, Katherine Yellin, Doreen (Sellers) Franklin, Anesh

202

Barua, Eddie Doukens, Jay James, Elias Rowe. He had drawn a red line through Kelly Podesto.

He tapped his pen rhythmically.

"How's it going, CSI?"

Liz was looking over from her desk, where Jules sat on a stool, coloring a cartoon elephant.

"Ahhhh." Sully exhaled, leaning back. "I'm trying to figure it out."

"Figure what out?"

"How someone could get so many details on these people."

"The dead people?"

Jules looked up.

"Discretion, please?" Sully said.

"Sorry."

"I know what dead means," Jules announced. "It's what happened to my mommy."

He put down a blue crayon and picked up a red.

"Listen, Jules—" Liz said.

"Mommy can still talk. She's gonna call me."

Liz sighed and walked to Sully, who felt a wince as he watched her awkward leg and hip movements. He wondered if there would ever be a cure for her. She was young enough. They could discover something.

"I *am* sorry," she said, sitting down next to him.

"Don't sweat it."

"The details you want. What about the obituaries?"

"What about them?"

"Whoever wrote the obituaries must know a lot about the subjects, right?"

"Way ahead of you. There's a woman—"

"Maria Nicolini."

"You know her?"

"Who doesn't?"

"She writes the obituaries. She has massive files."

"Right. And?"

"And what?" Sully gave a mocking smile. "Maria? If that woman is behind these voices, I'll eat my shoes."

Liz shook her head. "No. Maria would never do anything to anybody. Except talk their ear off."

"Like I said."

"But if she has all those files, who else sees them?"

"Nobody. They stay with her."

"You sure?"

"What are you getting at?"

Liz glanced at Jules, lost in his coloring.

"All I know is when I was in college, I took a couple of journalism courses. They said you always needed backup records if you ran a story, in case you ever got questioned. 'Save all your notes and research,' they said."

"Wait." Sully glanced at her sharply. "The newspaper? You're saying someone's got these files and could be running this whole thing — from the *newspaper?*"

She raised an eyebrow. "Where you work."

Had Jeff Jacoby known the mayor's job would be so demanding, he'd never have run for it. He had only done so because authority came naturally to him; he had it as president of the bank, he had it as president of his trade association, he had it at the country club over in Pinion Lake, where he was the senior board member.

Why not here in Coldwater? Heck, how hard could it be, being mayor? The job didn't even pay anything.

Who knew his term would coincide with the biggest news story to ever hit the county? But now that Coldwater had been given an international spotlight, Jeff was not about to lose it — not because little Kelly Podesto couldn't resist drawing attention to herself.

We could use some proof. That's what Lance, the TV producer, had said. And so, on Wednesday afternoon, Jeff organized a lunch meeting at Frieda's, inviting Lance, Clint, the police chief Jack Sellers (what Jeff had in mind would require security), and — the key to it all — Katherine Yellin, who, when Jeff asked her to attend, said she had to check with "her friend," the TV reporter Amy Penn, who said she had to check with her boss, the news director Phil Boyd, who said he had to check with his superiors at the network, which, Jeff happily discovered, was the same network that aired the national TV show that had brought Lance and Clint to Coldwater in the first place.

Jeff was quickly learning that the media had two sides; the side that wanted to get the news, and the side that wanted to make sure nobody else got it.

He could play to those desires. He was known in the banking community as the Rainmaker. By getting Katherine, Jack, Amy, Phil, Lance, and Clint all at one table, he was proving it. He noticed they all had their cell phones out. He glanced at Katherine's pink flip model. The one that started it all.

"So," he began, once Frieda had brought everyone ice water, "thanks to everyone for getting together today—"

"Can I ask something?" Katherine interrupted. "Why do we have to meet here? It's so crowded."

Frieda's was indeed packed, and despite sitting in the back, the group was the object of constant attention. Customers stared. Reporters snapped photos. Which was just what Jeff wanted.

"I just thought we'd patronize a local business."

"Frieda's doing OK without us," Jack snapped.

Jeff glanced at the police chief, whose left temple was bandaged. "Fair enough, Jack," he said. "But we're here, so, let's talk about *why* we're here, OK?"

At which point his plan was revealed.

One. Katherine had been planning to share a phone call with the world.

Two. The TV show needed to make sure this phenomenon was real.

Three. The other "chosen ones" were concerned that Kelly's lie would reflect badly on them.

Four. Channel 9 had been keeping Katherine "exclusive."

Five. Christmas was coming.

Jeff had plotted all these points together and had come up with what he called "a win-win idea." If Katherine could receive her call in front of the town and share the voice of her deceased sister with everyone, while being filmed for the national TV show, it would remove all doubt as to the true nature of the

Coldwater miracles. The others would be vindicated. Kelly Podesto would be forgotten. It would be a great Christmas story. And since the TV show was on the same network as *Nine Action News* in Alpena (and here was where Jeff imagined himself a TV executive), wouldn't it behoove Phil and Amy to join in? Don't they call that cross-promotion?

"Could we keep it exclusive in our market?" Phil asked.

"Doesn't bother us," Lance said.

"Amy could do the buildup pieces?"

"Fine," Clint said.

"Where would we do this?"

"How about the cider mill?" Jeff said.

"Outdoors?"

"Why not?"

"Weather issues."

"How about the bank?"

"You want this in a bank?"

"There's the churches."

"Could work."

"Which one?"

"St. Vincent's?"

"Harvest of Hope?"

"What about the high school?"

"The gym is an option—"

"We did it before when—"

"STOP! STOP! YOU CAN'T DO THIS! IT'S WRONG!"

The scream brought Frieda's to momentary silence. Lance and Clint glared. Jeff's mouth fell open. One might have suspected Katherine, who was being asked

207

to broadcast her dead sister's voice to the world, or Jack, being told of a huge public event with his head still bandaged from the last one.

But in fact, the voice that bellowed "STOP!" belonged to the woman who, in some ways, had started the whole thing.

Amy Penn.

"What are you *doing?*" Phil growled, under his breath.

Amy stared as if in a trance.

She didn't even realize the words had come from her mouth.

Elias Rowe watched the small waves hit the shore. He liked to stand at the edge of the Great Lakes. He could spend hours entranced by the water's movement. A friend who lived in Miami joked, "A lake is not an ocean, no matter how long you stare at it." But to Elias, who spent his childhood summers boating and swimming in these waters, a shoreline visit was like a pilgrimage.

It was Friday morning. He was on his way up north. He'd stopped for a few minutes to enjoy the solitude. He noticed icy patches near the water's edge, winter slowly taking control.

He dug his hands into the pockets of his vest.

He felt his phone vibrating.

It was the phone he had reluctantly purchased at that store in Coldwater. He and Sully were five days into their "experiment." He'd given no one the number. He looked at the display.

It read UNKNOWN.

Elias breathed out loudly, three straight times, like a man preparing to submerge for a dive.

Then he pressed a button and said, "Who is this?"

Three minutes later, his hands actually shaking, he dialed a number he had written on a folded piece of paper.

"You were right," he whispered when Sully answered. "He just called me."

"Who?"

"Nick."

That night Pastor Warren stood before a packed sanctuary at Harvest of Hope. It was Bible study, an event that just a few months ago might have drawn seven people. Now there were at least five hundred.

"I'd like to talk tonight about manna," he began. "Are you all familiar with what manna is?"

"Food from heaven," someone yelled out.

"Food from God," Pastor Warren corrected. "But yes, it came from the sky. Every morning. While the children of Israel were wandering in the desert."

"Pastor?"

A man had his hand raised. Warren sighed. He felt a bit light-headed, and he'd hoped to get through this lesson quickly.

"Yes, young man?"

"Does the soul need nourishment in heaven?"

Warren blinked. "I . . . I don't know."

"I've spoken with Tess. She said her mother never mentions it."

"Katherine never speaks about it either," someone else said.

"I'm friends with Anesh Barua," a middle-aged woman said, standing up. "I could ask him to ask his daughter."

"How did she die?"

"Leukemia. She was twenty-eight."

"When did you talk to him?"

"Everyone, *please!*" Warren yelled.

The congregation silenced. Warren was perspiring. His throat felt sore. Was he coming down with something? He had been letting his young deacon, Joshua, handle the Bible studies recently, but he'd felt compelled to make the effort tonight.

Earlier in the day he had heard about the mayor's plan: a televised broadcast of Katherine Yellin speaking with her dead sister. The whole world would be watching.

Every fiber inside Warren told him this was wrong, even blasphemous, that something terrible might happen to all of them. He'd tried to make an appointment with Jeff Jacoby, but was told his schedule was too full. He'd tried to call Katherine, but she didn't answer. Scripture reminded him to be humble, but a heat burned inside him; he felt as if he'd been slapped in the face. He'd been in this pulpit for fifty-four years. Did he not deserve the courtesy of being heard? What was happening to the people he knew? Katherine, who used to be his loyal congregant? Jeff, who used to welcome his input? Father Carroll? The other clergymen? They seemed to be leaving him behind, drawn to a light that Warren sensed was not godly in nature. He had even lost dear Mrs. Pulte to this madness, and volunteers had been making a mess of things in her absence. The tidy life he had known felt spilled and scattered. Even a simple Bible study was getting away from him. *Focus. Lord, give me focus.*

"Now then . . . manna," he said. "If you will read with me . . ." He squinted through his glasses. He wiped sweat from his brow. "Here . . . Exodus, chapter sixteen, verse twenty-six . . ."

Concentrate.

"God is speaking through Moses. 'Six days you are to gather it' — the manna — 'but on the seventh day, the Sabbath, there will not be any.'"

He looked up. "Do you know what happened?"

A small older woman raised her hand.

"They went out to get the manna anyway?"

"Precisely. In verse twenty-seven we read, 'And it came to pass, that some of the people went out on the seventh day to gather, and they found none.'"

He wiped his brow with a handkerchief. "Now, here you had a people who were being given the most amazing thing. Food from the sky. It tasted good. It satisfied them. It was the perfect nutrition. Who knows? It may not have even been fattening."

A few people chuckled. Warren felt woozy. His heart was racing ahead of his breath. *Keep going. Keep going.*

"But what happened? Some people still didn't trust God's word. They went out on the Sabbath — even

211

though he told them not to. Remember, manna was a miracle. A *real* miracle!"

Breathe in and out, he told himself. *Finish the lesson*.

"Even with this gift from God, they wanted more."

In. Out.

"And what did they get?"

"Nothing?" someone said.

"Even worse. God grew *angry*."

He lifted his chin. The lights seemed particularly harsh.

"God grew *angry*! We cannot demand miracles. We cannot expect them! What is happening here in Coldwater, dear friends, it is wrong."

The congregation mumbled.

"It is wrong!" he repeated.

The mumbling grew louder.

"Brother and sisters, do you know what the word *manna* means?"

People looked around.

"Does anyone know what it means?"

No answer. He exhaled.

"It means . . . 'What is this?' "

He repeated the words. The room began to spin. His voice went flat as a dial tone.

"What is this?"

And he collapsed.

The Sixteenth Week

Alexander Graham Bell created the telephone, but Thomas Edison created "Hello." Bell thought "Ahoy!" should serve as a standard greeting. But in 1878 Edison, his rival, suggested a little-used but phonetically clear word. Since Edison oversaw the first telephone exchanges, "Hello" quickly became the norm.

Edison also greatly improved the quality of the signal by introducing a compressed carbon disc to the transmitter.

Still, nothing Edison did with the telephone came close to inciting the original hysteria Bell inspired — until, perhaps, 1920, when Edison told a magazine that he was working on a "spirit phone," a device that might let people one day speak to the dead.

"I believe that life, like matter, is indestructible," he said. "If there are personalities in another existence . . . who wish to get in touch with us in this existence . . . this apparatus would at least give them a better opportunity."

The story prompted a furious reaction, six hundred letters to the editor, and multiple requests for the device. While Edison would later suggest he'd been less than serious, there are those to this day who search for clues to his mysterious invention.

Word that a live broadcast from Coldwater, Michigan, would feature, for the first time, a voice from heaven, set off a reaction that would have avalanched Edison. Roads to Coldwater were backed up for hours. The governor assigned dozens of state troopers, who positioned themselves every mile along Route 8 and every hundred yards on Lake Street. Caravans arrived. Station wagons and RVs and yellow school buses. Like a meteor shower, a solar eclipse, or a turn-of-the-millennium celebration, the event drew the curious, the devout, and those who simply wanted to be a part of something historic. It attracted religious zealots and nonbelievers alike, who felt it lunacy or sacrilege to treat heaven in such a fashion.

The event was set for Friday, three days before Christmas, at 1:00p.m. The location was the high school football field, outdoors, with a stage and loudspeakers, because no building in town could hold the anticipated crowds. Police chief Jack Sellers, who went on record as "totally against this whole idea," would not ensure the safety of an indoor filming. He envisioned a trampling of people trying to get inside and a fire hazard beyond description.

Amy Penn would not be covering the event. She had been sent home. Phil Boyd apologized for her lack of professionalism. No one knew what got into her, screaming "STOP!" and suddenly refusing to talk about a story she had cultivated for months.

214

"Probably exhaustion," Phil had said. "People do stupid things when they're tired." He assigned his top news anchor to take her place.

The green light for the entire plan had hinged, of course, on Katherine Yellin, who'd asked for a day to consider it. Friday morning, after praying for several hours at the foot of her bed, the phone rang. She knew it would be Diane. And it was.

"*Are you happy today, sister?*"

Katherine poured it all out. She expressed her frustration, the protesters, the doubters, the nonbelievers.

"Diane, will you speak with me in front of everyone? Let them know this is real? That we were the first?"

Static.

"*When?*"

"They want to do it next Friday. I don't know. These men. Is this good or bad, Diane? I feel so lost."

"*What do you truly want, Kath?*"

Katherine smiled through her tears. Diane, even in heaven, was concerned with her sister's needs.

"I just want people to *believe* me."

The static grew louder.

"Diane? . . . Are you still there, Diane?"

Finally, her sister answered her.

"*I am always here for you, Kath.*"

"You always were."

"*Friday.*"

Then silence.

The offices of the *Northern Michigan Gazette* were busier than ever. Recent weeks had seen the paper double in size, largely from ads aimed at out-of-town visitors. Ron Jennings had brought in freelance writers to help produce copy, and the two permanent reporters, sixty-six-year-old Elwood Jupes (who had been there for decades) and twenty-four-year-old Rebecca Chu (tabbed to replace him when he retired), each had at least five stories per edition.

In the two months he'd been working for the *Gazette*, Sully had never met anyone on the editorial side. He didn't want to. Given his past, and the nature of the news business, he only figured to encounter a bunch of questions he didn't care to answer.

But now he had reason to be here: Liz's sensible suggestion that someone at the newspaper might be privy to Maria's obituary interviews. With that much information about the deceased, and the access that reporters have to phone numbers, data, history, and backgrounds — what better perch from which to perpetrate a hoax?

"So, lets get started, folks," Ron Jennings said. He'd gathered the entire staff around a conference table — editorial and business. His enthusiasm could barely be contained. He stood by a white markerboard and tapped a blue Sharpie against it.

"This is going to be the biggest week we've ever had . . ."

When the meeting ended, Sully eased his way toward Elwood Jupes, the white-haired reporter with a boxer's nose and a rolling double chin that spilled over his buttoned collar and tight-knotted tie. Jupes glanced at

Sully through horn-rimmed glasses, then held out his hand and introduced himself.

"You're in sales, eh? I'm Elwood."

"Sullivan Harding."

"Mmm."

Sully paused. What was *that* about?

"How long have you been with us?" Elwood asked.

"Just a couple of months. And you?"

He chuckled. "Since before you were born, eh?"

"What do you make of all this? The phone calls, I mean."

"Damnedest thing I've ever covered."

"Do you think it's good?"

"Good?" Elwood narrowed his eyes. "Well. Let's see. People are behaving better, eh? We haven't even had a shoplifting incident since all this started. You talk to the ministers, every seat in church is full. People praying like never before. So what do you think, Mr. Harding? Is it good? Eh?"

Sully thought that if Jupes said "Eh?" one more time, he was going to slap him.

"I guess you've had to write about this an awful lot," Sully said.

"Nonstop since it happened." He sighed. "I barely get to cover anything else — except the Hawks games on Friday nights. I'm still a football nut, eh? We weren't too good this year. Only won three."

Sully changed the subject. "Hey. Did anyone ever find that Elias Rowe guy? Wasn't he one of the early ones?"

Elwood looked left and right, then leaned in.

"He's been in town this week. A few people spotted him."

"Why wouldn't he come forward?"

"Why? Maybe the person calling him isn't somebody he *wants* to call him, eh? Nobody ever thinks of that. But I do."

Sully felt his fists clench.

"So who's calling him?"

"Can't tell you. Have to protect my sources."

Sully forced a smile. "Come on. We work for the same side, right?"

"Oh, no," Elwood said. "The money and the news are never on the same side."

Elwood tapped him jokingly on his arm. Sully's mind was hurrying. He sensed the conversation was about to end; there was still so much he needed to know.

"Hey, speaking of business, I have to go to a client today. Davidson and Sons. You know them?"

"Know them? I'm sixty-six. Can you imagine how many funerals I've gone to? Anyhow, the owner is an old friend of mine."

Great, Sully thought. This guy and Horace. What a combination.

"I was speaking to a woman there. Maria. She told me she wrote our—"

"Obituaries. Yeah." Elwood made a face. "I never approved of that. You're taking money from an advertiser, and they're supplying you copy?"

"I know, right?" Sully said, thinking about Maria's files. "It seemed strange to me, too. How do we know what we're printing is accurate? Does someone check the details?"

Elwood cleared his throat. He studied Sully carefully, like a camera panning a horizon.

"You're pretty curious about this, eh?"

Sully shrugged.

"What makes you curious?"

"Doesn't matter."

Elwood rubbed his chin.

"Do you believe in heaven, Mr. Harding?"

Sully looked at the floor. The answer was no. He blinked and looked back at Elwood.

"Why?"

"No reason. But people have been wondering if heaven exists since man was created. Later on this week, we might get some proof of it. That would be the biggest story of all time, wouldn't it?"

Sully held still.

"As long as it was true."

"Mmm," Elwood said again. His lips tightened, fighting a grin. Sully decided to take a chance.

"Who's Nick Jos—"

He felt a whack on his shoulder.

"Are you boys getting to know each other?" Ron Jennings bellowed. "Maybe some other week, OK? We've got a load to do. Here's your call sheet, Sully. Let's go."

As Ron steered him away, Sully glanced over his shoulder and saw Elwood Jupes headed back to his desk. Ron walked Sully to the door, talking nonstop, reminding him that ad rates had been doubled this week in anticipation of the largest circulation ever for the *Gazette*.

"Tell everyone it's a once-in-a-lifetime opportunity," Ron said, opening the door. "They'll pay it."

And just like that, Sully was standing in the snow. He breathed out cold smoke and tried to process what had just transpired. Was he onto something, or further away? Up the street, he could see a bus unloading. More out-of-towners. He heard church bells chiming.

"Harding!"

He spun. Elwood Jupes was leaning out the door, grinning, saying nothing.

"*What?*" Sully said.

"You didn't turn that way when I yelled your name at the football game last month. How come?"

Sully swallowed.

"That was you?"

Elwood smacked his tongue on his teeth.

"You got a raw deal, kid. A lot of us know it. And never mind the idiot who yelled 'Geronimo.' He was drunk off his feet, eh?"

He shut the door.

The *Gazette* had indeed run a story about Sully's crash when it happened. It ran under the headline FORMER COLDWATER MAN IN MIDAIR COLLISION. Written by Elwood Jupes, it basically repeated most of the information in the Associated Press story, but added a quote from Sully's father, whom Elwood had phoned after the news.

"I know my son," Fred Harding had said. "He's a damn good flier. Somebody in that tower messed up, and I hope they get to the bottom of it."

No one ever did. Elliot Gray was dead, and all that was known about him was that he'd taken the job less than a year earlier, after similar work in three other states. The tapes of the tower transmissions were blank or distorted beyond comprehension. The suspicion at first was that Elliot Gray had somehow destroyed them, but such efforts would have taken time and expertise, and given how soon he crashed his Toyota into Giselle Harding's Chevy, it was quickly ruled impossible. The recording equipment had simply malfunctioned. No one else was in the tower, with all available personnel running outside to deal with the incoming Cessna, which made a belly-flop landing on the grass beside the runways after striking a telephone pole on its descent.

That plane suffered a dented fuselage and a split rudder — part of which likely had been sucked into Sully's engine, causing his crash. The Cessna pilot said he never saw the F/A-18, and that the tower had told him he was "cleared for final on twenty-seven right" — just as Sully had said he was told. There'd been considerable focus on this, until Sully's blood report became public.

The *Gazette* had written about that, too.

Sully never read those stories. But every night he sat in prison, he thought about that transmission, the words *twenty-seven right*, and how a human voice, speaking through wires — a technology unimaginable if not for the telephone — had changed his life forever.

Jack hadn't made pancakes in years, but it came back to him quickly enough, especially after the ninth batch. He was working two pans and a griddle. When the pancakes were ready, Tess took them on large trays and served them to the people in her living room.

Since Thanksgiving, her mother's old house had become a way station, filled with visitors (Tess forbade the word *worshippers*) who sat on the floor and questioned Tess about her conversations with heaven, what Ruth told her, what advice she gave. Tess did not allow anyone in the kitchen where the phone hung on the wall (except Samantha or Lulu and, now, Jack Sellers), and if it rang, she stretched the long cord into the pantry for privacy.

Jack had been coming every morning before work since last week. With all the insanity of the protests and the media, he liked being here for an hour or so, in an old-fashioned kitchen with plates clanking and silverware jangling. He liked how Tess didn't keep a television on. He liked how the place always smelled of cooking and how there were often children running back and forth.

Mostly, Jack liked being around Tess. He had to constantly push his eyes off her for fear he would betray his feelings. What most captivated him was how genuinely humbled she was by hearing her mother again. She struggled with it, as Jack did with hearing Robbie. She didn't want it to draw attention.

Which was why he tried to talk her out of the Friday event.

"Why be part of that fiasco?" he asked her in the kitchen.

She thought for a moment, then motioned for him to join her in the pantry.

"I know," she whispered, stepping inside. "But when I asked my mother, she said, 'Tell everybody.' I think I'm *supposed* to spread the word about this."

"You mean if you don't—"

"I'll be doing something wrong."

"A sin?"

"Kind of."

"Is that what Father Carroll said?"

She nodded. "How did you know?"

"Look, I go to church, too, but—"

"I wouldn't do what Katherine is doing—"

"No, that's crazy—"

"But if they want to ask me what I've learned, is it right to keep that to myself?"

Jack didn't answer.

"All the other people will be there, too."

She flashed her eyes. "Except you."

Jack looked away. "My ex stopped talking to Robbie. She said it makes her too sad."

"And you?"

"It doesn't make me sad. I love hearing his voice. But I have . . ."

"What?"

"I don't know."

"Doubt?"

"Maybe."

"Doubt is how you find God."

He stared at her. Hadn't Robbie said the same thing?

"Does this hurt?" she asked softly. She reached to touch his wound. Her fingers seemed to melt through his skin.

"Nah," he said, swallowing hard.

"It seems to be healing."

"Yeah."

They were inches apart.

"Why are you so worried about this show?"

"Because . . . I can't protect you."

It came out before he realized he was saying it. Tess smiled. She seemed to watch the words evaporate in front of her.

"That's sweet."

Then she kissed him. Once. Softly. They both pulled back awkwardly and said "Sorry" at the same time. Tess looked down and stepped outside the pantry and immediately heard her name called by the visitors.

Jack stayed where he was. But he was no longer where he was.

It was the last place in town to draw a crowd, but now even the Coldwater library was bustling. During the day, outsiders rifled through books and documents about the town's history. Magazine writers did research for major pieces. Others asked for maps. As the only librarian, Liz found herself in constant demand.

But after six in the evening, she would kill the outside lights and allow Sully to do his work in private.

On Tuesday night, three days before the scheduled broadcast, he came through the back door with another man, a beefy guy in a canvas coat and a wool cap.

"Hi," Sully said, not introducing him.

"Hey," she said.

"We're gonna talk over here."

They huddled in the corner by the computer. Sully took out his yellow pad. Slowly, methodically, Elias Rowe reviewed the conversation he'd had with Nick Joseph.

"*Where did you go, Elias?*" Nick's voice had begun.

"Leave me alone," Elias had said.

"*You need to do something for me.*"

"I don't need to do anything. Why are you calling me?"

"*You need to take care of something.*"

"What?"

"*You need to take care of Nick.*"

"I tried taking care of you. I gave you every chance!"

Sully stopped his note taking. "Then what did he say?"

"Nothing," Elias said.

"Did you ask him the questions we talked about?"

"I tried." Elias and Sully had worked out a list of inquiries they hoped might offer a clue about how this was happening. One was, "Where are you calling from?"

"*You know where,*" Nick had said.

"So he never said 'heaven'?" Sully asked.

"No," Elias answered. "I asked twice."

"And did you ask about the coworkers?"

"Yeah. I said, 'Tell me the guys from the old crew. What were their names?' And he didn't say anything. Just a lot of static and noise."

Why wouldn't he answer that? Sully wondered. It was a simple question for the real Nick Joseph. And how had he been able to call on a completely new number — on a phone that Elias had just gotten from Jason a few days earlier?

Sully put his chin in his hands. "What else?"

"I asked him, 'What does God look like?' Like we agreed. At first there was nothing. Just more noise. Then he said his name again. 'Nick.' And then . . ."

He paused.

"What?"

"And then, before I could say anything else, he said, 'Do what's right, Elias.'"

Elias began to tear up. "It really affected me. The guy was an ass, a total liability, you know? He took advantage left and right. But once I found out he was dead, there was always . . ."

"Always what?"

"A bad feeling. Like I'd done something wrong."

"But you c —"

"OH MY GOD!" Liz screamed.

"What?" Sully spun.

"There's somebody there!"

"Where?"

"At the window!"

Sully jumped, but whoever it had been was already gone.

226

Liz caught her breath. "Oh, man, sorry. It just startled me. There were two hands on the glass—"

But Sully was already out the door. He saw a blue car pulling away. He scrambled back inside.

"Man or woman?"

"Man."

"Old or young?"

"I couldn't tell."

Liz looked down. "I didn't mean to be such a baby."

"It's OK." Sully looked at the window. He looked at Elias.

"Did you ever meet Elwood Jupes?" he asked.

That same night, Katherine sat at her kitchen counter in a terry-cloth bathrobe, drinking a glass of cranberry juice and holding a framed photo. The photo showed a teenage Diane and Katherine, in bathing suits, standing on a sandy shore and holding up a first-place ribbon for Best Tandem Swim in the Lake Michigan One Mile Challenge. Their limbs were tan and lean, their faces bronzed.

"We're a good team, little sister," Diane had said.

"You were faster than me," Katherine said.

"No way! You're the reason we won."

Katherine knew it wasn't true. Diane could swim laps around any girl in Coldwater. But what mattered was boosting her kid sister's confidence. God, how Katherine longed for that. Sometimes what you miss the most is the way a loved one made you feel about yourself.

"Care for a little company?"

Katherine looked up to see Amy at the bottom of the steps. She wore a Yale sweatshirt and baggy blue sweatpants.

"Sure. Sit down."

"Thanks."

Amy slid onto a stool.

"Did you go to Yale?"

"An old boyfriend. This is all that's left."

"Well." Katherine stared at her cranberry juice. "That's more than my ex left me." She looked up. "Do you want something to drink?"

"More than you know," Amy said.

In the past twenty-four hours, Amy Penn had driven three hundred and twenty-six miles. After Phil dismissed her from the Coldwater story, she'd gone home to her rented duplex in Alpena, only to find it half empty. Rick was gone. He'd left some books, some dirty laundry, a wrapped sandwich in the fridge, and a box of Power Bars in the cupboard. Also a note. It read, "We can talk when you get some time. R." — a message she found ironic, since at that moment she had nothing but time. She picked up her cell to call him. She thought about how to apologize. She stared at the shape of the phone in her hand.

She never dialed.

Instead she got back in her car, drove all the way to Coldwater, parked on Guningham Road, and talked her way past two state troopers to knock on Katherine's back door.

228

"I'm going to see this through," she seethed when Katherine opened it. "I deserve that much. I don't care if they use me or not."

"I'll get the bed made up," Katherine said.

The truth was, Katherine had never wanted Amy to go. Amy was the only one she'd trusted since this started, and when Amy melted down at Frieda's — screaming "STOP!" and then shaking and not responding — Katherine had worried for her health and thought she needed some rest. It was only the next day, after Katherine had already agreed to do the program, that she found out Amy had been pulled off the story. The lead anchor in Alpena had been dying to get on the Coldwater thing, and Phil had to keep him happy, seeing as he brought in the ratings. Besides, Amy had served her purpose. Her righteous meltdown gave Phil justification to make the switch.

Now the two women sat in the quiet kitchen, Katherine with a cranberry juice, Amy with a bottle of wine. For once, with no camera in sight, the conversation turned away from heaven and phone calls and settled on relationships. Katherine spoke about her former husband, Dennis, who'd moved to Texas a year after their divorce. He'd managed to make himself look destitute on paper just in time for their settlement hearing. Katherine got almost no money. Later that year, Dennis bought a boat.

"How do men get away with that?" she asked.

Amy shrugged. Rick had been the third casualty of her working life. Her college sweetheart bailed when she took her first job in Beaufort, North Dakota, a station so remote it led with the crop report. Her second serious boyfriend actually liked the TV business — a little too much. While Amy was stuck in the editing booth at nights, he took up with the twenty-two-year-old blonde they'd hired to do sports. The two of them lived in Georgia now, on a golf course.

Rick was different, or so Amy thought. A professional himself, an architect, he understood long hours and office politics. But apparently he didn't understand following a story to the end. Or at least not this story.

"I'm so sorry," Katherine said.

"It's my fault," Amy said. "I was always weighing my career, getting mad at myself for not being far enough by this age or that age. It was so important to me, I thought it should be important to him. I thought that was love."

She ran a finger around the bottom of her wineglass. "Maybe that's what we tell ourselves when we really just want to get our way."

"Well, it's his loss," Katherine said. "I mean, look at you."

Amy squeezed her eyes shut and almost laughed. "Thanks."

"You know what Diane used to say?"

"What?"

"If you find one true friend in life, you're richer than most. If that one true friend is your husband, you're blessed."

She paused. "And if that one true friend is your sister, don't feel bad. At least she can't divorce you."

Amy smiled. "I didn't have time for friends."

"No?"

"Always working. You?"

"I had the time. But I turn most people off."

"Don't say that."

"I do. Too pushy. Always want to be right. Diane used to say, 'Kath, see if your shoes are on fire. I think you just burned another bridge.'"

Amy chuckled.

"I haven't had anybody talk to me that way since she died," Katherine said. "I've been walking around in a fog, almost waiting to hear her voice again. That's why, when these calls started, it made sense. She was my big sister. Anytime I needed her, she was there. Why *wouldn't* she come back to me?"

Amy bit her lip.

"Katherine, these people don't really care about you."

"Which people?"

"The TV people." She sighed. "Us."

A pause.

"I know," Katherine said softly.

"They just want a story."

"I know."

"Rick was right. We milk things until there's nothing left, then we go. Scorched earth."

"I know."

Amy turned her body. She looked Katherine in the eye.

"I'm a part of that."

"Not anymore." Katherine smiled. "You said 'Stop.'"

"Because I felt weird. I felt like we'd gone from reporting news to creating it." Amy exhaled. "But I wanted your story."

"Yeah."

"It was good for my career."

"I know."

"It's good for all these people here now. That's the only reason they're bothering with you. Do you understand?"

"I understand."

Amy seemed confused. "If you know all this, why go through with it?"

Katherine leaned back, as if to get a better view of what she was about to say.

"The day we buried Diane, I came home and stared at the walls. I asked God to send me a sign that she was all right. That if she couldn't be with me, at least she was with Him. I asked it every single day for two years straight. And then my phone rang. Diane's old pink phone with the high-heel sticker. The one I only kept to have another memory of her."

Amy stared blankly.

"Don't you see? God answered me. He gave me the greatest gift I could ask for — the voice of my sister. And if all He wants in return is to let people know that He is real, should I say no? Should I keep it to myself? In the old days, people stood on mountains and spoke to the people. But now —"

"Now we have TV?"

"Yeah, I guess."

"But what if," Amy said slowly, "she doesn't call?"

Katherine crossed her hands on the counter. "She will."

For a moment, both women just stared at their glasses, saying nothing.

"I lied to you," Amy mumbled.

"When?"

"When I said I was a believer. I'm not. Not really."

Katherine rocked slowly back and forth.

"Maybe Friday you will be."

The next day, Sully again timed a visit to Davidson & Sons with the lunch hour. He waited until Horace drove away. Then he hurried through the door and down the quiet hallway to Maria Nicolini's office.

"Hi, again," Sully said, poking his head in. "Is Horace here?"

"Oh, no, he's gone to lunch," she answered. "Boy. You must be wired in to his eating cycle."

"I can wait."

"Are you sure? He *just* left."

"We have a big issue coming up. He might want to be a part of it."

"Oh, I can imagine."

"Crazy, huh? What's going on in town?"

"It sure is. It took me twenty minutes to get to work this morning. I only live a mile awa —"

They were interrupted by the soft ring of chimes. Maria looked at a small security TV. "Excuse me," she said, getting up. "I don't know these people. They could let themselves in. The door is never locked."

A second later, Sully was alone.

He looked at her file cabinet. His breathing accelerated. He had come here to try and find out if anyone else — particularly Elwood Jupes — had access to Maria's transcripts, but suddenly that access was within his reach. He had never been a thief. He had never had a reason. But he thought about the broadcast on Friday and whoever was lurking at the library window and Elwood's odd line of questions and the fact that he simply didn't have enough information.

And Maria did.

He inhaled deeply. Either he was doing this or he wasn't. He pushed the faces of his father and mother and Giselle and Jules out of his mind, removing any wagging fingers of conscience.

He pulled open the drawer.

Moving quickly, he managed to find most of the original transcribed files — "Joseph, Nick," "Sellers, Robert," "Rafferty, Ruth," "Barua, Simone," and "Yellin, Diane" — and pluck them out before he heard Maria and the visitors approaching. He closed the drawer silently and clicked his briefcase shut. Then he jumped up and grabbed his coat.

"You know what?" he said, meeting them halfway down the hall. "I'll hit two more places and come back in a couple of hours."

"All right," Maria said. "You sure?"

"Yeah. I'm really busy."

"This is Mr. and Mrs. Albergo. This is Mr. Harding." They nodded.

"We're sorry for your loss," Mrs. Albergo said.

234

"Oh, no," Sully said, "I'm here on business, I'm not . . ."

The couple looked at each other.

"Mr. Harding did lose his wife," Maria said, "but earlier in the year."

Sully glanced at her. "Yeah. Yes, sorry, I did."

"We're here for my father," Mrs. Albergo said, quietly. "He's very sick. Bone marrow cancer."

"That's tough," Sully said.

"Very tough," echoed Maria.

"He doesn't have much time left. We're hoping when he passes, if he's buried here in Coldwater, we'll have a better chance of, you know, hearing from him again."

Sully gave a tight nod, resisting the urge to say something cynical. Then Mr. Albergo spoke.

"If you don't mind, can I ask you something?"

"OK," Sully said.

"Your wife. Has she ever . . ." He pointed to the sky. "You know . . . to you?"

"No." Sully swallowed. He looked at Maria. "It apparently doesn't happen to everybody."

Mr. Albergo lowered his finger. Nobody said anything. Sully felt his body tighten.

"I have to go," he mumbled.

In the parking lot, Sully unleashed his anger by banging on his car hood five straight times. *It never goes away! There's a reminder every damn hour, another little rip in your heart.* He threw the briefcase with the stolen information in the backseat. As he yanked open the driver's-side door, he caught a glimpse of a blue Ford Fiesta in the rear of the funeral home parking lot.

Someone was in it, watching him.

Pastor Warren, lying in the hospital bed, heard the tinny sound of cable TV news coming through the remote control. He pressed several buttons until it silenced. No more. He'd heard enough news to last him a year.

A mild heart incident. That's what the doctors said. He should be fine. Still, at his age, a few days of observation were needed. *Just to be on the safe side*.

Warren looked around the bland, antiseptic room — a rolling metal table, a maroon leather chair. He thought of how scared he had made everyone, collapsing on the pulpit, the emergency medical people rushing in. He recalled a line from Scripture: *Come to me, you who are weary and burdened, and I will grant you rest*. He had given his life to the Lord; he expected — in some ways hoped — the Lord would take it soon.

Earlier in the day, Father Carroll had come by. They'd spoken in generalities, about old age, health. Finally they addressed the upcoming broadcast.

"The network asked me to be available," Father Carroll said. "I think it will be good for the church."

"Perhaps."

"Do you think she can make it happen?"

"Who?'

"Katherine Yellin. Can she really summon her sister?"

Pastor Warren scanned the priest's face, hoping to see something he did not see.

"Wouldn't God do the summoning?"

Father Carroll looked away. "Of course."

He left a few minutes later. Warren felt worn out by the conversation.

"Pastor, you have more visitors," a nurse announced, entering with a new bag of fluid for his intravenous drip.

"More what?"

"Visitors. On the way up."

Warren pulled the sheet higher. Who now? Perhaps Mrs. Pulte? Or one of the other clergymen? The nurse left the room, and his eyes followed her out the door and to the hallway.

His mouth fell slightly open.

Elias Rowe was coming toward him.

History celebrates Alexander Bell, but his partner, Thomas Watson, the recipient of the world's first phone call, is much less known. Watson, who was indispensable to Bell, only worked with him five more years. Then, in 1881, he took the considerable money the telephone had earned him and pursued other interests. He took a long honeymoon in Europe. He invested in a ship-making business. He tried his hand at Shakespearean acting.

But thirty-eight years after their first phone conversation, Watson and Bell spoke again, this time over not twenty feet of wire but three thousand miles of it, with Bell in New York and Watson in San Francisco. It was the nation's first transcontinental call, and Bell began with the phrase he had uttered all those years ago: "*Mr. Watson. Come here.*"

To which Watson responded, "It would take me a week to get to you now."

It's a quiet theft, how time lures people away. Pastor Warren studied the face of Elias Rowe, whom he hadn't seen in months. He remembered Elias as a teenager, always around, always humble, always good with tools. He'd helped rebuild the church kitchen. Put new carpet in the sanctuary. For years he was a regular attendee at Sunday services — right up to the day Katherine Yellin made her announcement. *I have witnessed a miracle!* And Elias confirmed it.

Warren hadn't seen him since.

"I want to ask your forgiveness, Pastor," Elias said now, sitting alongside the hospital bed.

"You've done nothing that needs forgiving."

"I disrupted your service."

"Katherine beat you to it."

"Maybe so. But I want you to know I've been praying on my own a lot."

"God hears you, wherever you are. We do miss you in the sanctuary."

"Pastor?"

"Mmm?"

"Can I bring someone else in to see you?"

"Here? Now?"

"Yes."

"All right."

He motioned, and Sully entered from the hallway. Elias made the introductions.

"You see, Pastor, there may be something else I want to ask forgiveness for."

Warren raised his eyebrows. "What is it?"

Earlier that afternoon, Elias and Sully had sat in Sully's walk-up apartment, reviewing pages of Nick Joseph's file from the funeral home. In it, they found transcribed conversations of the relatives who had spoken to Maria — Nick's younger brother, Joe, and his older sister, Patty. (Both Nick's parents were deceased.) Along with the normal biographical details, his sister spoke about a "little Nick":

The thing that would make Nick saddest about dying is not knowing who's gonna take care of little Nick. The mother is a mess . . . I'm sure she won't even come to the funeral . . . When he stopped sending her money, she went crazy. She moved and didn't give him an address . . . But you can't write anything about little Nick, OK, Maria? That's between us.

Elias had never known about Nick having a child — or an ex — and neither had anyone on his crew. The way Nick drank and partied, they'd presumed he lived alone.

"Pastor, I know Nick used to belong to Harvest of Hope," Elias said. "I figured if anyone knew about this, you would. But when I went by the church, they told me what happened — you collapsing during Bible study."

"An unexpected adventure," Warren said.

"I'm real sorry."

"Don't be. The Lord has His plan. But about this son?"

"Yes?"

"I'm afraid I never knew he existed. And Nick used to come see me regularly. Patty, too."

"Wait. Nick visited with you?"

"He had terrible financial problems. The church would lend him what little it had."

Elias rubbed his forehead. "Pastor, I was the reason for those problems. I fired him. I took away his benefits."

"I know."

Elias looked away, ashamed. "He's calling me."

"Who?"

"Nick. That's who's been calling from . . . you know. Heaven. Wherever. He's angry. He wants me to do something. He said it was for Nick, and I thought he meant himself. But now I think it's his son."

Warren narrowed his gaze. "Is this why you went away?"

"I was scared, Pastor. I'm sorry. I didn't know he had a child—"

"It's all right, Elias—"

"I would never have fired him—"

"It's not your—"

"No matter how much he messed up—"

"It's all right—"

"These calls. His voice. They haunt me."

Warren reached for Elias's arm to comfort him. He caught Sully looking, and tilted his head toward him.

"What do you make of all this, Mr. Harding?"

Sully touched a hand to his chest. "Me?"

Warren nodded.

"Well, Pastor, no disrespect, but I don't believe in heaven."

"Go on."

"I think someone is manipulating these calls. Someone who knows a lot about the dead. If *you* didn't know about Nick's son, there can't be many who do, right? But the voice that Elias talks to, it knows. So either it's really Nick — even though he couldn't answer some basic questions that the real Nick would know — or it's someone with access to a lot of information."

Warren dropped his head into the pillow. He looked at the intravenous connection on the back of his hand, taped over several times so he couldn't see the needle or the fluid entering him. *Come to me, you who are weary and burdened.*

"Elias . . ."

He wiggled his fingers. Elias took his hand.

"You did not know about the child. God will forgive you. Perhaps there is a way to help the boy now?"

Elias nodded. A tear rolled down his face.

"And Mr. Harding?"

Sully straightened.

"I do believe in heaven. And I do believe God might grant us a glimpse."

"I understand."

"But not this way."

Sully blinked. A man of God was agreeing with him?

"Who do you think could create such a thing?"

241

Sully cleared his throat. "There's someone at the newspaper who has access to all this data."

Warren nodded slowly. "Newspapers," he whispered. "Very powerful things." He closed his eyes. "You know that firsthand, don't you?"

Sully felt a breath escape his chest. So Pastor Warren knew his story too.

"Yes, I do," Sully confirmed.

Winter nights fall early in northern Michigan. By five o'clock, Coldwater was dark. On the high school football field, under giant klieg lights, Jeff Jacoby inspected the stage. He had to admit, the producers were right; money could get anything accomplished. There was scaffolding everywhere, a huge white tent overhead, multiple lighting grids, portable heaters, and a smooth hardwood surface for the rolling cameras, which had been trucked in from Detroit. The whole thing was illuminated as bright as day, with the far stands closed off and the near ones covered with tarps in case of bad weather. Two massive projection screens stood to the left and right of the platform. In all his years living in Coldwater, there had never been such a setting. Jeff felt a surge of pride — followed by a wave of concern.

The schedule had been set. The "chosen ones" were to sit down with the famous host at precisely 1:00p.m., when the live broadcast would begin. They would be interviewed and take questions from the audience and from the nation via the Internet. All this would happen while Katherine waited for her call from Diane. A camera would be on her at all times. The producers had already tested her salmon-pink Samsung flip phone through the loudspeakers.

If a voice from heaven materialized, it would be clearly heard.

Of course, Jeff worried about the obvious: What if no call came? Katherine had assured them it would happen, but what proof did they have? To fatten the broadcast, the producers had brought in numerous "experts." There were clairvoyants who said they spoke regularly to the dead. There were paranormal specialists who had tapes of ghostly voices captured through radio frequencies. There was a woman who had suffered a near-death experience and now claimed she saw the spirits of the deceased all around her, even as she was being interviewed.

After a few hours of this, Jeff walked away wondering not whether the Coldwater phone calls were possible, but why they hadn't happened sooner. He'd heard Anesh Barua — in a "pre-interview" — speak about his daughter, who had told him heaven was "endless light." And Eddie Doukens, whose ex-wife described heaven as "our first house together, when our children were playing." Tess Rafferty claimed her mother, Ruth, told her that heaven is where "all is forgiven," where there are no "terrors of the night or arrows of the day."

This was powerful testimony. Still, Jeff worried. But when he pulled Lance aside and said, "What if Katherine's call doesn't come for three or four hours?" the producer grinned.

"We can only hope."

"I don't understand."

"No," Lance said, wryly. "You don't."

Lance knew the truth: it really didn't matter. The longer the program ran, the more ads were sold. The more ads sold, the more money was earned. In the end, the network treated proof of heaven no differently from a royal wedding or a reality-show finale: it weighed the costs of production versus the return on investment. Viewer interest in Coldwater was immeasurable; people would watch. And they would keep watching — as long as they thought a blessed voice was coming.

Whether heaven truly existed never entered the equation.

In the dream, Sully was in the cockpit. The plane was shaking. The gauges were dropping. He readied himself for ejection — and suddenly the sky went black. Sully turned to his right and saw, pressed against the window, the face of Elwood Jupes.

He burst awake.

From that gasping moment Thursday morning — the day before the broadcast — he'd been chasing his suspicion. He'd gone by the *Gazette* parking lot and peeked inside a blue Ford Fiesta — which, he had learned, was indeed Elwood's car. He saw boxes on the backseat, including several from Radio Shack.

Sully went inside and busied himself with fake ad-sales paperwork, glancing up several times to see Elwood staring at him. At ten-thirty, Elwood left the building. Moments later, Sully followed.

244

He trailed Elwood from a safe distance. When the Fiesta turned off Lake Street, Sully did the same. A few blocks later, he slammed on the brakes.

Elwood was pulling into Davidson & Sons, the funeral home.

Sully parked down the road. He waited over an hour. Finally he saw the blue Fiesta pass him, and he followed it down Cuthbert Road, to the home of Tess Rafferty. Elwood went inside the house. Sully waited down the street.

A half hour later Elwood emerged and drove to the high school field, site of the upcoming broadcast. When he parked and got out, Sully waited a minute, then did the same, ducking and hiding behind the production trucks. He saw Elwood examining the staging, the lights, and the control center — flashing his press credentials if anyone approached him. After an hour of this, he returned to his car and drove back to the *Gazette*.

Sully swung by the library and found Liz, who had a line of people at her desk. He motioned her into the back room.

"Elwood Jupes," he said.

"The guy from the newspaper?"

"Is there any way he could be more than that?"

"How do you mean?"

"Would he have a reason to be making these calls? Some kind of motivation?"

"I don't know. Maybe his daughter?"

"What about her?"

"She killed herself a few years ago. Drove off the bridge. It was terrible."

"Why'd she do it?"

Liz shook her head. "Why does anybody do it?"

"Do you have the story?"

"Give me a minute."

She left. Sully waited in the back. Ten minutes later, Liz returned empty-handed.

"It's missing. That whole edition. Not here."

The next few hours were a blur of activity. Sully sped to the Dial-Tek store to see if Elwood Jupes was connected to the phone plans of the chosen ones. While Jason started checking for him, Sully drove to the *Gazette* to search for the missing newspaper edition. Elwood was there, huddled over his desk, and he eyeballed Sully as he went to the stacks.

"Twice in one day," he remarked. "What're you looking for, eh?"

"One of the clients wants an original copy of an old ad."

"Mmm."

When he found the actual paper (Liz had given him the date) he barely glanced at the headline — DEATH ON BRIDGE BEING INVESTIGATED — before folding it and putting it in his briefcase. He didn't want Elwood catching sight of what he was looking at.

He then raced to the school, picked up Jules, dropped him at his parents', and drove quickly home to his second-story walk-up, where Elias Rowe was waiting on the steps.

Over the next few hours, they reviewed everything. They read all of Maria's transcribed discussions with the mourning families. They found out from Jason that Elwood was indeed on the same phone plan as the others. They read the old newspaper together, the tragic story of a twenty-four-year-old woman driving her car into the freezing November waters.

But most unusual was the byline.

The story was written by Elwood Jupes.

"He wrote about his own daughter?" Elias asked.

"Something's weird."

"But how does this connect to my phone calls?"

"I don't know."

"I'm telling you, it was Nick's voice."

"The others say the voices are real, too."

"It's spooky."

"He must be doing something."

They sat in silence. Sully glanced to the window; the sunlight was gone. In less than twenty-four hours, the whole world would be here in Coldwater, or virtually here, hoping to solve the greatest mystery in the world: Is there life after death?

Bumm-bummp-bummp!

Sully froze. He looked to the door.

Bumm-bummp-bummp!

His stomach tightened.

"You expecting someone?" Elias whispered.

Sully shook his head. He moved to the peephole, leaned in, and felt a shiver from his feet to the top of his head. A sick, familiar feeling enveloped him, one he'd promised himself the day he walked out of prison that he would never feel again.

"I'm Police Chief Sellers," said the uniformed man when Sully opened the door, "I need you to come with me."

Katherine and Amy stood on a small hill overlooking the football field and the massive stage. It was freezing, and Katherine pulled her scarf tighter.

"CHECK . . . CHECK, CHECK . . ."

The voice boomed, an audio man testing the microphones. The stage was lit in a wash of light that made it look as if the sun were hanging over it.

"What do you think?" Amy said.

"It's very big," Katherine replied.

"You can still back out."

Katherine smiled weakly. "This isn't up to me anymore."

The voice boomed again. "CHECK . . . ONE-TWO . . . CHECK . . ."

Amy saw at least half a dozen TV crews filming the final preparations, beefy men in parkas with cameras on their shoulders, pointed at the stage like bazookas. She felt an ache of injustice that she was not down there, breaking the latest news. Yet she had to admit she also felt some relief, like a student excused from a test.

"I can say something to them," Katherine offered.

"What do you mean?"

"I can say I won't participate unless you're doing the story."

"But that's not true."

"I can still say it."

"Why would you do that for me?"

"Don't be silly. I'd do it *because* it's you."

Amy smiled. For the first time since they'd met, she could envision Katherine's relationship with her sister Diane, and why Katherine felt such a deep loss. Loyalty ruled this woman's soul, but loyalty needs a partner.

"Thanks. I'm OK."

"Did you try calling Rick again?"

"He doesn't answer. He doesn't want to talk to me." Katherine looked down.

"You all right?" Amy asked.

"I was just thinking."

"What?"

"You can't get your phone to answer, and I can't make mine ring."

In the decade following the telephone's invention, Alexander Bell had to defend his patent more than six hundred times. Rival companies. Greedy individuals. *Six hundred times.* Bell grew so weary of lawsuits that he retreated to Canada, where at night he was known to sit in a canoe, smoke a cigar, and study the skies. It grieved him that people would accuse him of stealing the very things most precious to him — his ideas — and that the lawyers' inquiries suggested as much. Sometimes questions can be more cruel than insults.

Sully Harding sat in a back room of the Coldwater Police Department as Jack Sellers rifled such questions at him.

"What do you know about these phone calls?"

"What phone calls?"

"The ones from heaven."

"The ones people *say* are from heaven?"

"What is your involvement?"

"*My* involvement?"

"Your involvement."

"I don't have any involvement."

"Then why are you with Mr. Rowe?"

"We're friends."

"Friends?"

"New friends, yes."

"Is he getting phone calls?"

"You have to ask him."

"Why were you at the *Gazette* today?"

"I work there."

"You're an ad salesman."

"Right."

"Why would you be going through old newspapers?"

"Why are you asking me this?"

"I want to know your involvement."

"*What* involvement?"

Sully's head was spinning. Elias was somewhere outside, in another office. He'd seemed scared when the police arrived. Neither man had spoken to the other since.

"Are you arresting me for something?"

"I'm just asking questions."

"Do I have to answer them?"

"Not answering won't help your position."

"What's my position?"

"That you're not involved."

"I'm not."

"Why were you at Davidson's funeral home?"

"They're a client."

"Why were you at the football field?"

"Wait, how do you know all this—"

"Why are you following Elwood Jupes?"

Sully shivered.

"Were you ever in prison, Mr. Harding?"

"Once."

"What for?"

"A mistake."

"Why were you following Elwood Jupes? What is your involvement? What do you know about these phone calls?"

Sully swallowed; then, against his better judgment, he blurted it out: "I think Elwood may be making them."

Jack straightened. He pushed out his jaw.

"That's strange."

He stepped to a side door and opened it, revealing Elwood Jupes, standing with a notepad.

"That's what he says about you."

Jack did not watch cop shows. Most real cops don't bother. When you live in that world, false drama seems silly. Anyhow, things never go the way they do on TV.

Jack knew his line of questioning with Sullivan Harding was buckshot at best. He had no real right to interrogate him. He had only heard a complaint two hours earlier — Elwood, from the *Gazette*, who Jack knew well because any police chief in any small town is going to know the town's only reporter.

Elwood had called with a theory. This guy Harding, now an ad salesman, was hanging around with Elias Rowe, who had made himself scarce since announcing his call. Why? What did the two of them have in common? And Harding had been asking Elwood all kinds of questions. He talked about obituaries. He tried to find old newspapers. It was suspicious, no?

At other times, in other cases, Jack would have said, no, Elwood, it's not suspicious, and ignored the whole thing. But what he couldn't say — yet desperately wanted to know — was, could it be true? Could this whole thing be a hoax? It mattered too much. To him. To Doreen. To Tess. To everyone in town. He had his son back. Tess had her mother back. People shouldn't play with those emotions. That, Jack felt, was criminal in a way nothing on the books could be.

So he brought in Sully, on a flimsy premise, and he grilled him — until he realized Sully was thinking of Elwood what Elwood was thinking of Sully. It degenerated into an almost comical exchange of finger-pointing.

"Why were you at the funeral home?" Sully said.

"I was asking them about you," Elwood said. "What were you doing after hours in the library?"

"I was researching you. Why were you at the football field?"

"I was seeing if you'd been there."

And on and on. Finally Jack scratched his head and interrupted them, saying, "Enough." He was worn out from listening. And it was clear that neither man had anything more than suspicions.

Same as Jack did.

"I'm sorry to barge in on your place," he said.

Sully sighed. "Forget it."

"It's not generally how we do things in Coldwater."

"Coldwater isn't Coldwater anymore."

"You can say that again," Elwood interjected.

"My son thinks he's gonna get a call." Sully was looking at his feet. He surprised himself. Why did he just say that?

"From his dead mother?" Elwood asked.

Sully nodded.

"That's tough."

"It's why I wanted to prove this wrong."

"Don't want to give him false hope?"

"Exactly."

"Like some ghost is gonna call and say everything's all righ—"

"It's not like that," Jack interrupted. "Hearing someone you thought you lost . . . It just feels . . . like *relief*. Like the bad thing never happened. I mean, it's strange at first, you look at the phone, you think it's a joke. But you'd be amazed at how normal it is to talk to him again . . ."

He realized both men were staring at him.

"Doreen told me that," he said, quickly.

"Your wife?" Sully asked.

"Ex-wife."

For a moment, nobody said anything. Finally, Elwood flipped his notepad closed. He looked at Sully. "Well, you might have missed your calling."

"How's that?"

"You could have been a reporter."

"Why?" Sully half chuckled. "Because I got the story wrong?"

Elwood chuckled back. They were all suddenly very tired. Jack looked at his watch and said, "Let's get out of here." He opened the office door to the outer area, where Elias got up from a desk and exchanged looks with two state troopers who were watching him.

Moments later, they all drove off. Jack stopped at Tess's house, and he smiled when she opened the door. Elwood stopped at Pickles and drank a beer. Elias headed to his brother's place to sleep in the guest bedroom.

Sully drove home in silence, staring out the window at the bright glow coming from the football field, and two massive spotlights that seemed to scrape against the heavens.

The Day of the Broadcast

NEWS REPORT
ABC News

ANCHOR: Good morning. It's Friday, December twenty-second, and later today, the small town of Coldwater, Michigan, will be the focus of international attention as it wrestles with an attempt to contact heaven. Alan Jeremy is on-site. Alan?

(Alan in snow.)

ALAN: As you can see around me, Coldwater has already received one delivery from above, a lake-effect storm that came overnight and dumped five inches of snow on the ground. Plows can't get through due to cars parked everywhere. School has been canceled. Many businesses are closed. The town is at a literal standstill as it waits, along with much of the world, for what one woman claims is the soul of her dead sister contacting her from heaven.

ANCHOR: What do we know about this woman, Alan?

(Images of Katherine.)

ALAN: Her name is Katherine Yellin; she's a forty-six-year-old real estate agent, divorced, mother of two.

Apparently she and her sister were very close. Diane Yellin died from an aneurysm two years ago. Katherine says she has been talking to her sister regularly since September — through telephone calls that, she claims, are from the afterlife.

ANCHOR: Others make that claim as well, right, Alan?

(*Images of the others.*)

ALAN: Yes. Six others, ranging from a day care director to a dentist. Most of them will also be part of the national TV broadcast today. But the focus will be on Yellin, her sister, and what a voice from the "other side" may sound like. Yellin will be monitored live, and any contact she gets will be broadcast in real time. Not since Alexander Graham Bell demonstrated the telephone for the Queen of England in 1878 has the world sat in such anticipation of a single phone call.

ANCHOR: This one might have bigger ramifications.

ALAN: Indeed. In Coldwater, I'm Alan Jeremy for *ABC News*.

"Can't we get more plows?" Lance yelled, over the din of blowers and industrial-size generators.

"I'm trying!" Jeff yelled back. "I've called five different towns!"

Lance shook his head in disgust. They were supposed to be prepping the broadcast. Instead, wherever he looked, people were clearing snow — volunteers brooming the stands or wiping down the set with towels. Jack Sellers was leading dozens of officers through deep drifts, stepping into and out of each

256

other's boot prints. Jeff Jacoby was trying to locate more plows.

Of all the nights for a storm. Lance pressed the button on his walkie-talkie and said, "Clint, are the ambassadors on their way to the guests?"

He heard static. Then, "We told them ... *zrrzylp* ..."

"Again?"

"We ... *mzyrrrp* ... o'clock."

"What?"

"*Zrrrrp* ... what?"

"Are they on their way, Clint?"

"—them ten o'clock."

"No. Not ten o'clock! Now! You see all this snow? Go get them early!"

"*Zmmzzpt* ... them now?"

"Yes. Now. Now!"

Static. "Copy th—"

Lance hurled the device into a snowdrift. *Are you kidding me?* In four hours they were hoping to broadcast a call from another dimension, and they couldn't even make their walkie-talkies work.

Sully poured a bowl of cereal for his son. He splashed milk over the top.

"Can I have some sugar, too?" Jules asked.

"There's enough sugar in it already," Sully said.

They sat by the window overlooking the ravine. The snow-drifts were like lumps of frozen cream, and the trees sagged with heavily frosted branches.

Sully gulped his coffee, extra strong, trying to rally some energy. He couldn't remember when he'd felt so tired. He'd chased his theory; his theory was wrong. He felt like a fool. An exhausted fool. Had it not been for Jules, he'd have slept all day.

"Listen, school's called off today, so I'm gonna take you to Grandma and Grandpa's, OK?"

"Can we play in the snow first? Can we make a Studley?"

Sully smiled. That was Giselle's nickname for a snowman — one with muscles. "Let's make a Studley!" she would yell, bursting from the front door holding Jules's hand, high-stepping in her winter boots. Sully looked at their son and felt a welling in his chest, as if he owed him a massive apology. All this time chasing Elwood, Maria, Elias, the obituaries, this whole obsession with disproving a miracle, and every day his son just kept on loving him, a small miracle in itself.

"Sure," Sully said. "We'll make a Studley."

"Cool!" Jules said, and then he shoved a giant spoonful of cereal in his mouth, the milk dripping down his cheeks. Sully took a napkin and dotted his face as he chewed.

"Daddy?"

"Mmm."

"Don't feel sad. Mommy is gonna call you."

Sully lowered the napkin.

"Let's just make a snowman, OK?"

"A Studley," his son corrected.

An hour later they had a three-layered, muscle-bound snow sculpture near the front porch, with a stick for a nose and pretzel nuggets for a mouth and eyes. Sully's father, Fred, pulled up in his truck and got out, smiling.

"Is this your new security guard?"

"Grandpa!" Jules said, clomping through the snow and hugging his legs.

"Thanks for picking him up," Sully said. "He wanted to do this first."

"No problem," Fred said.

Sully wiped the snow off his gloves and sniffed. "It took you a while. Lot of traffic?"

"Ridiculous. They have troopers everywhere, don't know what they're doing. And there aren't enough tow trucks in the world to clear the parking mess."

"Are you and Mom . . ."

"What? Going to the show?"

"Is that what they're calling it?"

"What would you call it?"

"A show sounds right."

"Your mother wants to."

Sully sighed. He nodded toward Jules. "I don't want him being a part of that, OK?"

"I'll keep him home with me," Fred said. "If heaven wants to talk to us, I imagine we'll hear it in our house."

Sully snorted, remembering where he had inherited his cynicism. He pushed his ski cap higher on his forehead.

"I gotta get to work."

"Is anybody working today?"

"Money collection. Gotta pick up a check from the funeral parlor."

"Davidson's?"

"Yeah."

"Cheery place."

"Tell me about it. That owner is a piece of work, huh? Like talking to Lurch the butler."

"Sam?"

"Hmm?"

"Sam Davidson? He's kind of small and fat. Not much of a butler."

Sully paused.

"Who's Sam? I'm talking about Horace."

"Oh, that guy. Nah. He's not the owner. He bought a share of the place so Sam could retire."

Sully stared at his father.

"When was that?"

"Maybe two years ago? He gives me the creeps. Who wants to run a funeral home?"

"Horace isn't from Coldwater?"

"I think we'd remember a face like that. Nah. He came in from out of state. Why?"

Sully looked at the chunky snowman, its pretzel eyes gazing back at him.

"I gotta go," he said.

Katherine finished her morning prayers and did her makeup. She heard Amy in the kitchen and went to greet her in her bathrobe.

"Good morning."

"Morning. How are you feeling?"

"Nervous."

"Yeah."

Katherine had Diane's phone in her right hand.

"Can I make you some breakfast?" she asked Amy.

"You don't have to bother."

"They say breakfast—"

"Is the most important meal of the day."

"Well, they do."

Amy smiled. "I can't afford the calories. This business is not very nice to fat people."

"You could never be fat."

"Oh, give me a month."

They laughed.

"You know, when—"

The doorbell rang.

Katherine looked at her watch. Her face fell. "They said they'd come at ten. It's only nine twenty!"

"Let me handle it."

"Really?"

"Get dressed. Don't pop out."

"Thank you!"

She darted back to her bedroom. Amy went to the door.

"Yes?" she said to the three men on the porch.

"We're with the show."

"Katherine's not ready yet."

"We want to get her wired, get the phone hooked up."

"She'll be ready at ten."

They looked at each other. All three were young, dark-haired, and wearing parkas with the network patch. Behind them, along Guningham Road, were news vans with painted logos — EYE-WITNESS 7, LOCAL 4, ACTION 6. A small band of cameramen was on the sidewalk, pointing lenses at the house like a firing squad. Amy suddenly felt a million miles from her old life.

"Could we just get her wired up now?" one of the young men asked. "The sooner the better. All this snow."

Amy crossed her arms. "You told her ten, she'll be ready at ten. You can't keep pushing her. She's a human being."

The men made funny shapes with their mouths, different ways of biting their tongues.

"Wait, didn't you do some of the original reports?" one asked.

"Yeah, yeah," another continued. "Amy Penn, *Nine Action News*. I've watched all of your stuff."

"Katherine's not supposed to be doing other media—"

"We had her exclusive—"

"Did you run this through Lance?"

"You know how much money they're spendi—"

"This is a violation—"

"You better not—"

Amy shut the door.

Sully inched the Buick through traffic. He had never seen the streets of Coldwater so congested. No one

262

had. Cars crawled. Many blocks remained unplowed, with drifted snow as high as your knees. Vans and buses, their exhaust pipes blowing dirty smoke, slowly shuttled several thousand passengers on their pilgrimage to the football field.

By the time Sully reached Davidson & Sons, it was eleven thirty. The broadcast would begin in ninety minutes. He hurried from the car, took two steps, and slipped clumsily on an icy patch, falling forward into a snowbank, his face impacting the cold and wet. He pushed himself back up awkwardly, wiping the dripping snow from his nose and cheeks, and stumbled to the front door.

Inside the hallways were empty, the soft music playing. Sully's pants and jacket were soaked. He moved around the corner and saw Maria in her office. She had her coat on.

"Mr. Harding," she said, looking at him. "What happened?"

"Slipped in the snow."

"Oh, my. You're all red. Here."

She pulled tissues from a box.

"Thank you. Maria, where's Horace?"

"Oh, dear, you missed him again."

"Ahhh."

"Well, at least he's not at lunch."

"Is he over at the broadcast?"

"That's where I'm headed. I don't really know where he is, to be honest."

"He didn't tell you?"

"He never does on Fridays."

"Why not?"

"He doesn't work on Fridays."

Sully swallowed so hard, it felt as if an egg were passing down his throat.

"Since when?"

"Oh, for a while now. Since the summer, anyhow."

Fridays. All those calls on Fridays.

"Maria, I need to ask you something. It may seem weird."

"All right," she said, cautiously.

"When did Horace start working here?"

"Oh, I remember that. It was a year ago last April. My grand-daughter's birthday."

A year ago last April? A month after Sully's crash?

"Where did he come from?"

"Someplace in Virginia. He's always been pretty quiet about it because, well . . . you would know."

"Why would I know?"

"That's how military people are, right?"

Sully bit his lip.

"And what did Horace do . . . in the military?"

"I'm not sure. He and Mr. Davidson talked about it. Virginia. Fort something in Virginia."

"Fort Belvoir?"

"Yes. Goodness. How did you know that?"

Sully clenched his fists. Fort Belvoir was the army's command center for military intelligence. *Wiretaps. Phone intercepts.*

Maria looked at her watch. "Ooh. I'm late."

"Wait. One more thing."

"All right."

264

"Those transcripts you do of the families, for the obituaries?"

"Yes?"

"Does Horace see them?"

She seemed perplexed. "Why would you ask—"

"Does he *see* them?"

His tone made her draw back.

"I . . . I guess he *can*. It wouldn't make much sense."

"Why not?"

"Because he sits in on all those meetings."

"What?"

"That's his policy. He sits in on everything. He talks to everybody. He gets copies of all papers."

Sully's eyes went far away. He remembered the first time he met Horace. *It was a lovely ceremony.* Horace attended everything. He read everything. He knew about everyone who had a funeral in Coldwater — Nick Joseph, Ruth Rafferty, Robbie Sellers.

Giselle.

He knew about Giselle.

Sully stepped in toward Maria.

"Where does he live?" he whispered.

"Mr. Harding, you're frightening me."

"Where does he *live*?"

"Why—"

"Please," he said, his jaw clenched. "Just tell me *where he lives*."

Her eyes widened.

"I don't know. He never told me."

By noon, every seat in the stands was occupied. Generators cranked up heat blowers. The bright lights made the stage warm enough to keep a coat unbuttoned.

Jack had already briefed the police force, met with the state troopers, and distributed walkie-talkies to dozens of auxiliary officers. Now he escorted Tess through the high school doors and down to the teachers' lounge, which served as the holding area for the show's guests. Tess gripped her purse, which held a new cell phone to which her home phone had been forwarded — Samantha's idea — in case her mother should make contact while she was out of the house.

"You still don't have to do this," Jack whispered.

"It's all right," Tess said. "I'm not afraid of questions."

Jack knew that was true. He had watched her many mornings with the followers who sat in her living room, answering anything they wanted to know.

"I'll be on the stage the whole time," he said.

"Good," Tess said, smiling.

He had gone by her house last night after the whole ordeal with Harding, Jupes, and Elias Rowe. He needed to unwind. When he told her the story, she listened attentively, occasionally pushing her long, blond hair back behind her ears.

"So there was no conspiracy," she said when he finished.

"Just two guys suspicious of each other," he said.

She seemed happy. In a way, he was too. The heavenly calls had withstood a challenge. That somehow made them more believable.

After that, Tess made him hot chocolate with real milk and they sat on the couch and talked for a while about the broadcast and the hysteria and what to expect today. At some point Jack must have dozed off; when he opened his eyes, he was still on the couch, but with a blanket over him. The house was dark. He felt like sleeping there until morning, seeing Tess come down the stairs, feeling that old sense of starting the day like a couple, but he knew that with everything going on, that was unwise. He folded the blanket, left it on the couch, drove home, took a shower, and went out to the high school, where he'd been ever since.

He escorted Tess now to the VIP zone, and she approached a woman with a clipboard. "Hi, I'm Tess Rafferty."

"Great," the woman said, putting a check next to her name. "There's coffee and snacks back there if you like. And we have some paperwork."

She handed her the clipboard. A man's voice suddenly bellowed.

"Good morning, Tess."

Tess turned to see Father Carroll, wearing a heavy wool coat over his clerical outfit. Next to him was Bishop Hibbing.

"Father," she said, taken aback. "Good morning. Good morning, Bishop."

She shot Jack a glance. He introduced himself, then stepped back and dug his hands into his police parka. "So. I've got a million things to do. You're good to go?"

"I'm good," Tess said.

"I'll see you out there."

Jack left the building, trying to flush his personal feelings and focus on the biggest logistical challenge he'd ever faced. He approached the giant stage, where he would be stationed for the entire broadcast. The crowd was streaming in, and people were already sitting on the hills behind the stands. *In the snow?* Jack thought. Thankfully, the storm had passed and the sun was actually poking through the clouds. He wondered what this town would be like tomorrow — better or worse?

As Jack neared the stage steps, his cell phone rang.

"Yeah, Chief Sellers," he said.

"*Dad . . . It's Robbie.*"

He froze.

"Son?"

"*Tell them about me, Dad . . . Tell them where I am.*"

Sully had reached Liz and told her to meet him at the library, as fast as she could. He ran through snowdrifts, his car useless on the crammed Coldwater streets. His breath came in gasps, and the cold air made his lungs feel as if they were being scraped from the inside.

"What happened?" Liz said when he pushed through the library's back door.

"I need an address." He tried to catch his breath. "Have to find out . . . where Horace lives."

"Who's Horace?"

"From the funeral home."

"OK, OK," she said, moving to the computer. "There's public records, mortgage stuff, but we'd have to have some basics."

Sully bent at the knees, heaving in and out.

"Start with 'Horace' . . . What the hell is his last name? Put in the funeral home, see what comes up."

She clicked the keys quickly.

"Bunch of stuff about Davidson and Sons . . . Davidson and Sons . . . Horace Belfin, director."

"Look for a home address!"

"I don't think . . . hang on . . . No, nothing."

Sully looked at his watch. It was nearly twelve thirty.

"How do we find out where someone lives in this town?"

Liz continued to type rapidly — then stopped and looked up.

"There might be a faster way," she said.

Ten minutes later, they pushed through the chiming front door of the Coldwater Collection real estate agency. The receptionist's area was empty, but there was one man sitting at a back desk.

"Can I help you guys?" Lew asked.

"Maybe," Sully said, catching his breath. "It's gonna sound strange."

"What could be strange in Coldwater? Just don't tell me you want a house where your dead relatives can call you. I'm fresh out."

Sully looked at Liz.

"You're skeptical?" he asked.

Lew glanced back and forth, as if someone might be listening.

"Well, I'm not supposed to contradict the great Katherine Yellin, our beloved sales partner, but yes, I'm — what did you say? — skeptical. This has been the worst thing to ever happen to us here. Actually, I don't believe any of it, but don't tell anyone." He sniffed. "Anyhow, are you looking for a house?"

"Yeah," Sully said. "One that might prove you're right."

Lew touched his chin.

"Keep talking."

At five minutes to one, the host of the show emerged from a heated tent to massive applause from the crowd. She was dressed in a fuchsia coat, with a black turtleneck, a knee-length skirt, black tights, and knee-high boots. She took her seat on a stool. From the other side of the stage came Tess Rafferty, Anesh Barua, Eddie Doukens, and Jay James. They too sat on stools, arranged in a straight row.

Finally Katherine Yellin emerged, wearing a Persian blue pantsuit that Amy had helped her choose. She was holding the pink phone in her left hand. The crowd erupted into a cacophony of shrieks, applause, and excited conversation. She was guided to a chair, off to the side, flanked by — at Lance's last-minute suggestion — the Coldwater police chief, Jack Sellers, who wore a stunned expression, having just spoken to his dead son.

270

"Thank you all for coming!" Mayor Jeff Jacoby bellowed into a microphone. "We're about to get started. Remember, everyone, we will be live, beaming around the world. So please, no matter what happens, let's make sure Coldwater looks good, right?"

He turned and motioned to the white-haired priest.

"Father Carroll, would you bless the crowd before we start?"

Sully bounced the Buick over snowy lawns, cutting around parked cars in an effort to reach Route 8. Every bump jerked him forward and back, some nearly slamming him into the dashboard. He went up curbs and down curbs, the chassis banging in protest. He had no choice; if he slowed down, the car might sink in the snow.

He had a street address and a hastily drawn map on a piece of stationery. According to real estate records, Horace had purchased a home on the outskirts of Moss Hill fifteen months ago, a large property with an old farmhouse and a barn. He'd paid cash. Because the transaction had been handled by their group, a copy of the deed was in the files at the Coldwater Collection offices. Lew had happily handed it over, noting, "I never believed Katherine, even when she got that call here."

Sully spun the car off a lawn and onto a passable street, bouncing as it hit the flattened snow. He kept seeing Horace's long, haggard face, and he mentally rifled through every conversation they'd had for some clue as to how he was involved.

It was a lovely ceremony. I imagine the family has told you.

I am the family.

Of course.

Sully's stomach was churning. He careened onto Route 8, which was actually plowed, and the Buick's tires gripped the road gratefully. Sully slammed the accelerator. On his left was creeping traffic, backed up for a mile coming into Coldwater. The road out of town was empty.

How are you doing, Mr. Harding?

Not so good.

I understand.

He glanced at his watch.

It was ten after one.

The broadcast had begun.

Upon royal request, Alexander Graham Bell agreed to an event of worldwide significance: a demonstration of the telephone for Queen Victoria. It took place at her personal palace on the Isle of Wight, January 14, 1878, less than two years after the emperor of Brazil had exclaimed, "My God! It talks!" Already the phone was much improved, and the Queen would receive the most elaborate show yet. Four locations were to be connected, so that Her Majesty would hear, through the receiver, all of the following: a spoken voice from a nearby cottage; four singers in the town of Cowes; a bugle player in the town of Southampton; and an organ player in London.

Reporters from newspapers would chronicle the event. Everyone knew that if the Queen was impressed, the phone would be assured a rich future throughout the British Empire. But moments before the scheduled start time, Bell discovered that three of the four lines were not functioning. With no time to address the issue, he looked up to see the regal party entering the room. He bowed slightly as he was introduced to Her Majesty Queen Victoria; her son, the Duke of Connaught; and her daughter, Princess Beatrice.

The Queen asked, through her gentleman-in-waiting, if the professor would be kind enough to explain "the device he calls the telephone."

Bell picked up the receiver, took a breath, and privately prayed that the one remaining connection was there.

At the county hospital, with the television softly playing, Elias Rowe placed his hand on Pastor Warren's slender wrist.

"It's started, Pastor," Elias said, softly.

Warren opened his eyes.

"Mmm . . . all right."

Elias glanced down the hospital corridor. It was nearly empty, owing to the many missing staffers who were attending the broadcast, some of whom had declared the day a religiously excused absence. Throughout Coldwater — and much of the country — there was a palpable feeling that this date in history, three days before Christmas, might bring a change to life as we knew it, like the morning of a major election, or the night man walked on the moon.

Elias had come to visit Pastor Warren because, after last night's craziness with Sully and Elwood, he needed to clear his head. The two men prayed together. Now Elias sat in a cushioned chair next to Warren's bed, and they watched the culmination of the strangest four months of their lives as the TV host introduced the "chosen ones" and Katherine Yellin. The cameras kept cutting to people in the crowd, many of whom were holding hands or had their eyes closed in prayer.

"Katherine," the host asked, "you have asked your sister Diane to contact us today, is that right?"

"Yes," Katherine said.

She looks nervous, Elias thought.

"Did you explain to her why?"

"Yes."

"How did you explain it?"

"I told her — I asked her — if the Lord wanted the whole world to know that heaven was real, could she prove it to . . . I guess, the whole world."

"And she said she would?"

Katherine nodded, glancing at her flip phone.

"You have a list of questions that people around the world have voted on — the questions about heaven they most want answered?"

Katherine fingered the clipboard they had given her. "Yes."

"And everyone else here," the host said, turning to the others, "you have all brought your phones, I understand. Can you show them to us?"

They all took out their phones, and held them in their laps or in front of their chests. The camera closed in on them, one at a time.

"Now, the phenomenon of voices from the other side is not new," the host said, turning as she read a teleprompter. "We want to bring in an expert, Dr. Salome Depawzna, who specializes in paranormal communications. She joins us from Houston, via satellite. Dr. Depawzna, thank you."

On the giant screens appeared the image of a middle-aged woman with streaky gray hair, sitting before a backdrop of the Houston skyline.

"I'm happy to be here," she began.

"Can you tell us, Doctor — in the past, have other people been able to make contact with—"

Drrrnnnng.

The host stopped. The guests turned left and right.

Drrrrnnng.

On the stage, Tess looked down.

Her new phone was ringing.

"Oh, God," she whispered.

Drrrrnnng.

Then . . . *Bddlllleeep* . . .

Then . . . *Ole-ole* . . .

First one, then the next, each phone in each of the chosen ones' hands was going off. They looked to each other, paralyzed.

"Hello?" Dr. Depawzna said on the screen. "Did I lose you?"

The audience, realizing what was happening, began to yell. "Talk to them!" "Answer them!" Tess looked to

Anesh, who looked to Jay, who looked to Eddie. Across the way, Jack Sellers, standing by Katherine, saw a shocked look on her face, then saw it turned on him.

Because his phone was ringing, too.

Sully found the house at the end of an unpaved, unplowed road. He stepped from the car. There was a high chain-link fence around the exterior, and the farmhouse was set deep on the property. The barn was even farther behind it. Sully saw a front gate, but he did not intend to announce his arrival. He took a breath, then charged the fence and leaped onto it, curling his fingers around the links. A decade of military training had taught him to scale barriers; years away from duty left him gasping at the effort. He managed to reach the top, flop a leg over the protruding wires, then whip himself up and over, letting go as he braced to break his fall.

Do you remember me?

Mr. Harding.

Call me Sully.

All right.

Sully trudged ahead, anticipating the encounter. The snow was high, and every step he took was like lifting weights with his knees. His eyes watered. His nose ran. As he approached the farmhouse, he saw a large, boxlike structure next to the barn. A tall pole protruded at least sixty feet up from it, with what looked like broken steel candelabras attached. Branches and green leaves hung near the top, as if someone had tried to

276

make it look like a tree. But the other trees around it were bare, and these leaves were brighter than those of the nearby evergreen pines.

Sully knew camouflage when he saw it.

It was a telephone tower.

"Anesh? What did your daughter say?"

" 'We are here.' "

"Tess? Your mother?"

" 'We are here.' "

"Jay? Your partner?"

" 'We are here.' "

"Eddie? Your ex-wife?"

"Same thing."

"And Police Chief Sellers?" The host looked at Jack as he stood awkwardly, midstage, between Katherine and the chosen ones, like someone pulled out of line. "What did the voice tell *you*?"

"It was my son." Jack heard his amplified voice echo over the crowd, as if he had yelled into a canyon.

"What is your son's name?"

Jack hesitated.

"Robbie."

"When did he die?"

"Two years ago. He was a soldier."

"Has he called you before?"

Jack lifted his chin. He wondered where Doreen was, how she would take all this. He wanted to apologize. He looked across the stage at Tess, who nodded slightly.

"Yes. He's been calling me all along."

An audible gasp went through the crowd.

"And what did he say just now?"

Jack swallowed. " 'The end is not the end.' "

The host looked into the main camera and crossed her hands on her lap, flushed with the glow of having just broadcast history. All the phones ringing at once? Each of the heavenly voices passing on one brief remark, then going silent? *The end is not the end?* She tried to maintain the gravitas of the moment, believing this tape would be seen by generations to come.

"So, let's review what we've witnessed here—"

"WE DIDN'T HEAR ANYTHING!"

The voice bellowed from the stands. The host tried to locate it. She put a hand to her forehead, shielding her eyes from the bright lights.

"WE DIDN'T HEAR ANYTHING! HOW DO WE KNOW?"

People turned, craning their necks. A camera operator spun and zoomed in on the man standing by the front row of bleachers, white-haired, in a long coat, wearing a jacket and tie. His image appeared on the giant screens.

"THEY COULD ALL BE LYING!" Elwood Jupes yelled.

He looked both ways, his hands out, imploring the towns-people.

"WE DIDN'T HEAR ANYTHING, DID WE?"

Sully placed his gloved hands on the wooden barn exterior and pressed his ear against it. He heard muffled sounds, nothing he could make out. The large front door was twenty feet away, but Sully thought better of banging on it. If Horace was really behind all that was happening, nothing would suffice but catching him in the act.

The base of the barn was stone, the roof tin, the sides cedar planks. There were no windows. Sully moved from the south end around to the back. He was shivering, exhausted; his lungs were burning. Only when he envisioned Jules, his little boy, picking up a phone and hearing a make-believe call from Horace, creepy Horace, emotionless Horace, ghostlike, too-thin Horace, did he find the strength to push on, slogging into and out of snowdrifts until he came around the north side, where he saw a metal rail about ten feet high.

And beneath it, a sliding access door.

"So what are you saying?" the host asked now, standing on the edge of the stage. "That all these people are making it up?"

"For all we know, yes," Elwood said, speaking into a microphone that had been handed to him. His challenge had disquieted the crowd. They had come to witness a voice from heaven, he reminded them, yet all they had seen was five people answering their phones and telling them what they'd heard.

"Do you live here?" the host asked.

"My whole life, eh?"

"And what do you do?"

"I'm a reporter for the local paper."

The host glanced at her director.

"Why aren't you with the rest of the media?" she asked.

279

"Because before I had a job here, I was a resident here. I went to school here. I got married here. I raised my little girl here."

He paused. "And she died here."

A mumble from the crowd. Elwood's voice choked.

"Folks here know it. She took her life on a bridge. She was a good kid with a bad disease, and she didn't want to live anymore."

The host gathered herself. "I'm very sorry for your—"

"No need to be. You didn't know her, and you don't know me. But a few months ago, I got one of these phone calls, eh?"

"Wait. You got a phone call from your dead daughter?"

"It was her voice."

The crowd gasped again.

"What did you do?"

"I told whoever it was not to play around, that next time I'd tape it and go to the police."

"And?"

He looked down.

"And she never called again."

He wiped his face with a handkerchief. "So I want to hear it, that's all. I want to hear another *real* voice talking about heaven and let everybody here be the judge. Let them decide. Then I'll know . . ."

His voice trailed off.

"You'll know what?" the host asked.

Elwood looked away.

"If I made a mistake."

He wiped his face again. He handed back the microphone. The crowd had fallen silent.

"Well, we're here for just that," the host said, walking back to her chair. "And Katherine Yellin—"

She turned to where Katherine was seated, a designated cameraman hovering just a few feet away.

"We're counting on you for that."

Katherine squeezed her sister's pink phone. She felt as if the eyes of the entire planet were on her.

Sully held the edge of the door. Everything he had, he summoned to his grip. He knew he'd get one chance to surprise Horace, and he needed to do it fast. He exhaled three puffs of air, then, without hesitation — just as he'd pulled the ejector handle — he yanked the door hard and came charging in.

It was dark, and his eyes took a moment to adjust. There were large machines, small red lights, power supplies, snakelike cords. Equipment was rack-mounted, but he couldn't tell what it was. There was a large metal desk and an empty chair. The noise he'd heard was a flat-panel TV.

It was showing cartoons.

"Horace!" Sully yelled.

His voice wafted up to the barn rafters. He slowly circled behind the machinery, his eyes darting left and right.

"Horace Belfin!"

Nothing. He approached the desk, which was neatly arranged with stacked papers and yellow highlighters in a coffee cup. Sully pressed a lamp button, and the surface was illuminated. He pulled open one of the drawers. Office supplies. Another drawer. Computer cables. Another drawer.

Sully blinked.

Inside was something he'd seen before. Maria's files. Her color-coded tabs. Up front, he saw familiar names.

Barua. Rafferty. Sellers. Yellin . . .

He froze.

The last file read, *Harding, Giselle.*

"Mr. Harding!"

Sully spun around.

"Mr. Harding!"

The voice came from outside. Sully's hands shook so badly, he couldn't close the drawer.

"Mr. Harding! Please come out!"

He followed the sound to the barn entrance, inhaled, then peered out from behind the door.

"Mr. Harding!"

Horace was standing by the house, in a black suit, waving.

"Over here!" he yelled.

When Katherine gave birth to her first child, Diane was in the delivery room, as Katherine had been with Diane when her first daughter was born. The sisters held hands as the contractions increased.

"Just a little longer," Diane said soothingly. "You can do it."

Sweat poured down Katherine's face. Diane had driven her to the hospital two hours earlier — Dennis was at work — weaving through cars at breakneck speed.

"I can't believe . . . we didn't get . . . pulled over," Katherine said between breaths.

"I wish we had," Diane said. "I always wanted to tell a cop, 'It's not my fault, this lady's gonna have a baby!'"

Katherine nearly laughed, then felt the sharpest pain yet.

"My God, Diane, how did you stand it?"

"Easy." Diane smiled. "I had you, remember?"

Katherine thought about that moment as she held her pink phone and gazed at the crowd. The show was in the midst of a commercial break, the lights had been lowered, and she suddenly wished she could slip away and go back home, be by herself, waiting for Diane's voice, instead of this — all these people, all these cameras, those phones ringing, that crank, Elwood Jupes! And now the countless eyes staring up at her, waiting, waiting.

She glanced around the stage. A makeup artist was working on the host's face. Production assistants pushed space heaters closer to the guests. Jack Sellers stood a few feet away, staring at his feet.

Katherine studied him. She had met him once or twice, back in the days when folks in Coldwater were known by their first names and their jobs — "Jack, the police chief," "Katherine, the real estate agent" — before the town was divided by whose phones were ringing and whose weren't.

"Excuse me," she said.

Jack looked up.

"What do you think he meant? Your son?"

"How do you mean?"

"When he said, 'The end is not the end.' What do you think he meant?"

"Heaven, I guess. At least that's what I hope."

He looked off.

"I didn't plan to tell anybody."

She followed his gaze to the crowd.

"It's too late now," she whispered.

And with that, her phone rang.

Sully entered the farmhouse carefully, touching the porch's doorframe before passing through it. Horace had waved him inside — "Over here!" — then disappeared. If this was some kind of trap, Sully thought, he was ill prepared. As he inched forward, he looked for something he might pick up to defend himself.

The hallways were narrow, the floors old and scuffed, the walls painted in dull hues; every room seemed small, as if from a time when people were smaller, too. Sully passed the kitchen with flower-patterned wallpaper and light oak cabinets, a pot of coffee sitting on the counter. He heard voices coming from below and spotted, at the end of the hallway, a railing that led to a basement. Part of him wanted to run. Part of him had to go down there. He slid out of his heavy coat, letting it fall silently on the floor. At least now he could maneuver.

He reached the railing.

He thought about Giselle.

Stay with me, baby.

He began to descend.

Nine years after he invented the telephone, Alexander Bell was experimenting with sound reproduction. He recorded his voice by speaking through a diaphragm that moved a stylus and cut grooves into a wax disc. He recited a series of numbers. At the end, to authenticate it, he said, "In witness hereof, hear my voice . . . Alexander . . . Graham . . . Bell."

For over a century that disc sat untouched in a box in a museum collection — until finally technology involving computers, light, and a 3D camera allowed the sound to be extracted from the wax. Researchers heard the dead man's voice for the first time; they noted the way he pronounced his name, with the faint trace of a Scottish accent — "Alex-ahhnder Gray-ham Bell."

Today people create voice imprints countless times each day — most commonly by leaving telephone voice mails. Bell's precious invention, through which human conversation once traveled over a short wire, can now transmit to satellites and transform our words into digital data — data that can be preserved, replicated, or, if so desired, manipulated.

As Sully stepped into the basement, he did not know he was staring at such technology. He simply saw Horace in a high-backed chair, amid a bank of TV screens showing the stage at Coldwater's football field. He was surrounded by computer monitors, several keyboards, and multiple racks of electronic equipment. Cords, dozens of them, were bound together, running up the wall and out through an opening toward the barn.

"Sit anywhere you like, Mr. Harding," Horace said, not turning around.

"What are you doing?" Sully whispered.

"If you didn't know, you wouldn't be here." Horace tapped several keys. "Here we go."

He pressed a final key, and on the screen, Katherine Yellin could be seen looking at her phone. It rang once. It rang twice. The TV cameras closed in as she flipped it open.

"Hello . . . Diane?" she said.

Her voice boomed over the basement speakers, making Sully snap back. He saw Horace reading from a list on a screen. He tapped several keys.

"*Hello, sister.*"

It was Diane Yellin's voice.

Sully heard it in the basement. Katherine heard it in her ear. The crowd heard it in the stands. And people worldwide heard it on their TV sets or computers — thanks to a signal being sent from Horace's equipment, received through a cell phone, bounced through an amplified board, and cast out through a network audio feed.

Alexander Bell's dream of humans speaking from far away had come to a full and bizarre circle.

A dead woman's voice, re-created, was now having a conversation with the living.

"Diane, it *is* you," Katherine said.

Horace typed something quickly.

"*I am here, Kath.*"

"There are people here listening."

More typing.

"*I know . . . I see . . .*"

"Diane, can you tell the world about heaven?"

Horace snapped his hands up, like a pianist finishing with a flourish. "Thank you, Katherine Yellin," he mumbled.

He flicked a key, and a monitor filled with words. He spun around and looked straight at Sully.

"It helps when you know a question is coming," he said.

What the world heard next was a fifty-four-second explanation of life after life — all in the voice of a deceased woman. It would be transcribed, memorized, printed, and repeated more times than anyone could possibly count.

This is what it said:

"*In heaven, we can see you . . . We can feel you . . . We know your pain, your tears, but we feel no pain or tears ourselves . . . There are no bodies here . . . there is no age . . . The old who come . . . are no different than the children . . . No one feels alone . . . No one is greater or smaller . . . We are all in the light . . . the light is grace . . . and we are part of . . . the one great thing.*"

The voice stopped. Katherine looked up.

"What is the one great thing?" she whispered.

In the basement Horace nodded slightly, the question expected. He tapped another key.

"*Love . . . You are born in it . . . you return to it.*"

On the screen, Katherine was crying, holding the phone as if it were a trembling bird.

"Diane?"

"*Sister . . .*"

"Do you miss me like I miss you?"

Horace paused at his keyboard, then typed.

"*Every minute.*"

Katherine's tears flowed. The others onstage could only watch in silent reverence. The host pointed to the clipboard, and Katherine lowered her head and began to read the questions.

"Does God hear our prayers?"

"*Always.*"

"When will we get the answers?"

"*You already have them.*"

"Are you above us?"

"*We are right next to you.*"

Sully stepped closer to Horace in the chair. He could see, on the man's thin, haggard face, tears rolling freely down his cheeks.

"Then heaven is really waiting for us?" Katherine asked.

Horace inhaled and typed one last thing.

"*No, sweet sister . . . You are waiting for it.*"

What happened next in the basement was violent and sudden. Sully would only later remember the details — the cords he ripped from the electrical outlets, the monitors he swept from tabletops, the rack of equipment he plowed into with a football block, knocking it to the ground. He was blinded by fury, as if a film were over his eyes and a buzzing sound in his head that he had to make stop. He threw himself into anything he could, panting heavily, his muscles taut as cables. When the rack of equipment crashed, he spun and saw Horace watching him — not angry, not scolding, not even visibly surprised.

"STOP IT! NO MORE!" Sully screamed.

"It's done," Horace said, softly.

"Who *are* you? Why are you doing this to people?"

Horace seemed taken aback.

"I'm not doing anything to anyone."

"You are! It's terrible!"

"Really?" He motioned toward the screens. "It doesn't look terrible."

Although the sound had been lost during Sully's rampage, the monitor images remained: people cheering, hugging, on their knees in prayer, crying on each others' shoulders. Katherine was being embraced by the others. The host was beaming and moving between them all. Watching it in silence made it even more surreal.

"This is insanity," Sully whispered.

"Why?"

"It's a huge lie."

"Heaven? Are you sure about that?"

"You're giving them false hope."

Horace crossed his hands on his lap.

"What is false about hope?"

Sully steadied himself on a table. His throat constricted, and he was gasping for breath. A pain behind his eyes was so severe it nearly blinded him.

Horace turned a knob, and the screens went blank.

"Now we'll see," he said.

"You can't get away with this."

"Please, Mr. Hardin—"

"I'll tell everyone."

Horace pursed his lips.

"I don't think you will."

"You're not going to stop me."

Horace shrugged.

"Don't try anything — I'm warning you."

"Mr. Harding. You misunderstand. I hold no strength over you. I am not a well man."

Sully swallowed hard. At that moment, staring at Horace's near-skeletal frame, his drawn expression, the eyes underlined by dark circles, he realized that, indeed, the man must be ill. Until now, Sully had associated his faint pallor and unhealthy look with the undertaking job.

"So . . . what are you?" Sully asked, eyeing the electronics. "Military intelligence?"

Horace smiled. "Can we use those words together?"

"Phones? Intercepts? Hacking?"

"Beyond that."

"International? Spy surveillance?"

"Beyond."

"Is that how you pulled this off?"

Horace raised an eyebrow. "This?" He motioned to the equipment. "This is not very difficult anymore."

"Tell me! Explain, damn it!"

"Very well."

In the minutes that followed, Horace detailed a process that stunned Sully with how far technology had evolved. Phone messages left by the deceased. A certain provider that stored years' worth of them on servers. Hacked acquisition. Voice recognition software. Editing programs. People leave dozens of messages a day, Horace noted. With so many to work with — thus, so much vocabulary — one could create almost any sentence. Sometimes they came out trailing off or disjointed, so keeping conversations short was key. But knowing about the people who were speaking, their histories, their family issues, their nicknames — all conveniently provided by the Davidson & Sons obituary interviews — made the task much easier.

By the time Horace finished, Sully understood enough to see how a mass deception was possible. What he did not understand was the reason.

"Why did you do it?"

"To make the world believe."

"Why does that matter?"

"If it believes, it behaves better."

"What's in that for you?"

"Penance."

Sully was taken aback.

"Penance?"

"Sometimes you sit in a cell and don't deserve it, Mr. Harding." He looked away. "Sometimes it's the other way around."

Sully felt lost. "Why those people?"

"It could have been others. These were enough."

"Why Coldwater?"

"Isn't that obvious?"

He lifted his palms.

"Because of you."

"Me? What do I have to do with this?"

For the first time, Horace looked surprised.

"You really don't know?"

Sully straightened. He clenched his fists defensively.

"I am sorry," Horace said. "I thought that was clear by now." His eyes drifted. "How did you find my home?"

Sully explained — Maria, the library, the real estate office.

"Then you read the deed?"

"Yeah," Sully said.

"Read it again."

Horace sighed deeply and placed his hands on the desk, rising like a dazed fighter lifting off the canvas. He seemed more frail than ever.

"You're not going anywhere," Sully said.

"That is beyond your control."

"I'll call the police."

"I don't think you will."

Horace moved to the back wall. "Your wife, Mr. Harding. I'm sorry you never got to say good-bye. I know how you feel."

292

He tugged on the bottom of his black suit coat. His knuckles protruded from his thin, veined hands. "It *was* a lovely ceremony."

"Don't talk about Giselle, damn you!" Sully screamed. "You don't know anything about her!"

"I will soon enough."

Horace pressed his palms together as if in prayer. "I'm going to rest now. Please forgive me."

He pressed a button on the wall, and the room fell into blackness.

In ancient times, stories traveled from lips to lips. A messenger running over mountains. A man riding for days on horseback. Even the most wondrous event would need to be spoken of again and again — mouth to ears, mouth to ears — spreading so slowly you could almost hear the planet conversing.

Today we watch the world together, seven billion people staring at the same campfire. What happened on the stage of the Coldwater football field was relayed to the most remote corners of civilization — not in weeks or months, but in hours. And for one night on earth, the idea of heaven was as close as it had ever been.

PROOF! some headlines read. HEAVEN SPEAKS! read others. People gathered in the streets from Miami to Istanbul, cheering and hugging and singing and praying. Churches, synagogues, mosques, and temples were overflowing with followers wishing to repent. Cemeteries were packed with new visitors. Terminally ill patients breathed differently as they closed their eyes. There were doubters — there are always doubters —

but for one night, more than any piece of news since news was first gathered, a single story was the start of nearly every conversation on the planet.

Did you hear?

What do you think?

Can you believe it?

Is it a miracle?

Only one man, speeding an old Buick along a two-lane road, knew the truth and was making plans to reveal it. He gripped the wheel, fighting exhaustion. He realized he had not eaten anything since the night before. His legs were soaked from the thighs down, the result of trudging through snow-drifts, looking fruitlessly for Horace, who had somehow disappeared.

It had taken Sully a while to escape the basement darkness. Horace had killed the power to the entire property. Sully banged and bumbled until he found the steps, and he searched the house and later the barn. He wandered through the nearby woods. There was no sign of the old man. As the afternoon light faded, desperation overtook him — a need to share what he had seen before something or somebody could stop him. He retreated from the property, clomping through the snow until he reached the fence, which he climbed again, sheer adrenaline carrying him over the top. His car was cold, and it took several attempts before the engine turned over.

Now he drove in the early-evening darkness, his headlights battling the thick mist that had descended. As he came around a bend and approached the outskirts of his hometown, he saw a line of red taillights that stretched for a mile.

"Ahh no," he said to himself. "God, no, no, no."

The broadcast had sparked a mass pilgrimage to Coldwater, and entry was slow and clogged. Sully felt adrift, locked out. He suddenly wanted to hold his son so badly, his eyes filled with tears. He remembered the cell phone in his pocket. He pulled off his glove, found it, and dialed his parents' number. It rang twice, and then . . .

"Mommy?" Jules's voice said.

Sully's heart sank. The boy had been fooled too. He'd seen something, heard something, been told something. Sully's voice caught in his throat.

"Mommy?" Jules said again. Sully heard his father in the background: "Jules, give me the phone now—"

Sully pressed the red button, disconnecting them.

I don't think you will, Horace had said.

Could he have been right? Was the knowledge of a hoax of heaven as paralyzing as proof of heaven itself? Sully could hear his breathing accelerate. He stared at the line of taillights. He banged his naked hand on the dashboard. No. *No!* He would not lose to this creepy, delusional maniac. He flicked on his interior light and rifled through the papers on the passenger's seat until he found a number and, fingers shaking, dialed it.

"Jupes?" he said when the voice answered.

"Who's this?"

"Sully Harding."

"Oh. Hey. I didn't—"

"Listen to me. It's a hoax. The whole thing. I have proof."

There was a long silence.

"Are you still there?" Sully said.

"I'm listening," Elwood replied.

"It was computers. Software. The dead people left phone messages that were used to re-create their voices."

"*What?*"

"It was a fake the whole time."

"Wait—"

"You have to tell them."

"Whoa, whoa, hold on. Who did it?"

"It was—"

Sully stopped. He swallowed. He thought of what he was about to say. One sentence would change everything. He envisioned hordes of media sweeping down on the funeral home, police, too, and he realized that there was something he needed to find before they did.

"I'll give you everything when I see you," Sully told Elwood. "I'm coming into town. The traffic is just —"

"Listen to me, Harding, I can't do enough here. We don't even publish until next week. If what you're saying is true, you need someone who can handle it right now. I know a guy at the *Trib*."

"Where?"

"The *Chicago Tribune*. We worked together years ago. You can trust him. Can I call him? Can he call you?"

Sully pressed the phone against his ear. He felt more alone than he had ever felt in his life.

"Yeah," he said. "Have him call me in an hour. I have to do something first."

Christmas lights hung on nearly every house in Coldwater, but porch lights were now on as well. There was an animation to the streets, and revelers, bundled in their winter coats, went from home to home, ignoring the cold. There were no strangers. If you were in town, you were part of the miracle. Doors were flung open. Meals were served. Laughter was abundant, car horns honked, and many blocks heard the sounds of Christmas music.

Although the broadcast had ended several hours earlier, the football field was still bathed in light, and hundreds of people milled about, not wanting to go home. The famous host was giving interviews, as was Jeff Jacoby, the mayor. Katherine Yellin had no fewer than ten state troopers around her, as people mobbed to yell her name or pepper her with questions. She spotted Amy Penn, looking up from below the stage.

"Amy!" Katherine hollered. "Please! Will somebody let her up here?"

Meanwhile, Jack Sellers had found Tess, and she stuck close as the crowds sucked into them, too, shouting everything from "Thank you!" to "God is great!" Despite his uniform, people were grabbing for Jack, to shake his hand, to rub his coat, to touch him in some way. Someone yelled, "Chief Sellers, please bless us!" Jack felt a hard grip on his shoulder, and he spun to see Ray, with Dyson standing beside him.

"We got you," Ray said.

They each took a side.

"I need to go home," Tess said, leaning into Jack. "Please? This is too much."

"Come on," he said, pushing through the crowd, and Ray and Dyson yelled, "Clear the way, please . . . Clear the *way!*"

At the county hospital, Elias sat alongside Pastor Warren. They had been mostly quiet since Diane Yellin's words from heaven. At one point after the call had abruptly ended, Elias asked his pastor, "Does this prove what we believe?" and Warren softly said, "If you believe it, you don't need proof." Elias didn't say much after that.

A nurse changed the IV bag again and made a comment about the "the wonderful news." She left, smiling. The two men watched her go. The heart monitor machine made a small humming noise.

"Would you hold my hand, Elias?" Warren asked.

Elias slipped his big palm over the pastor's bony fingers and squeezed them tight.

"You are a good builder," Warren said softly.

"You, too," Elias said.

Warren looked at the ceiling.

"I'm going to miss Christmas service."

"Maybe not," Elias said. "Maybe you'll be out of here by then."

Warren smiled weakly. His eyes closed.

"I will be."

298

Sully remained trapped in the long line of traffic entering Coldwater. It had been over an hour, and he had only advanced half a mile. The *Chicago Tribune* man had not called. Sully turned on the radio. Nearly every channel was reviewing the event, replaying Diane's words. It was everywhere. One station. The next station. Up and down the dial, a dead woman's voice.

"In heaven we can see you . . ."

Sully snapped it off. He felt helplessly frozen — inside this car, inside this traffic, inside the knowledge of something the rest of the world did not have. He reviewed everything Horace had said in the basement, searching for some clue. Why did he choose Coldwater? What did this have to do with him?

Then you read the deed?

Yeah.

Read it again.

What was there to read? It was a legal document, full of complicated jargon, the same thing anyone would sign when buying a property.

He thought about calling Liz. She might be able to read it to him. But something protective made him hesitate, as if, once he told her what he knew, bad people would try to pry it out of her.

Instead he held up the phone and sent her a text.

Are you there?

A few seconds later, his phone buzzed.

Yes. So worried. Are you OK? Where are you?

Am OK. Do you have property deed?

For Horace's house?

Yes. Where is it?

A few seconds passed.

I gave it to you.

Sully froze. He read the words again. Then he grabbed the pile of papers on the seat next to him. He flipped and threw each one aside as he scanned their headings. *Not that one. Not that one. Not that one . . .*

There it was.

Deed of Property. He held it up. Reading small print was difficult in the car's interior light. Sections about recitals, provisions, description of property, lot numbers. How could any of this matter? He scanned to the bottom, a line for the seller to the left, one for the buyer to the right.

Sully squinted to read the buyer's signature.

He read it again.

A shiver passed through his body.

The signature read, "Elliot Gray."

The car behind him honked, and Sully nearly sprang off his seat. He cursed. He read the deed again. A thousand thoughts ran through his mind. *Elliot Gray? Impossible!* The name that had haunted him since the plane crash? Elliot Gray, the air traffic controller who, with a single blunder, had destroyed the best part of

Sully's life? Elliot Gray was dead! Why would Horace toy with him this way? Why did—

His phone rang. He looked at the display. A number he didn't recognize. Sully pressed the green button.

"Hello?"

"Yeah, this is Ben Gissen from the *Chicago Tribune*. I'm calling for Sullivan Harding?"

"This is him."

"Yeah, uh, I got a kind of odd call from an old friend of mine, Elwood Jupes. He writes for a paper in Coldwat —"

"I know —"

"OK, good. So, he said you had some information about the phone calls thing? He said it was important. What really happened up there?"

Sully hesitated. He lowered his voice. "What do *you* think happened?"

"Me?"

"Yeah."

"I'm not here to think anything. I'm just here to listen to what you have to tell me about it."

Sully exhaled. He couldn't clear his head of Elliot Gray. *Elliot Gray?*

"Where should I begin?"

"Anywhere you want," the man said. "Why not—"

The line died.

"Hello?" Sully said. "*Hello?*"

He looked at the phone.

"Damn it."

He held the display up to the small light. There was still battery power.

He turned it over in his hand.

He waited.

He waited.

Moments later, it rang again.

"Sorry," Sully said, answering. "Did I lose you?"

"*Never*," a woman's voice said, softly.

He stopped breathing.

Giselle.

What do you do when the dead return? It is the thing people most fear — yet, in some cases, most desire.

He heard his wife say, "*Sully?*" It sliced through him, cut him open, he bled sadness and joy. So clearly her voice. From her mouth, her body, her soul. *Her voice.*

But.

"I know it's not you," he mumbled.

"*Baby. Don't.*"

"I know this isn't real. I know Horace is doing this."

"*Please. If you love me. Don't.*"

Sully swallowed. He could not hold back his tears. He did not want this conversation, but he so longed for a conversation.

"Don't what?" he finally whispered.

"*Tell him*," she said.

And the line fell silent.

The next few minutes were a private hell for Sully Harding. He buried his face in his hands. He screamed. He pushed his fingers into his hair and yanked it so hard he felt the roots cry in pain. He grabbed the phone. Threw it down. Grabbed it again. He hollered

302

his wife's name, the sound bouncing flatly off the car's windows. The cruelty of this Horace! The depths of his lie! He felt violated and sick, as if something were rising from his gut and he would choke on it if he didn't swallow it back.

When the phone rang again, Sully physically shook — he grabbed his elbows as if he were freezing — and it rang twice more before he answered with the barest of whispers.

"Who?"

"It's Ben Gissen. Mr. Harding?"

His body deflated. Even knowing it was a deception, he wanted to hear Giselle again.

"Hello? It's Ben Gissen? We got cut off?"

"Sorry," Sully mumbled.

"So, OK, go ahead — you were gonna tell me something?"

Sully stared at the car in front of him, his eyes refocusing, as if awakening from sleep. He saw the shape of heads in the backseat. Children? Teenagers? He thought about Jules. He thought about those people in Coldwater being manipulated, as Horace was trying to manipulate him now. Something ugly began to stir inside.

He told Ben Gissen, "Can you get here in person? I don't trust talking over the phone."

"You really have proof this is a fake? I can't get all the way up there just to—"

"I have proof," Sully said flatly. "All the proof you need."

"I'm in Chicago. It would take a few hours—"

But Sully had already hung up. He steered his car off the road, made a U-turn in the snow, and headed the other way.

Elliot Gray, I will kill you, he thought.

He slammed the accelerator.

Jack opened the squad car door and helped Tess get out.

"Watch the ice," he said, taking her arm.

"Thank you," she said.

The ride to her house had been noticeably quiet. They shook their heads or occasionally mumbled, "Maaaan," or "Unbelievable," the way people do after surviving something calamitous. On the streets, countless strangers were celebrating and singing behind blue barricades. The car's headlights briefly illuminated their faces — under parka hoods or ski caps — then left them behind in the dark.

"I used to recognize almost everyone in Coldwater," Tess said.

"I used to know where they all lived," Jack added.

Now, as they walked to her door, it was the quiet that felt strange. They reached the porch. They looked at each other. Jack's walkie-talkie squawked.

"Jack, you there?" a man's voice said.

Jack pressed a button. "Yep."

Static. "Can you talk?"

Button press. "Give me a minute."

Jack hooked the device back on his belt. He sighed and looked again at Tess. It felt as if something were coming to an end.

"I'm so tired," she said.

"Yeah."

"You must be even worse. God. You've been up for how long?"

He shrugged. "Can't remember."

She shook her head.

"What?"

"I was just thinking about tomorrow."

"What happens tomorrow?"

She looked away. "Exactly."

Jack knew what she meant. He'd had this nagging feeling all evening that by having told the world about Robbie, he had somehow completed the task.

"Didn't your mother say it wouldn't last?"

Tess nodded and closed her eyes, as if exhausted. She leaned forward into his shoulder, rested there for a moment, then opened her eyes and kissed him lightly on the lips. His walkie-talkie squawked again.

"Sorry," he grumbled. "What did we do before we had these things, huh?"

Tess smiled. "I'll be fine. Thanks for seeing me home."

She entered her house and shut the door. Jack returned to his car. He knew he needed to call Doreen — explain the calls from Robbie, why he'd kept them a secret. It was only right. First he pressed the button on the walkie-talkie, a wireless device that would have impressed even the great Alexander Bell.

"Jack here," he said. "I'm clear."

"Jack, you need to get up to Moss Hill fast."

"Why? What's up?"

"You need to see for yourself."

Desire sets our compass, but real life steers our course. Katherine Yellin had only wanted to honor her sister. Amy Penn had only wanted a big career. Elias Rowe had only wanted to run his business. Pastor Warren had only wanted to serve God.

Desire set their compasses, but the events of the last sixteen weeks had steered them far off course.

So Katherine, Friday night, was hustled from the giant stage, wondering why she had never heard Diane call her "sweet sister" before.

Amy Penn was trailing behind her, staring at the media as if coming out of a cult.

Elias Rowe now felt obligated to Nick Joseph's son — a boy he'd never met.

And Pastor Warren, whose church had grown too full for his mission, would meet the Lord alone, after taking his final breath in a hospital bed late Friday night.

Sully Harding had one desire as well: to kill a man named Elliot Gray, or Horace Belfin, or whoever he was, to make him pay for the ways he had haunted Sully's life. He drove four miles at a breakneck speed with this fury burning inside him, his muscles taut, his hands ready to do the deed, every breath in his lungs oxygenated by revenge.

But when his Buick pulled down the street, real life changed his course. He slammed the brakes. He recoiled.

Red lights were flashing silently. The house was surrounded by police cars. There were troopers walking

306

the perimeter, and a cluster of dark, unmarked vehicles that Sully figured for government.

"Jesus," he whispered.

Desire sets our compass, real life steers our course. Sully Harding would kill no one tonight.

He shifted the Buick into reverse.

After Midnight

The Coldwater celebration continued into the night, and Lake Street was as crowded as a parade route. The mill served free cups of hot cider. Plates of pies and cookies were laid out on bridge tables. A church choir stood in front of the bank, singing an old hymn:

> High in the heavens, eternal God,
> Thy goodness in full glory shines . . .

Two miles out of town, Sully Harding, who had once again been halted by the inbound traffic, surrendered his last ounce of patience and yanked the wheel harshly to the right. He steered the Buick out of the long line of cars, then hit the gas, speeding along the rocky shoulder between the road and Lake Michigan. He had to get home. Had to get to Jules. Had to find some answers.

What had all those squad cars been doing at that house? Did the police know that he'd been there? Was everything going to come out? Would they be looking for Sully next?

Why Coldwater?

Because of you.

Me? What do I have to do with this?

You really don't know?

Who was Horace? Was Elliot Gray alive? *It can't be Elliot Gray!* Sully tried to focus, but his head was pounding and he was unable to string more than two thoughts together. As the car sped along, he began to perspire. His neck hurt. His throat was dry. He heard the words *you should slow down* in his brain, but they were like something yelled from far away.

He blinked hard, then blinked again. His car bounced, and a rock flew up and cracked the windshield with a sharp *thwock*. Sully lost focus for an instant. The road curved left, and when he steered that way, his headlamps threw light onto three people — man, woman, child — who had gotten out of their car to gauge the traffic. They froze. Sully's eyes widened in horror. He jerked the wheel as he slammed the brakes and the car swerved wildly to the right and skidded uncontrollably before flying off the bank, soaring over low brush that poked up from the snow. For a brief and silent moment it hung in the air, more airplane than automobile. Just before it crashed onto the frozen lake, Sully's instinct was to reach over his head and eject.

And then — impact! The car smashed down and spun backward. His body was tossed across the front seat and slammed into the passenger-side door, his head smacking the window, turning his world black. The car reeled on the ice in rotations, as if someone were using it to wipe the surface, around and around and around again, finally coming to a groaning rest —

four thousand pounds of steel atop a few inches of frozen water.

And Sully, bleeding, slumped on the front seat.

What in life can love not penetrate? Mabel Hubbard, deaf since childhood, gave Alexander Bell a piano as a wedding gift and asked that he play it for her every day, as if his music could pierce her silence. Decades later, at Bell's deathbed, it was his wife who made the sounds, saying the words, "Don't leave me," while he, no longer able to talk, used sign language to answer, *No*.

What in life can love not penetrate? Sully's consciousness had lapsed into darkness; no earthly sound could have stirred him free. Yet somewhere beyond everything, as the ice beneath his car began to buckle, he heard the words of the first phone call ever made.

Come here. I want to see you.

What happened next could never be explained. But it was clear and real and would remain Sully's most indelible memory for the rest of his life. He heard three words.

Aviate.

He felt himself lift from the wreck.

Navigate.

He drifted swiftly like a spirit through the darkness. He was suddenly inside his apartment, coming down the hallway and turning into the doorway of Jules's bedroom. There he saw, sitting on the edge of the boy's bed, his wife, Giselle, as young and radiant as she had ever been.

Communicate.

"Hi," she said.

"Hi," came the sound off his lips.

"It's only for a moment. You have to go back."

Sully felt nothing but lightness and warmth, complete relaxation, as if lying in summer grass when he was ten years old.

"No," he said.

"You can't be stubborn." She smiled. "That's not how it works."

Sully watched her lean over Jules.

"So beautiful."

"You should see him."

"I do. All the time."

Sully felt himself crying inside, but there were no tears, no change in his facial expression. Giselle turned as if she sensed his distress. "What is it?"

"You can't be here," he whispered.

"I'm always here."

She pointed to a shelf, where the angel urn containing her ashes now sat. "That was sweet. But you don't need it."

He stared. His eyes could not blink.

"I'm so sorry."

"Why?"

"I wasn't there when you died."

"That's not your fault."

"I never said good-bye."

"Such a needless word," she said, "when you love somebody."

Sully trembled. He felt old wounds opening wide.

"I was ashamed."

"Why?"

"I was in prison."

"You still are."

She came toward him then, close enough that he could feel a glow coming off her face, and in her eyes he saw every day they'd ever had together.

"Enough," she whispered. "Forgive. I didn't suffer. Once I knew you were alive, I was happy."

"When was that?"

"At the start."

"What start?"

"When I died."

"That's the end."

She shook her head no.

And with that, Sully felt himself being jerked backward, as if someone had the tail of his shirt. Emotion was returning. A tingling cold. A distant pain.

"Don't tell him, please."

He had heard her say that before. Only now he realized whom she was talking about.

Their son.

She looked over at Jules, who rolled to his side, revealing the blue toy telephone snuggled beneath his shoulder.

"Don't tell him there's no heaven. He needs to believe. He needs to believe you do, too."

"I do," Sully said.

He added, "Love you."

"I do," she repeated, smiling, "love you."

He felt her beside him then, around him, behind him, all over him, like the complete immersion of a crying child in his mother's embrace. As the room became a blur of glows and darkness, he was whisked backward, beneath the most incongruous of sounds, the words *pull* and *the handle*.

The next thing he knew, he was falling out of the car. The cold air was bracing. He dragged himself along the snow-covered ice until he was a few yards away, and struggled, woozily, to get to his feet. His head was bleeding. He looked to the sky. He looked for any sign of his wife. He heard only wind and a distant honking.

"Giselle!" he rasped.

Just then the ice gave way with a roaring crunch, and Sully watched with a stunned expression as the Buick dropped into the dark water and began to sink.

The Next Day

NEWS REPORT
ABC News

ANCHOR: A startling development in the Coldwater, Michigan, story. Alan Jeremy reports.

(Alan in front of Horace's property.)

ALAN: That's right. This has all come out in the last hour. According to local police, a man named Horace Belfin, who worked here as a funeral director, may have been involved in creating the phone calls that riveted the world yesterday — phone calls that so many believed were coming from the afterlife. Belfin was found dead in his home on Friday evening. Cause of death is still unknown. Jack Sellers is the Coldwater police chief.

(Image of Jack Sellers.)

JACK SELLERS: It appears that Mr. Belfin may have been involved in some kind of communications interception activity. We're still piecing together the details. I can't really tell you what was done — only that there was a lot of equipment.

ALAN: We're told the federal authorities are involved. Why is that?

314

JACK: You'd have to ask them.

ALAN: Chief, you were the recipient of phone calls from your deceased son. How does this make you —

JACK: My story is not important here. Right now we're just trying to figure out what — if anything — was going on.

(Alan standing by the protesters.)

ALAN: Reaction from nonbelievers was swift.

PROTESTER: We told everyone! What did you people think? That you could just pick up your phone and talk to dead people? It was so obviously a hoax. Right from the start!

(Aerial view of Horace's property.)

ALAN: Belfin lived here on this five-acre farmhouse property. He purchased an interest in the Davidson and Sons Funeral Home less than two years ago. He was unmarried and, according to government sources, had no family. This is all we know at this time. We'll have more reaction from people here as the day goes on. But right now, it seems the "Miracle at Coldwater" may be in doubt . . .

Two Days Later

A dusting of new snow fell on Christmas morning. Here and there in Coldwater you heard the scrape of shovels on church steps and saw smoke wafting from chimneys. Inside houses, children tore open their presents, oblivious to the melancholy looks on their parents' faces.

A midmorning holiday service was held at Harvest of Hope Baptist Church, which also served as the memorial service for Pastor Warren. A eulogy was given by Father Carroll. The other clerics paid their respects. Elias Rowe made his first appearance since that day he stood up in the sanctuary; he stood once again, this time to declare, "No matter what anyone says, I know Pastor's in heaven today."

Katherine Yellin attended the service, along with Amy Penn, whom she introduced as "my friend." For the first time in four months, Katherine kept her phone in her purse and did not check it every few minutes.

Tess Rafferty hosted a houseful of visitors, more people than her mother had ever assembled for a holiday. But the tone was subdued, and as they handed out plates of pancakes together, Jack caught Tess glancing at the silent phone in the kitchen, and he gave her a smile as she blinked back tears.

In the living room of his parents' house, Sully Harding watched Jules open the last of his presents — a pack of coloring books from Liz, who sat on the floor next to him, her streak of pink hair now dyed a Christmas green.

"You feeling OK?" Fred Harding asked his son.

Sully touched the bandage on the side of his head. "Only hurts if I think," he said.

After a few minutes, with Jules fully engaged in his gifts, Sully entered his childhood bedroom and closed the door. His parents had converted it to a guest room, but still kept his varsity letter certificates and a few football photos on the wall.

Sully reached into his pocket and took out a crinkled envelope. His name was typed on the front. He thought back several nights to the lake and the spinout and the way he'd wobbled to the shore, slipping and sliding as the Buick slowly disappeared beneath the icy surface. He fell into a snowbank, exhausted, and lay there until he heard the siren of an ambulance. Someone had called 911, and Sully was taken to the hospital, stitched up, and diagnosed with a severe concussion. The emergency room doctor could not believe he'd regained consciousness quickly enough to escape the car's sinking. How long could it have been? A minute?

Sully stayed overnight for observation. Early the next morning, still groggy, he opened his eyes to see Jack Sellers enter the room and close the door behind him. He was wearing his uniform.

"You gonna be OK?" he asked.

"Think so."

"What can you tell me about him?"

"Who?"

"Horace."

"Not much," Sully lied.

"He was into a lot of stuff," Jack said. "He had equipment I've never seen. And twenty minutes after we get there, about a dozen Feds show up. They told us to keep quiet about everything. They took it all."

"How did you find him?"

"He called us."

"He *called* you?"

"At the station. Friday afternoon. He said there was a dead man at his property. When we got there, we found him in a hidden 'safety' room in the back of the basement. He was lying on the floor."

Jack paused. "The dead man was him."

Sully leaned back into the pillow. He felt dizzy. None of this made sense. Dead? Horace — *Elliot Gray?* — was dead?

"Look," Jack said, reaching into his pocket. "I'm breaking about a million laws here. But I found this in his desk before anyone else and, well, I took it, because if I didn't, they would have. I took it because whatever he was doing to you, he might have been doing to me, too, and some other people I care about, and I want to know and I don't need the whole world to know with me, you understand? This has been hard enough."

Sully nodded. Jack handed him an envelope. He folded it in half.

"Don't let anyone else see it. Read it when you get home. And then . . ."

"What?" Sully said.

Jack blew out a mouthful of air.

"Call me, I guess."

Sully had waited until after Christmas morning. He kept seeing Giselle in his mind, on the bed, sitting next to their son, smiling.

So beautiful.

You should see him.

I do. All the time.

He'd wanted to be with Jules every minute since then, as if being alongside him brought the three of them together. He had turned away the *Chicago Tribune* reporter and Elwood Jupes, telling them he was wrong, he'd been drunk and confused and upset about the broadcast. They finally gave up on him and chased other leads. But now, with Jules's laughter coming from the next room and his trusted new playmate, Liz, keeping him company, Sully felt ready for whatever was in this dead man's envelope, perhaps an explanation of the madness that had shadowed Sully for months.

He tore it open.

And he read.

Dear Mr. Harding,

I beg your forgiveness.

My real name, as you now likely know, is Elliot Gray. I am the father of Elliot Gray Jr., my only child, with whom you are also tragically familiar.

319

On the day of your plane crash, it was I who destroyed the flight recordings at Lynton Airfield, a relatively simple task for someone with my background.

I did so in a foolish attempt to protect my son.

We had been estranged for many years. His mother died young, and he did not approve of my occupation. In hindsight, I cannot blame him. It was clandestine, deceitful work that often took me away for long periods of time. I did it in the name of country and government, two things that mean surprisingly little to me as I write this.

That morning, because he refused to take my calls, I arrived unannounced at Elliot's home. I had come to settle affairs with him. I was sixty-eight years old, and had been diagnosed with an incurable cancer. It was time to resolve our differences.

Unfortunately, Elliot did not receive me well. We argued. It is a father's naive belief that he can always make things right in the end. I could not. Instead, he rushed out agitated and angry. An hour later, he gave you the wrong clearance.

On such moments do lives turn.

I believe it was my presence that put him in a distracted state. I knew my son. He had his weaknesses. But his work, like mine, was impeccable. I had driven to the tower to hand him a letter that contained my final wishes. I could have left it at his home, but I suppose, deep down, I wanted to see him once more. I arrived in time to hear the faraway sound of your jet crashing.

There are no words to describe that moment. My training prepares me for controlled behavior in chaotic situations. But I'm afraid my son panicked. I found him alone in the tower's control booth, yelling, "What did I do? What did I do?" I told him to lock the door and let me handle things as I moved quickly to erase all data — thinking, like an operative, that with no flight recordings, he could not be proven at fault.

For some reason, as I did this, he fled the facility. To this day I do not know why. That's the thing when people leave us too suddenly, isn't it? We always have so many questions.

In the confusion that followed, I left the tower undetected, another thing I am trained to do. But after learning of Elliot's car crash, his death, and your wife being left in such terribly fragile condition, I was consumed with regret. I come from a world of checks and balances. My son, I am responsible for. You and your wife were strangers, crossfire victims. I became desperate to make amends.

A few days later, at Elliot's funeral, I witnessed friends I didn't know he had. They spoke lovingly about his belief in a better world after this one. They said he trusted in the grace of heaven. I never knew he felt that way.

For the first time in my life, I wept for my child.

I came to Coldwater to settle my debts — to him and to you. With access to your military records, I was able to study your background. I tracked your return here, how you'd moved your son in with your parents as you dutifully visited your wife in the hospital. When I learned of the charges you faced, I felt grave concern, knowing no evidence would be found to defend your actions. The ongoing case meant Elliot's death was constantly in the news. My conscience found no rest.

I have always been a man of action, Mr. Harding. Knowing my life was drawing to a close, I purchased a nearby home, took on a new identity (again, a simple matter with my government background), and, by fortuitous accident, met Sam Davidson, who was hoping to retire from his life's work at the funeral home. As you approach death, its mystery takes on a mournful appeal. I bought an interest in his business, and discovered that the grieving of others gave me comfort. I listened to their stories. Listened to their regrets. Nearly all of them had a single desire — the same desire, I suppose, that led me to the airfield that day: to speak with their loved ones at least once more.

I decided, for a handful of them, to make it so. To make my last act one of empathy, and perhaps give you and your son something hopeful after your wife's passing.

The rest — how I did it, the eight voices, the timing, the details — I am fairly sure you will have figured out by this point. Do not count on discovering much evidence. My former employers will cover any important tracks. When you do what I did for so long, you are never truly retired; as my identity could be an embarrassment to them, they will reduce my significance and ensure I remain mostly a mystery.

But I am sharing this with you, Mr. Harding, because to you I can never repay my debt. You may think someone with my background would have no belief in God. That would be inaccurate. It was with fierce belief in God's support that I justified my actions all those years.

I did what I did in Coldwater as penance. I will die, as all of us do, without knowing the outcome of my works. But even if my methods are revealed, people will believe what they choose to believe. And if a few more souls have come to faith because of these calls, perhaps the Lord will show me grace.

Either way, by the time you read this, the mystery of heaven will be solved for me. If I could truly contact you and tell you of its existence, I would. That would be the smallest of debts I could repay.

Instead, I end this as I began it, asking your forgiveness. Perhaps, soon, I will be able to seek the same from my son.

Good-bye —
Elliot Gray Sr., aka Horace Belfin

How do you let go of anger? How do you release a fury you've been standing on for so long, you would stumble were it yanked away? As Sully sat in his old room, holding the letter, he felt himself lifting off from his bitterness, the way one lifts off in a dream. Elliot Gray, an enemy for so long, was now seen differently, a man forgivable for his mistake. The missing flight recordings had been explained, as had the elusive deception that had consumed Coldwater for months. Even Horace had become humanized, a grieving man trying to make amends.

Sometimes you sit in a cell and don't deserve it, Mr. Harding. Sometimes it's the other way around.

Sully read the letter again. His eyes fell on the words *the eight voices*, and instinctively he went through them in his mind. Anesh Barua's daughter, one. Eddie Doukens's ex-wife, two. Jay James's business partner, three. Tess Rafferty's mother, four. Jack Sellers's son, five. Katherine Yellin's sister, six. Elias Rowe's former employee, seven. Elwood Jupes's daughter, eight.

Eight.

What about Giselle — the last voice Horace had manipulated? Did he not count her? Had he left her out on purpose?

Sully grabbed his phone and scrolled through the call log from Friday night. He found the one from the *Chicago Tribune* reporter. It read 7:46p.m. He scrolled back one more call, which read UNKNOWN. That was the one with Giselle's voice.

The time stamp was 7:44p.m.

He scrounged through his pockets and found the number Jack Sellers had given him at the hospital. He dialed it quickly.

324

"Yeah, this is Sellers," he heard a voice say.

"It's Sully Harding."

"Oh. Hey. Merry Christmas."

"Yeah. Same to you."

"Look, I'm with friends—"

"Yeah, no, I'm with family—"

"Did you want to talk somewhere?"

"I just need to ask you one thing."

"All right."

"It's about Horace."

"What about him?"

"Time of death."

"He was dead when we found him. Ray was first in. He had to record it. Six fifty-two p.m."

"What?"

"Six fifty-two p.m."

Sully felt every part of him shiver.

7:44p.m.

"You're sure?"

"Positive."

Sully felt dizzy.

He hung up.

Did I lose you?

Never.

He ran to the living room and gathered Jules in his arms.

Two Months Later

Small towns have their own heartbeat, no matter how many people come or go. In the weeks and months that followed, that heartbeat returned to Coldwater, as trucks departed and stands were dismantled and visitors peeled away like layers of onionskin. Frieda's Diner had empty seats. Parking was plentiful on the snow-cleared roads. In the back of the bank, the president — and mayor of the town — could be seen tapping a pencil on his desk.

No more phone calls were received. Christmas passed. New Year's, too. Katherine Yellin never heard from her sister again, nor did Tess Rafferty hear from her mother, nor Jack Sellers from his son, nor any of the other chosen ones from anyone else. It was as if the miracle had blown away, like seeds of a dandelion.

The news about Horace Belfin and his mysterious death gave rise to wild speculation for several days. Many postulated that the calls were an elaborate hoax, staged by this strange old man who, according to a military spokesman, had retired from a low-level clerk position in a Virginia office after being diagnosed with inoperable brain cancer.

But there were precious few details. The equipment from Belfin's home was seized by the government, which issued a report saying only random data was found. For a while the media pushed for more information, but without the voices from heaven, interest in the story faded, and they ultimately moved on, like a child who leaves a half-read book on the table.

In time the worshippers left the lawns and the open fields. And with nothing to protest, the protesters left, too. Bishop Hibbing and the Catholic Church closed their file on the case. The world absorbed the Coldwater phenomenon the way a shaken snow globe lets its white flakes settle to the bottom. Many took the words of Diane Yellin and studied them as gospel; others dismissed them as fiction. As happens with all miracles, once life goes on, those who believe retell them with wonder. Those who do not, do not.

Although the town was largely saddened by the loss of the heavenly voices, no one seemed to notice how, in their own way, the calls had steered people to just what they needed. Katherine Yellin, so alone since Diane's death, had made a sisterly friend in Amy Penn. And Amy, once consumed by her TV career, left the station and rented a small house in town, where she had coffee daily with Katherine and worked on a book about what she'd witnessed in Coldwater, Michigan.

Tess Rafferty and Jack Sellers found comfort in one another, patching the holes left by the deaths of their loved ones. Father Carroll and the other clerics saw a boost in church attendance, something they had prayed

327

about for years. Elias Rowe, honoring his conversations with Pastor Warren, made amends with Nick Joseph's family, built them a small house, and gave Nick Jr. his first summer job, in construction, where over the years he would earn enough to help pay for college.

Sully Harding took the ashes of his wife, Giselle, from the apartment to a niche at a cemetery.

He came home and had his first restful night in years.

It is said that the earliest spark for the telephone came when Alexander Bell was still in his teens. He noticed how, if he sang a certain note near an open piano, the string of that note would vibrate, as if singing back to him. He sang an A; the A string shook. The idea of connecting voices through a wire was born.

But it was not a new idea. We call out; we are answered. It has been that way from the beginning of belief, and it continues to this very moment, when, late at night, in a small town called Coldwater, a seven-year-old boy hears a noise, opens his eyes, lifts a blue toy to his ear, and smiles, proving heaven is always and forever around us, and no soul remembered is ever really gone.

Author's Note

This novel takes place in a fictional town called Coldwater, Michigan. There is an actual Coldwater, Michigan, and it is a fine place and I encourage you to visit it. But this is not that town.

Acknowledgments

This book was written with God's grace, lots of coffee, a morning table by a Michigan window, and love from family and friends.

It was birthed at a difficult time, and many people helped me through that. A sentence is meager payback, but as deeply as ink can express it, my gratitude to Janine, for every precious minute; to Kerri Alexander, for her partnership and loyalty; to Ali, who shared many a Skype conversation; to Phil McGraw, for efforts above and beyond; to Lew C., for understanding; to David Wolpe and Steve Lindemann, two men of God who showed divine patience; to Augie Nieto, a pal through and through; to Eileen H. and Steve N., whose bravery inspired me; to the kids at HFH in Haiti, where I went to keep my perspective; and hugely to, in a way only they can appreciate, two true friends, Marc Rosenthal (since I was twelve) and Chad Audi (since I was forty-seven). There are no words except "The day finally came!"

Also, Mendel is a bum.

David Black has now passed the quarter-century mark with me, which should earn him a medal. I thank him for his tireless belief, and all the great folks in his office — Sarah; Dave; Joy; Luke; Susan, who rules the globe; and Antonella, who rules cyberspace.

My deepest thanks also to my new family at HarperCollins, who have welcomed me so warmly, from sales to marketing to publicity to design. Particular appreciation to my new creative chum, Karen Rinaldi, who hung in for a mere eighteen years to make it happen, and whose loving touch is all over this book, and to Brian Murray, Jonathan Burnham, and Michael Morrison, for taking a big leap of faith.

A special overseas thanks to David Shelley, of Little Brown UK, whose always-thoughtful notes make me feel like I know what I'm doing, and to Margaret Daly, the best friend an American writer could ever have in Ireland.

My father said everything would end up OK — "Just keep working on your book" — and he was right, as usual. My love for my parents knows no bounds. My earliest readers, Ali, Trish, and Rick, gave me reason to go on.

And every Giselle, Alli, or Marguerite I write is really just Janine. How else could I imagine a love so deep?

I would also like to pay tribute to the numerous books and articles that helped in my research of the telephone and its colorful history. And to the state of Michigan, which I love, and where I was happy to finally set a story, even a fictional one.

Finally — and firstly — anything created by my heart or hand is from God, by God, through God, and with God. We may not know the truth about phones and heaven, but we do know this: in time, He answers all calls, and He answered mine.

MITCH ALBOM
Detroit, Michigan, June 2013

THE MAGIC STRINGS OF FRANKIE PRESTO

Mitch Albom

At nine years old, Frankie Presto is sent to America in the bottom of a boat, his only possession an old guitar and six precious strings. Frankie's ability is unique, and his amazing journey weaves him through the musical landscape of the twentieth century, with his stunning talent impacting upon numerous stars along the way, including Elvis Presley, Carole King and even KISS. Frankie becomes a pop star himself. He makes records. He is adored. But his gift is also his burden, as he realises: through his music, he can actually affect people's futures — with one string turning blue whenever a life is altered. Then, at the height of his popularity, Frankie Presto vanishes, and his legend grows. Only decades later does he reappear to change one last life . . .

FOR ONE MORE DAY

Mitch Albom

This is the story of a man named Charley who loses his job, leaves his family and decides, one night, to end his life. Somewhere between this world and the next, he encounters his mother, who died years ago, and he spends one last day with her — a day he never had on earth. This "ordinary" day covers the whole of their existence, and reveals how Charley, like many children, was constantly forced to choose between his mother and his father. He gets the chance many of us yearn for — to ask the questions never asked while our parents are alive. In the end, Charley learns how little he really knew about his mother, how her love saved their family and how deeply he wants the chance to save his own.

TUESDAYS WITH MORRIE

Mitch Albom

An emotional and intellectual ride with Morris Schwartz, teaching us about life and ourselves. To Mitch Albom the rediscovery of the college professor who had taught him nearly twenty years ago was a magical find. This older and wiser man had been his patient mentor when he was young and impassioned, helping him to see the world as a more profound place. Mitch got his second chance to meet Morrie in the last months of the older man's life. Their rekindled relationship turned into one final "class" of lessons in how to live.

THE FIVE PEOPLE YOU MEET IN HEAVEN

Mitch Albom

From the author of the phenomenal *Tuesdays With Morrie*, comes this enchanting, beautifully written novel that explores a mystery only heaven can unfold. Eddie is a grizzled war veteran who feels trapped in the toil of his father before him, fixing rides at a seaside amusement park. The war left him wounded and his days tumbled into one another, loneliness, regret and sad dreams of what could have been. Then on his eighty-third birthday, Eddie dies in a tragic accident, trying to save a young girl who is in the path of a falling cart from the "Free Fall" ride. With his final breath, he feels two small hands in his — and then nothing. He awakens in the afterlife, where he learns that heaven is a place where your earthly life is explained to you by five people who were in it. As each of his guides lead him through heaven, Eddie discovers a little bit more about what his time on earth meant, what he was supposed to have learned, and what his purpose in life truly was. The answer is as magical and inspirational as a glimpse of heaven itself.

SPECIAL MESSAGE TO READERS

THE FIRST PHONE CALL FROM HEAVEN

In the small town of Coldwater, Michigan, a handful of bereaved residents start receiving phone calls from beyond the grave. Some call it a miracle; others are convinced it's a hoax. Regardless of opinion, one thing is certain: Coldwater is now on the map. People are flocking to this tiny, remote town to be part of this amazing phenomenon . . . Sully Harding's wife died while he was in prison, and he now cares for his young son — who carries around a toy cell phone, believing his mommy is going to call him from heaven. But Sully soon discovers some curious facts: the calls only come in on a Friday, and each recipient happens to have the same cell phone plan. Something isn't adding up, and Sully is determined to keep digging until he uncovers the truth . . .